I WISH I WAS LIKE YOU

By
S.P. Miskowski

JournalStone Publishing

JOURNALSTONE
YOUR LINK TO ARTISTIC TALENT

M
Miskowski

This is a work of fiction. All of the characters, names, incidents, organizations, and dialogue in this novel are either the products of the author's imagination or are used fictitiously.

JournalStone books may be ordered through booksellers or by contacting:
JournalStone
www.journalstone.com
The views expressed in this work are solely those of the authors and do not necessarily reflect the views of the publisher, and the publisher hereby disclaims any responsibility for them.

ISBN: 978-1-945373-78-7   (sc)
ISBN: 978-1-945373-79-4   (ebook)

JournalStone rev. date: July 7, 2017

Library of Congress Control Number: 2017942713

Printed in the United States of America
1st JournalStone Edition

Cover Art & Design: 99designs - Chameleonstudio74
Images - https://www.123rf.com/photo_44384898_urban-background-brick-wall-under-the-lamp-light-at-night.html?term=dark%2Bstreet&vti=o88n22op8ukcbx9ndc
https://www.123rf.com/photo_33889707_full-length-portrait-of-young-woman-isolated-on-white-background.html?fromid=aVBaUkpkcWhTZ0Vrd0c2VWFRdnVWZz09
https://pixabay.com/en/beautiful-girl-hair-model-portrait-1850115/
Author Bio Photo: Denise Jarrett

Edited by: Dan Mason

I WISH I WAS LIKE YOU

Something more goes to the composition of a fine murder than two blockheads to kill and be killed, a knife, a purse, and a dark lane.
- Thomas De Quincey

A dead man is the best fall guy in the world. He never talks back.
- Raymond Chandler

In the end I will forget you.
I'm sorry
to have to say that.
But, I will forget myself,
too,
so don't feel bad.
– Steven J. Bernstein

Part One

"First rule. Never open your story with a corpse. It's a cliché. More important, I don't *like* it, so don't do it. If you do it to be ironic, I'll throw your manuscript in your face. If you do it to piss me off, I'll flunk you. And then you can explain to your parents, who pay your fucking tuition, how you wrecked your grade point average with a lame-ass workshop in *crime fiction*." - Lee Todd Butcher, RIP

Chapter One

On a Friday afternoon, at the end of a shitty week, after waiting for a bus in merciless rain for a quarter of an hour and giving up, trudging the final six blocks and stomping up three flights of stairs to my lousy, cramped apartment in a building reeking of mouse turds and tomato soup, the last thing I expected to find waiting for me was a dead body. Facedown on the living room floor, sprawled across the cruddy tangerine carpet that came with the place.

By the way, I'm using the term 'facedown' loosely. The corpse lay torqued at a sharp angle, one arm extended toward the window and the other pinned beneath the torso. Most of the face had traveled across the room and now decorated the mantel and fireplace in fading streaks. A thin plume of brain matter curled out of the demolished forehead with a comical flourish. A revolver rested quietly, as if ashamed, under the coffee table.

Given the circumstances, some people might scream. Other people would cry. Here's what I did. I stepped over the body and made for the pack of American Spirits on the mantel. Because fuck moderation at a time like that; I needed a cigarette.

Three cigarettes, a glass of Burgundy, four tokes of weed—about an *hour* later—I'd had time to calm down and think. Most of my thoughts took the form of questions.

First, if not most alarming, why was there no response to a gunshot inside my Capitol Hill apartment? Had the novelty of it confused my neighbors...?

"Druida, did you hear a loud bang?"

"Did you say 'bang' to me?"

"I'm not kidding. Did you hear it?"

"A bang? An actual...? Like a noise?"

"*Druida, please. A noise. Like a bang.*"

"*I have no idea. Listen, I taped last week's* X-Files, *do you want to watch it before the new episode? Or do you want to investigate a so-called bang? I can't handle both right now...*"

Second, and still not the worst part, at what time did it happen? I was at work all day. How long did the corpse lie there on the carpet?

I tried to remember precisely when I'd left the apartment. It was that morning, yes, and before dawn thanks to my soul-sucking job at a photocopy center. I recognized the acrid coffee grounds moldering in a French press on the black and white kitchen counter. From the carpet came the scent of dried blood, a bitter tang of rust. Also a lingering and gag-worthy trace I recognized from the salon around the corner. Burnt hair like sweet, toxic caramel.

I sat on the floor and stared at my corpse and wondered how long I'd been dead. This was the worst part. Not the first or second thing that occurred to me, but the most upsetting circumstance.

I smoked and drank and considered what to do next. I wandered around my squalid living room. I leaned against the window with its view of an ATM alcove across the street, a place where people slept and ate and peed and offered outrageous services for a dollar. Where I once observed a schizophrenic homeless man knighting a drunk Seafair Pirate with a samurai sword.

I was gazing down at the ATM when it hit me. The craving, the insistent urge to find a crowded room with crisp white linen, steaming cups of coffee, warm bodies, and the buzz of conversation—to immerse myself in all of those human sounds and delicate motions.

As a warning sign, a taste of things to come, almost as soon as I felt the familiar longing for coffee, I was staring through the window at B & O Espresso...

The downpour had subsided to a drizzle. I saw *you* at a table inside the café, studying the view. You were scanning the traffic sluicing up and down Olive Way. Your eyes reflected the rain on glass. You sighed, fascinated by the drifting clouds. I watched you lift a cup of espresso to your lips. I wondered what the hell you were thinking. And then I knew.

You congratulated yourself for being patient and staying put. You were waiting, yes, but this was a test. You were plotting against your lover, the 'married with two children' tax attorney you described to girlfriends as your 'paramour.'

The really twisted tale is always a love story, isn't it? Tears before cocktails and a quick screw at a downtown hotel every other Friday. The tax attorney wanted to break up with you but he was afraid. He was taking the coward's route, pointing out all of your flaws and hoping to make you leave him, but you were tenacious.

Some would have called you a stalker, although you thought of your life in more heroic terms. You were bravely ignoring your lover's criticism—of your impatience, your scattered nature, and your shallow opinions. You wanted to kill him because he didn't love you. More than you wanted him dead, you wanted to hurt him. You wanted to break him. You wanted to twist the necks of his pre-school children until they snapped in your hands. Well, well!

I turned my face left and right, no reflection captured in the object of your attention, the rain-spattered window between us. The patterns folded and refolded, a lace veil of rain and darkness. Designs kept opening in further and further seams beyond reach...

All the way down the crooked spine of Denny Way, beyond bumbling traffic and breathless pedestrians, the aftermath of the storm, biding its time south, churned up the tide against a battery of splintered piers. Diners chattered over plates of fried clams and bowls of salmon chowder behind steamed restaurant windows at the Market.

I felt the breeze like a cold blade across my back.

A late afternoon ferry, lights glowing from the car and passenger decks, glided across Elliott Bay, a slender point of separation between water and sky. I knew this without looking. Just as I knew a girl in a paisley dress had pulled a Swiss Army knife on the driver of a #7 bus, and the downtown Metro line had temporarily screeched to a halt...

B & O Espresso turned out to be chock-full of mistresses that Friday. I allowed my attention to wander to another table.

At first glance I knew the man *you* were waiting to see wasn't going to show up. He was with a co-worker in a seedy room at the Ever Spring Inn, six miles north, on Aurora Avenue. The co-worker was laughing, blinded by thick strands of champagne blonde hair across her face, a whiff of jasmine rising from her abdomen each time he thrust inside her.

I studied your smile. I saw you were too wound up, too desperate, too *you*, to be happy. You were impatient with others. You saw yourself as a significant person, and other people as scenery. Your impulse was always to move, to exit, to leave the door squeaking on its hinges.

In a couple of years, purely seeking attention in the most dramatic way, you would eat a fistful of Valium. The resulting fog would surround you, hold you as tightly as a winter coat, and you would step onto the railroad tracks to greet the train from Portland. On a blistering cold night your sister would drive to the morgue to identify the pieces of you retrieved at the scene.

That was where I left you, my brief second encounter, a slightly chubby Anna Karenina sipping coffee and grieving like a million other lonely fools. Convinced you were right to spend your life this way, in a melodramatic haze, too self-absorbed to know you were doomed...

Since that night I've felt a constant urge, an itch to tell my story. I've wanted to feel words forming on my tongue or flowing from my fingertips. I wanted that whole day, the whole year before it, my entire existence, to be a story I could *use* because that's how desperate people are and how calculating. Even dead people. We want our lives to add up to something, despite all evidence to the contrary.

When the police eventually responded to my landlord's call, when they broke down my door to pinpoint that *new* terrible smell permeating the building, it would have been nice if someone, somewhere had known a couple of things about me. Things they could never read in a newspaper.

For example, I was never part of a 'publishing scene,' whatever the hell that might be. Any 'scene' going on in Seattle, trust me, I was not part of it. If anything cool or great was happening while I was alive, I was not involved in any way. The 'scene' bypassed me like a rock in the middle of the freeway.

One thing both dailies got wrong was my taste in music. I was not a club-hopping local. I wasn't even a huge Nirvana fan. If asked (and I never was), I would say I was more of a Gas Huffer, Pixies, Cramps, Velvet Underground, Robert Johnson on Sunday, and occasional

Butthole Surfers gal. So the implication that I would copycat Cobain's suicide pissed me off more than anything. Almost anything.

As time went on—as time goes on—facts mean less than the relief I feel on those occasions when I cross paths with a soul mate. Because bitterness, it turns out, is eternal; it gathers momentum. Feed it an occasional sacrifice and it doesn't subside. It feels better, deeper, and more luxuriant.

Of course I hated my life, but my fate—to become a composite sketch of a 1994 twenty-something with a terrible job living in a grubby apartment in a city best known for suicide, rain, and serial killers—this was too much.

The trouble was, despite my newfound ability to read bits of information from random strangers, I couldn't remember exactly what happened in my own apartment on that first day. Oh, after a while the blast, the explosion of light and darkness, returned, but not the face staring at me from behind the barrel. The face of my stupid enemy remained a mystery for some time.

That first night I only knew my memory was becoming selective, a tiny door etched into an immense wall running as far as I could see. It wasn't possible to observe what I wanted when I wanted, but once I opened that door, the random view was spectacular.

None of which mattered to the cops when they started kicking down the door to my apartment. They had to go by what they could see. The first thing they saw was my corpse. The second was a gun I never owned, with my fingerprints on it. Third was a notebook, lying open on the coffee table. The fourth thing was this journal entry, written two days prior:

Have you ever hated someone? Not the parking-space-stealing kind of hate. Not the ex-lover and his corset-wearing, skinny new girlfriend kind of hate. I'm talking about bile surging in your belly and a taste of sulfur at the back of your throat. Ordinary objects become alluring. They seduce your imagination—the steak knife poised in your hand above the plate, paralyzed by a desire to find its real purpose in your companion's heart.

In the throes of hatred, you might forget to bathe. You might start your day with a face that feels like it's lined with wet sand because you forgot to sleep. At two a.m. you start talking back to the clock on the nightstand. You bitch that clock right out. For half an hour you address the clock by the name of your nemesis.

Brilliant! To the cops and the newspapers I would be nothing but a nut case, another hysterical girl who couldn't handle life in the city. When people glanced at the brief, perfunctory articles in the dailies they would learn I was an unpublished writer; a twenty-something deadbeat; a liar and a plagiarist. That Friday in 1994, I became everything my former boss, Eve Wallace, said I was.

I don't know if my downward spiral started with my job at a crummy weekly paper, or stealing another writer's story, or losing a contest, or moving to the city, or having sex with my writing teacher, or being born in the dullest suburb in the Northwest. On one level, I realize it didn't begin with Eve. I only associate her with my failure. All of the ugliness I'd sown really came alive once I knew her name and accepted the job she offered me.

And who was this person, this fulcrum of all my petty disappointments? She was nothing. Eve Wallace was the kind of woman Lee Todd Butcher wouldn't have noticed if they were alone together in a bathtub. She was the epitome of middle-aged womanhood, a sagging vessel, a ship heading to port for the last time. She enjoyed nothing. Her life was over. When we met she was in her mid-thirties, by her account; late thirties, according to gossip; or forties, to guess by appearance. She was as close to invisible as it's possible for a living person to be. If she sat in a café with her back to a complicated wallpaper pattern, and I sat opposite her, a moment would inevitably arrive when my vision couldn't separate Eve from the wallpaper.

Eve and I were not alike in any way. Lee Todd once told me I was "a killer by nature, a pragmatic sadist; both the wound and the salt in the wound." If his description was accurate, several things make sense. But why would I take the word of a loser, a cranky-ass poet, a hack Raymond Chandler who ran out of time? Lee Todd warned me not to move to Seattle and I told him to go to hell. It's funny how things turn out.

Who knows? Maybe in another month or two I would have made up my mind to leave the city. Maybe I would have stopped obsessing over Lee Todd's fucked-up advice (both taken *and* rejected). Maybe I would have been ready to find out who I was, and what I wanted to do. I might have traveled, maybe to India, maybe Europe.

Well, never mind, as they say. Apparently I'll be rotting in the cold mist and mildew for whatever passes for eternity these days. I'm stranded in the rain in a port city crowded around a bay of skeletons. For centuries, everybody's wanted a piece of this place. I can't figure out why. Crows own the land, seagulls own the water, and the gray people scuttle back and forth under low skies, clutching paper cups of coffee, ducking raindrops and bird shit. Below the surface, tectonic plates grind at one another, edges bulging, compressing, threatening to break open and drag the landscape under.

No matter what's left, after the tsunamis roll in and the ocean pulls everything natural and man-made into a roiling grinder of dirt, rock, and foam—I'll probably still be here. Perched on a rock, reclining on the limb of an ancient redwood, or sipping an espresso and waiting for the next thing to happen.

Until then I bide my time by following strangers and making friends.

A series of Carpenter Gothic houses on 23ʳᵈ Avenue huddle in the shadows like a row of silent monks on a sullen summer night, too humid for comfort, too late for a walk; a night for keeping the windows ajar.

You must be a cutter. I can see the skittish little scars on the inside of your arms. Fading as unevenly as adolescence.

Yours is the surname of a Seattle founding father. 'So embarrassed' by the fact, you go by a less conspicuous moniker and tell yourself you're being humble and real, hiding under your grandmother's maiden name, living in the Central District, waving to neighbors who regard you with a wary shake of the head and a shrug. You're the weird white lady in the house on the corner with the messy yard, and no one likes you.

You grew up in the Pacific Northwest, attended the Bush School then Cornish for a semester, and then Evergreen State College, an artistic haven your daddy hated. "It's make-it-up-as-you-go-along-and-give-yourself-an-A-for-malarkey-education," he said. He wanted you to be a sensible, dutiful caretaker of the family legacy. Alas.

You wanted to be a textile weaver or a folk musician. You lost interest as soon as your mother bought you a loom and a guitar. Your childhood drifted from the dock in gloomy silence as you wandered in the fog from port to port around Puget Sound on your step-daddy's yacht.

Your parents and their fussy, silver-haired friends are full of rules and pretensions; their ice-cold houses teem with hideous heirlooms; they never let you talk about anything real. They smirk and chuckle when you rant about human rights, and animal rights, and the planet, and space travel. They live in quaint piles of Victoriana perched on the crumbling edges of Mercer Island.

A reporter for the *Post-Intelligencer* once profiled your step-daddy for the weekend edition and described your home as 'picturesque.' After you read the article you hid under the bed all day and fell asleep angry because no one came looking for you.

Lonely child with a trust fund and no need to accept reality, at thirty-five you still believe in spirits, wood sprites, and fuzzy-haired druids. All imaginary friends are welcome in your world. You burn noxious white candles to ward off negative energy.

You cried for two days over a blue heron crushed by a friend's motorboat—a heartbroken, overgrown girl with no boundaries. You're crying about the heron again when I find you sitting cross-legged on the floor of your living room. The floorboards gleam because a maid comes to clean and polish them bi-monthly. Your square fingertips are poised on the planchette of the Ouija board, scanning the arc of letters.

"Souls who roam, feel free to come and settle here," you whisper to the gloom. "Settle here beside me…"

Marvelous smoky clouds roam the night sky, some as low as the rooftops visible through your windows. You imagine ghostly spirits riding those clouds to your doorstep. You long to be connected to those entities, anyone, any sign of a living cosmos beyond your insipid friends with trust funds, yachts, and portfolios. Anything real, you believe, will make *you* real, too. A bolt of truth from the heavens will render the tedious comforts and illicit dreams of your dowdy life somehow significant. This is what you want, you tell yourself. You tell me.

I consider your weight, the way the flesh of your feet strains at the leather straps of your sandals. You've spent years in therapy, and more years being regimented and counseled by bodywork professionals, to no avail. You can't find happiness as you are; and you can't alter your physique, not as your parents want you to do.

With infinite delicacy and patience I slide my hands over yours. I note the widening of your eyes and the quickening of your pulse. I allow the rough contours of your stubby, childlike fingers to absorb mine, and we begin to sweep the planchette in a pattern, forming my name and a greeting.

"G-R-E-T-A," we write. "H-E-L-L-O."

Your hands slip from mine, and you scream. You snatch the planchette from the board and fling it across the room to shatter against the window ledge. You keep on screaming despite my efforts at calming you, and then you crab-walk clumsily over the polished floor to the corner. Still screaming, siren-like, you clasp your knees to your chest. The contortion of your plain, sad face tells me this will be your next excuse for medication. Also a month-long stay at your uncle's farm on Vashon Island; the housekeeper will feed you creamy delicacies three times a day.

You will give away your books on the occult and take up Jane Austen. You will finally obey your mother and marry a stockbroker, give excruciatingly painful birth to a child you can't love, and spend your days planning dinner parties and boating trips. And every night you will swallow a tiny pill for seven blissful hours of dreamless sleep. Until the night when you finally feed your soul by swallowing all the pills and washing them down with a bottle of Beaujolais Blanc—all to forget me.

Chapter Two

"Keep background information about your characters to a minimum. The quaint childhood habits and adolescent adventures of your protagonist are of no interest to people who read crime fiction. If you're into *that kind of thing*, take a walk down the hall in the English Department and don't stop until you spot a sign with the word 'Literature' on it. Bye!" – Lee Todd Butcher, RIP

Like most people of my generation, I grew up a little bit lazy and extremely bored. I spent thousands of hours doing nothing, skulking in my shredded jeans and Siouxsie T-shirt around the outlying middle-class suburbs of Otisville, in eastern Washington State. The sky is misshapen above my hometown, or at least the clouds and light form an optical illusion so the sky appears to arc downward and then roll up again. The disorientation caused by this legendary natural occurrence is blamed for the higher than average number of traffic accidents.

My life was ordinary. I rode my bike to school, stole cassette tapes from the music department at Fred Meyer, and drank gin behind trash dumpsters in the alley. I went to school with kids who believed they were a lot cooler than me. A few of them shot heroin or huffed spray paint and died before graduation. Comparatively speaking, my teen years were uneventful.

I could lie to create a more flattering portrait, but what's the point?

Facing an eternity of parenthood, my mom and dad resisted their natural impulse to flee. Instead they wasted their youth paying off a third mortgage on a ranch-style house with three bedrooms, two baths, and a dining area lined in fake wood paneling.

We lived on a street where all the neighbors could see through one another's living room window, and nothing ever happened. People went to work and to school. People celebrated holidays with barbecues and fireworks. People met at motels and bars and pretended to be mysterious. A father of four was arrested for indecent exposure at the park. A woman drove drunk through her neighbor's roses and somebody killed her cat the next day. This was life in the suburbs.

Nobody murdered anybody, at least nobody who got caught. Families knew one another, or pretended to, from a safe and civil distance. They didn't discuss anything more controversial than the local football scores. A natural death on our block justified the entire population shambling outdoors in pajamas to drink coffee and watch the paramedics strap down and ferry away one of our own. Afterward, minus information, we speculated.

"Hal was out of shape. I offered to take him to the gym as my guest. Said he didn't have time. Look at him now…"

"He was under too much pressure at work. All that overtime! Stress is a killer. I told him to slow down and spend more time with the family but he didn't listen. Look at him now…"

"His marriage was coming apart. I urged him to see a lawyer and get free of the whole mess. Look at him now…"

Regardless of the slant our gossip took, one thing was consistent; we blamed the dead guy. People always do. It's a way of siding with life, with energy and bouncy tits, a way of stepping back from death, mocking anyone who seems tired, weak, depressed, or just too goddamn eager to lie down. It's a way of pretending to be on friendly terms with good fortune.

Good old good fortune! She'll never let us down!

It's a classic M.O., self-delusion. Mortality comes to shoot us all in the head one day. Speculation and blame won't make any difference. Yet sanity craves answers. People demand explanations, even if those explanations are ridiculous. Our ability to screech through mundane disasters on a shopping cart of bravado relies on the belief that it *matters* how we live and where and for how long. The only thing keeping us going is self-importance.

No wonder suburban kids crave violence. Sugar, too, but mostly violence. Not toward ourselves, necessarily, but we long for something bloody and real, a loud *bang* to break the tedium and sharpen the senses.

By my sophomore year I'd seen kids overdose in the public pool; crash into a wall with a motorcycle; shine sunlight through a magnifying glass and blow up a cartridge of shotgun powder at close range; and set a teaching assistant's wig on fire with a Bunsen burner and a can of hairspray.

Death occurred often enough but not murder. Where I came from, a murder would have been a blessing. We could have talked about a murder for years. Death without murder seemed naked and over-advertised.

Murder was one of the few subjects that held my adolescent attention. I pored over the gruesome details in magazines. I thought of both perpetrators and victims as people I knew, maybe because I didn't have friends. I watched crime dramas on TV and made up elaborate fantasies around them. I read books by an FBI profiler who developed a theory about serial killers. He proposed a plausible combination of factors—prefrontal lobe damage in childhood, early exposure to extreme violence and emotional abuse—indicating higher than average risk. I read all of his case studies and dreamed about turning into a killer. I fell asleep each night reading the most frightening tales of brutality, and woke with a smile on my lips.

"Trouble," my mother used to say when she saw me reading my awful books. "Always trouble." She liked to tell a story about a girl named Finch, and how I'd dislocated her shoulder by dragging her off a swing set in kindergarten. Also a girl named Lana I'd stabbed in the left butt cheek with an unsharpened pencil for cutting in line at lunch. I don't remember any of this. I know there were no consequences, no counseling or time out, none of the attention afforded 'special kids' of my generation. All of which makes me wonder if my mom invented these stories in a misguided attempt to explain empathy to her poker-faced only child.

My parents urged me to study forensic science, or psychology, or even mortuary management; anything related to my interest that might lead to an income. One way or another I ended up wandering through high school without distinguishing myself. It was hard to believe all the great things our blathering valedictorian claimed he was going to do as soon as he was released upon the unsuspecting world. The thought of someday sharing an office with a guy like that made me want to fill a backpack with candy bars and walk into the woods, hoping to be eaten by bears.

I didn't want a practical application for my prurient interest. Its illicit nature was its primary appeal. I didn't want a degree in a field that would help me find a job. I didn't want a job. In fact, I didn't know what I wanted. I didn't care what I wanted. It didn't bother me that I didn't care.

While my classmates grudgingly followed their parents into corporate accounting and civil engineering, I maintained my habit of dabbling in coursework and gliding through with a grade point average no one bragged about. After high school I chose a community college instead of a university because it was cheap and located three miles from home. This way I didn't have to admit it was time to grow up and move on. I had no intention of growing up *or* moving on. When I tried to picture what a life of mine would be like, I could only see patterns of shifting light and muted colors, fuzzy at the edges, the same way I imagined heaven.

I inherited a piece-of-crap Gremlin from my mom's brother when he finally bought a real car. I registered for classes with the faint hope of stumbling onto a subject I could stand to be immersed in for more than a month. Besides murder, of course. Over the dull ensuing days I sampled and gradually stopped attending Creative Mathematics, French, Anthropology, Shakespeare, Spanish, Biology, Latin American History, German, and Humanities.

I spent my nights drinking Rainier beer and making out with a guy named Jack Brinkerhoff who had a part-time job uninstalling solar panels. We grappled in his Corvette as many times as it took to admit the absence of any attraction between us. It's hard to say, sometimes, which is the more powerful force: lust or boredom.

On the drives home, by myself, I let the black shadows flanking the road envelop me. Moonlight faded to a pinpoint and then expanded, stretching across my vision, revealing the night version of our warped, uneven sky.

The semester before I quit community college I signed up for a class in crime fiction appreciation. The elective course description clicked with the morbid inclinations of my suburban soul, and I figured nothing could be less practical than appreciating gruesome, made-up stories. I thought it would be an easy grade and nothing more.

The teacher was named Lee Todd Butcher, and my absolute first thought the moment I saw him was: *That guy doesn't know he's dead.* His paperback bio note made him sound like a combination badass martial artist and soldier of fortune. In the cover photo he squinted from beneath a fedora, a poor man's Clint Eastwood sucking on a Pall Mall cigarette. The guy wore at least three layers of pretentiousness. Yet I couldn't stop staring at his picture, at the cold blue-gray irises and the shadows under his eyes. Where did he get the nerve?

The actual Lee Todd was a ghost of his photograph. He leaned a lot and stooped at both shoulders and hips, a once vain man resigned to turning silver and balding in equal measure. Maybe he was heroic when he was younger. Under the fluorescent lights of a classroom, etched against a green chalkboard, he was a middle-aged guy wearing department store sweatpants that barely clung to his narrow hips. His threadbare Iron Maiden T-shirt must have shrunk a couple of sizes, judging from the way it strained against his chest. The rippling effect made him appear more muscular and I wondered if this was why he favored the shirt; he wore it almost every day.

He said the first session would be an introduction to him and his story, and how he operated. A show of hands revealed less than half the class recognized Lee Todd's name before showing up, and less than one quarter had read any of his books. So the first order of business, he said, was to tell us all about his career and how he ended up 'in a shithole like Otisville.'

Lee Todd had written eight crime novels in the 1970s and early

'80s. Three of them, *Rage of Death*, *Long Way Back*, and *Whiskey Fever*, made the *New York Times* Best Seller list for their genre. After that he told his friends he was hard at work on a real masterpiece, a hell of a book, a surefire crossover. He was going legit, adding a literary smirk to his signature style. He assured his friends he would finally win an Edgar, and probably a National Book Award for this one.

Meanwhile he scratched out a few stories for *True Detective* and *Ellery Queen*, and managed to stay alive in a Brooklyn apartment where he waged war daily with cockroaches, ants, and writer's block. He completed the first ten thousand words of his new novel. Then he threw out the pages and wrote five thousand words 'so bad they held their noses at their own stench.'

He threw away page after page, day after day, until he ran out of ideas. Then he decided a great idea would come if he didn't try so hard. He wrote book reviews for a couple of months. He drank and smoked and soon realized he'd written nothing but reviews for a year and a half. Gradually, with a fading sense of purpose, he stopped talking about awards. Then he stopped talking about his novel. Then he stopped answering his agent's phone calls.

When Lee Todd finally admitted he couldn't write another novel, everything went to shit. He'd spent the book advance on cocaine and a piece of land in his home state of Washington. This last he planned on turning into a mud bog for modified-car races, a scheme his accountant Vince Devon insisted was 'a peerless investment.'

The land was over-priced. The only person who made a profit from the deal was the accountant. Vince Devon was last seen boarding a plane for the Cayman Islands.

Casual coke had become a habit though not an addiction, eating up the last of Lee Todd's savings. In one nightmarish weekend he realized he was broke, he was unemployed, and he would have to hang onto the property in Washington for years, just to see a return.

When Lee Todd's publisher canceled his book contract and demanded repayment of the advance, he was forced to give up his grubby apartment and his life in New York. Since his childhood dream had been to conquer the Big Apple as a famous author, this was pretty depressing. He moved back home to a state he despised and settled into a doublewide trailer with a pair of deer antlers over the door and clay wind chimes rattling in the carport. The day his bank account hit zero he called in a favor from a colleague, a writer whose books he had favorably reviewed back in the day.

"Can you teach?" the writer asked.

"Who *can't* teach?" Lee Todd answered.

"This is community college," said the writer. "It won't pay much."

"Great, I'll take it," said Lee Todd, knowing his only alternative at this point would be the night shift at 7-Eleven. Thus began what he hoped would be a temporary career, one that had lasted four years when I met him.

He recounted this fall from grace, from semi-fame to semi-academia, in the cadences of a world-weary private dick. He included unnecessarily grisly details, and promised an A if we didn't rat him out to the English Chairman for chain-smoking in class.

He also proposed a list of rules for crime fiction, and made us swear to honor them for all time. These idiosyncratic preferences, I assumed, were all he had left from his glory days. Adhering to the list of rules was a vow I took — not at all seriously — when I chose to be one of his acolytes. I agreed but I was lying, keeping my fingers crossed in my pocket, so to speak.

This was a long time ago. Certain moments I can recall as if they happened yesterday. Others, once crucial, have all but evaporated.

Lee Todd Butcher died in a hospital bed with pinholes dotting his liver and a face the color of pumpkin guts. But his words went on resounding in my head. He was the first person I ever met who said what he thought while he was thinking it.

"Here's the thing to remember, people. You're only, what, nineteen years old? What could you possibly know? Your brains aren't even formed yet. Your writing is crap. Okay? I don't care how clever your mom thinks it is. It's crap. Accept that now, today, before you leave this fucking classroom. Or you can all go to hell. Those are your options."

The 'Aurora Bridge' arches upward, a massive metallic monster in the gray-blue light of a crescent moon. Quick flashing beams of automobiles cut the pale night like blades.

You wear an expression of mild disappointment. I don't blame you. The view should be breathtaking but it isn't. There's nothing much to see from a passing car until it comes flying around the suspended curve approaching over the western shoulder of Queen Anne. By then the show is almost over. Like so many structures, the George Washington Bridge on Aurora was intended to be more impressive than all that had gone before, and ended up another source of irritation and misadventure. What to do about all the lonely-hearts and forgotten friends and neglected artists who flock there to die?

In my opinion the engineers who designed the bridge would have been brilliant with roller coasters. Every passing vehicle goes humming through the air like a giant insect on speed. Even sober a pedestrian could easily fall on the footpath on hands and knees, giddy and sick from the height and the speed of the cars whipping past.

If you fell, would you gain a minute to think? Would the postponement and further reflection change your mind?

Every day at 1 a.m., after wiping down your workstation in the kitchen, stacking the dish racks, and turning off the lights, you walk to the bus stop in a trance, exhausted. Luxuriating in fantasies of flying, soaring, sailing to the moon on gossamer wings. Turning your face toward the black voluminous clouds while the rest of the world goes silent.

No one notices when you board the bus for your work shift every afternoon. Even if you forget to pay for a ticket, no one questions it. No one notices you. The driver stares into the asphalt void. The other passengers sit hunched over and tired, making their way home at the hour when your night is only beginning.

In the bathroom in the cement block motel where you rent a room by the month, you are compulsive about leaving no traces. You wipe your fingerprints and stray hairs off the sink and shower as efficiently as you scrub grease off pots and pans all night long.

When you started at the restaurant you were told to wear elbow-length rubber gloves. You took them off one night and no one cared. Even with the gloves you feel blisters rising on your fingers. You don't care anymore.

You wonder how badly the fall will hurt and for how long but you've heard of people dying of shock during the fall itself. You wonder what shock feels like, what impact and catastrophe striking your body simultaneously will feel like. Will your numbness spare you, or will the hard slap of mortality bring you to life for an instant? If so, will you want to live? Your eyes continue to search the sky, although you say you've given up.

I tiptoe a little closer. Hanging from the metal rail, both hands overhead, lightly gripping the rail by my fingertips, I stare at you and lean forward. Menacing? Perhaps. Trying not to smile.

"What are you doing?" I ask.

Your face turns quickly away from the moon, away from the clouds, toward me. Your eyes open, flashing white in the light! You see me for less than a second before you let go and scream, less than a second before you plummet to the ground far below.

Chapter Three

My mother had a favorite saying I hated. I knew it was paraphrased from a Rolling Stones song of her youth. She pretended she'd made it up.

"We get the things we crave," she used to say with a smarmy grin, often in the direction of my dad and usually over TV trays bearing Microwave dinners, "not the things we think we want." This raggedy hippie wisdom was certainly apt in relation to Lee Todd Butcher.

"See, it doesn't matter where a writer comes from," he said one day in class. "What matters is being able to imagine the worst thing that can possibly happen, and then build a plausible story around it. The best gift a crime fiction writer can have is a diabolical mind, and that's not a product of experience. It just happens."

He was sitting on the corner of his desk with one leg hiked. This was a default position that reminded me of a broken-down dog leaning against a fence to pee. He seldom left his desk during class. He never paced; given his hacking cough, a stroll across the room might have worn him out. He never tried to democratize the seating arrangement by having us pull our chairs into a circle.

"Sitting in a circle is for cowboys and children," he said to the student who suggested it. "Do you want to study westerns, read Louis L'Amour and Zane Grey? Should we build a campfire? No? Then I'll sit up here and you sit out there where you can receive all of this fucking wisdom I'm offering."

He lectured on research, structure, devices and clichés, characters and motivation, story versus plot, pacing, complications, climax, resolution, and denouement. He also gave reading assignments. To his credit not all of them were his own books. Dashiell Hammett, Raymond Chandler, Cornell Woolrich, Charles Willeford, Chester Himes, John D. MacDonald, and Elmore Leonard were included. Absent from the list were most of Lee Todd's successful friends and rivals. And he never included women.

"They're, uh, sort of a different breed," he said. Then he moved to kill the subject. "Hey, if you want to read and write cozy mysteries set in a fanciful English village in the 1930s, have at it, kids! But that's not my thing. If the story doesn't have any grit to it, I lose interest after the first page. Know what I mean?"

One of the two other girls in class raised her hand.

"Yeah, uh, Pauline?" Lee Todd said.

"How about Mary Higgins Clark?" she asked.

The two girls were sitting next to one another. They exchanged glances. I noted this collusion peripherally.

"Like I said," Lee Todd explained. "Feel free to read what you enjoy, suburban domestic drama, women's lib novels from the 1960s, whatever turns your crank. Not in my class."

The last thing I wanted was to become a member of the Cozy Girl Club. From that day on, I paid no attention to the other girls.

Up to this point I hadn't given any thought to being a crime fiction *writer*. For me the class had been a way to buy and kill time. Staying busy at school kept my parents believing I was learning a trade during a period when I had no prospects and no way to support myself. At the same time I found it more entertaining than drinking beer all day, to study the myriad ways an author might contrive to slaughter human beings.

When I realized Lee Todd believed females weren't supposed to care about these things, I decided I cared about them. I plowed through the recommended reading list, and steered clear of female authors. It wasn't that I wanted the guy to like me. I wanted him to envy me. I wanted to break his code and then steal it.

I began to daydream about making a name for myself, earning a living doing what my teacher and negative inspiration could no longer do. I had a vague notion of rising in his estimation only to leave a few skid marks across his ego. Maybe my animosity sprang from latent attraction but I doubt it. Butcher was a guy whose best years were over. I was young enough and experienced enough to see him as fair game, a pelt to be tanned and worn as a souvenir.

Moving on from Lee Todd's list I read Jim Thompson and James M. Cain, finding the latter preoccupied with domestic drama, opera, and American aspirations. Thompson was a different matter. Gritty, amoral, and messed up in ways I'd never imagined. After every trip down one of those dusty, grim, nasty roads I felt like I needed a shower and a night alone.

"You reading that, Gloria, or just trying to look tough?" Lee Todd asked when he spotted my tattered copy of *Wild Town*.

We were the last people exiting the classroom on a Wednesday afternoon. For only the second time all semester I'd caught his full attention and I wasn't sure what to do with it.

"Greta," I said.

"Huh?"

He squinted at me like he thought I was speaking a language he didn't recognize. I was going to explain when his face split into a wide grin and he tapped me on the arm.

"Just playin' with ya, kiddo," he said. He turned quickly and was gone, sauntering away from me down the waxed floor of the fluorescent hall toward the parking lot.

Pike Place Market bustles and crackles in winter. Shoppers dressed in three layers of clothing sidestep one another and offer thin smiles of apology for taking up too much space.

You like the market best at night. Oily fragrance of Alaskan halibut and cod fading on the breeze, boardwalks creaking under your footfalls, you can't get enough of the slop-slop-slop of the tide against the pier. When you were a child you dreamed of growing up to be a fish, swimming deep, tempting the fisherman's net with your flashy scales. You woke up sad to be a child again.

Your mouth grew fishlike with the years, pulled down at the corners. When anyone asked why you were sad you answered, "I was born sad." Prompting ahs and ohs and sighs and cheer-up gifts. Your mother lavished presents upon your dear tiny self and held your hand and went on spoon-feeding you until you were seven. Your friends worried for your health. Your girlfriends worried for your state of mind. They were right to do so.

I track your descent from one ragged wooden ramp to another, and follow you outdoors. I know you must hear the echo of your journey, the shadow catching up to you on the icy boardwalk. Beside you the silhouettes of steamships climb, as gigantic as the whales of your slumbering mind.

You take one faltering step. You regard the endless cold of the deep, and the endless sorrows of the shore, and you consider your mother. Her eyes fringed with tears, her wishes ignored by everyone. On the pier you stand alone in a mist-shrouded stasis, almost unaware of a hand extending, taking your shoulder in a calm, decisive grip, turning you ever so firmly toward the gray blackness of the freezing, poisonous void, the dark-watered bay, the empty sky, and me.

Chapter Four

Lee Todd Butcher wasn't my first whatever-you-call-it. 'Boyfriend' sounds like one of those sitcoms set in the 1950s. 'Lover' is a word from a romance novel, and there wasn't much romance between us. 'A dude I screwed' speaks for itself, a crass tribute to something that doesn't deserve credit.

There had been Gordon, the drummer, whose cover band, Corrosion, I followed for two months in high school. Gordon was five years older than I was and he succeeded in 'cracking the seal' of my apparently super-resilient hymen on the floor of his van between gigs one Saturday night. I can never smell wet dog without remembering the moment, or the blood, or the grimace Gordon made while wiping the floor with a filthy beach towel.

Once the technicalities were out of the way, I was ready to practice my new skill. Unfortunately Gordon was one of those guys for whom sex means a tiny portion of what it actually means. I lost interest the second time he insisted on a rim job without taking a shower. Nose six inches from the crinkled flesh of his anus, noting how the raw pink alternated with brown flecks in the folds, I just said no. Later I commemorated the day with the word 'fuck-brain' scratched with a silver dollar on the back door of his van, a sort of warning sign for his future dates.

I got over Gordon by having sex with Jimbo, a computer science major with shoulder-length Jesus hair and a Five-Year Plan to marry a rich girl, 'even if she's fat and ugly,' so he could start his own business. I wasn't fat, I wasn't really ugly, and I definitely wasn't rich. But I knew what Jimbo liked and I was pretty sure the coddled princess he hoped to marry wasn't going to hit his ass with a wooden paddle and make him lick her toenails until he came in his Pac-Man boxer shorts. But who knows? I've been wrong plenty of times.

I got over Jimbo by having sex with Stephen, who was born in south London, a fact he shouted to every person who ever remarked on his accent. He was okay in bed, never asked me to play dress-up or anything, and didn't mind taking turns with the orgasms. But Stephen never stopped talking. Mostly about how superior everything British was, compared to everything American—education, housing, childcare, films, theater, conversation, history, geography. One time he got into an argument with a bank teller over the mandatory charges on a checking account.

"You don't understand what I'm asking," he explained at least five times to the harried teller. "Can you tell me *what* I'm paying for, in terms of added service? Because it seems to me you're making a profit from my money simply residing in your bank. Do you follow? I am, in effect, *lending* you my money and you make a profit from it in the marketplace and give me *nothing* in return except the use of *my* money. Then you want to *charge* me for it. Do you see what I'm saying? Do you understand what I'm saying?"

The teller sputtered between sentences. "Sir… Sir… Excuse me, sir…"

"You've charged me to print my cheques and in England the printing is *included*. Yours is an *inferior process*, in the States, do you see? *Do* you understand?"

Stephen's contempt for all things American made it surprising when he proposed marriage. But I figured he was angling for a green card. At nineteen this was a lot more than I could handle.

I knew a girl named Kiki who married a Dutch guy who kept her locked in the bedroom all day. She told me this over lunch at McDonald's. Her story of being dragged by the hair and slapped around was so detailed and intense, it was only later I wondered how she escaped long enough to eat a cheeseburger, and why she didn't have a mark on her.

"Why did you marry this guy?" I asked Kiki.

"Pieter," she said, contorting the vowels into sounds I couldn't reproduce.

She studied the view from the grimy window at McDonald's. Across the street a jeweler advertised wedding rings as a specialty 'for over sixty years.' Flanking the jeweler's were a pawnshop and a rundown furniture store. Both were consumed by mold and ivy.

"He's crazy about me, absolutely *insane with passion*," Kiki said. "I was afraid he might hurt himself if I didn't marry him."

I thought about this while Kiki finished her vanilla shake. She licked a drop of white cream from the corner of her lips and watched me with owlish eyes. Her thin, placid smile and pixie haircut were her best features. I wondered how much of what she called passion was nothing but a craving for drama.

"Don't be bloody *stupid*," said Stephen when I turned down his proposal. "You could have a *British passport*, you fucking cow. You could travel and see the world and *learn* something instead of dying of ignorance in the same town where you were born. What's *wrong* with you?"

Stephen wasn't the only guy who thought something was wrong with me. Most of the men I met had a list of things I ought to do, from taking better care of my hair and skin and nails, to learning how to cook what they liked, to giving them blowjobs while they watched their favorite movie for the twelfth time.

None of these so-called relationships worked. Not because the men were wrong and not because I was independent but because I didn't know what I wanted to do with the vast number of unclaimed years that stretched before me. I didn't know what or who I was, or how I wanted to wear my hair, or whether I wanted to cook or have children or travel. All I knew was that these questions were exhausting and I was tired of thinking about them.

This is when I met Lee Todd Butcher, a man who wanted nothing. He would be easy to land and easy to forget. Or so I thought.

His house was slightly cleaner than the back of Gordon the Rim Job's van. A squat, bulky trailer home, it stood on a patch of dry grass at the end of a quarter-mile-long dirt road. The wooden fence surrounding the property was useless, designed to contain cows back when the area was mostly farms and ranches. Only indigenous plants grew nearby and they were parched. Lee Todd didn't believe in wasting water if he had to pay for it. Whatever could thrive on rainfall could stay; the owner was content to let the rest expire and decorate the ground with shriveled amber stalks and tattered leaves. The land on all sides could have served as an atomic test site in a bygone era, a wasteland of dead grass, dying boxwood, and dust.

Inside, the trailer had a surprisingly high ceiling with a couple of crossbeams for decorative effect. An eclectic set of firearms lined the walls. An elk head stared from its place of honor above the living room sofa.

"Gilda, take your time, and figure out what you want," Lee Todd told me over a Budweiser. "You're, what, almost twenty? When I was your age I was trying to lose a finger to get out of the fucking Army. Seems like a century ago."

"God. How old are you?" I asked, feeling a spaghetti strap of my silk camisole as it fell from my shoulder. I pretended not to notice, knowing he noticed, seeing it register in the pale blue and gray flicker of his eyes. I wanted to lean back and gaze at the elk head from underneath but I didn't move.

"Never ask an old man how old he is," he said with a wink so immeasurably swift and light I wondered if I'd imagined it.

"Fifty?"

"Jesus."

"Sixty?"

"Fucking Christ!"

"Tell me and I'll stop guessing," I said.

The afternoon sun transported a cloud of dust motes to the center of the living room. The couch and lampshades were lemon yellow and spattered with something that might have been beer. I couldn't tell if this was their original color or if the sun had robbed them of a bolder hue.

"What do you want out of life, Greta?"

"So you do know my name," I said. I tried to lift one eyebrow in the cocky manner of a woman from one of the novels assigned in class.

Lee Todd barely suppressed a laugh. He took hold of my wrists and held them with such mild warmth I would have swooned if I'd known how. I slid closer, slipped one leg over his lap, and straddled him. We sat like this for a minute, the bright flint of his eyes meeting my stare with no hint of coyness.

When he kissed me, this too was different from the fumbling, pecking, and grunted negotiations I'd known with other guys. When he lifted me up and walked to the bedroom carrying me, still straddling his hips and holding him by the shoulders, he was almost the guy in the photo on his books.

Lee Todd never rushed anything. He let every lazy gesture arrive in its own time. Making love was unhurried and as natural as the sensual draws of a cigarette afterward. He lay naked, stretched out across the sheets, one hand behind his head, smoking, watching me.

"What are you studying besides hack writing?" he asked.

"Not much."

"This thing I teach, it's nothing, Greta. It's an appreciation class: How to recognize crime fiction when you see it."

"Are you urging me to drop out?"

"I'm urging you to take more classes."

"I'm leaving, going home to my parents who are less boring than you are tonight. Thanks."

"No. Thank you."

"No, thank you."

"No, thank you…"

This thing between us, whatever it was, went on for a few months. I spent hours driving out to his house in the middle of nowhere to drink cheap beer and make love. Class time was about Lee Todd's dead career and the rules of crime fiction. Our personal time was direct, simple, without rules and without plans.

I can't say how long we might have lasted if I'd quit the class — or if I'd never turned in the required short story for my final grade. Maybe he would have become bored and asked me to leave, or maybe I would have wandered away. We were doomed regardless but who knows when it would have ended, or under what circumstances. Here's how it actually ended.

A quarter of our class credit depended on the one and only story we had to turn in, a week before the semester ended. Lee Todd didn't believe in leading group critiques. The idea of handing out copies of a student's story to everyone in the class and having a discussion about it made him laugh and cough and laugh again.

"The blind leading the blind in a mud wrestling match," is how he described students analyzing one another's stories. "Writers are jerks, even amateur ones. Everybody wants to win. Everybody wants to be the best one, the prize pig. And none of you know what you're talking about. That's why a group critique gets vicious. It gets ugly. Feelings get hurt. People cry and call their parents and somebody gets fired—and it ain't gonna be me. Nope. You'll hand in your lousy amateur story to me, the only authority in the room. I'll meet with each of you privately, to give you the bad news about how terrible it is."

We all laughed. Because I guess each of us expected to be the exception to the rule, even me, with no experience other than basic composition and a few essays in high school. I thought I was smart enough to absorb all of the rules and examples and then crank out a convincing story.

I based my narrative on what I'd gleaned from the recommended reading, including Lee Todd's books. I followed his advice obsessively. I avoided as many clichés as I could recognize. I mined the stories of famous writers for clever plot twists and what I thought were sterling conventions and startling moments of truth. I revised and revised. I revised so much, even my parents noticed and began to think I was taking an interest in something.

"I always knew you'd end up being a writer," my mom said one day and shook her head as if to say, "Oh well."

I had no idea where she came up with that pronouncement. In time, her words would haunt me like a wicked refrain. I would hear them mocking me after I moved to Seattle, after I failed to get published, after Eve judged my words and found them inadequate. I would begin to wonder why I'd ever wanted to write fiction of any kind. Maybe I only wanted to prove I could do what my teacher did, better than he had done it.

"Greta, your appointment is at 11:15," Lee Todd said. He was calling off each student's name in class and setting his office hours for the next two days. I waited until we broke for the afternoon before approaching his desk.

"We could just talk about my story at your house," I told him and shrugged. The prospect of hearing my first critique should have sent ice water through my veins but it didn't. That's how ignorant and confident I was.

"I have office hours scheduled," Lee Todd said. "So we'll meet here."

"It's really okay," I said, still not getting it. "I don't mind." Here I attempted what I later knew to be a mortifying parody of adult casualness. "You're a pro, the setting won't matter." I winked.

His eyes held mine with a sharpness I hadn't seen before.

"No," he told me. "It does matter. This is about your grade. 11:15 and don't be late. The next person's slot is 11:45."

The pivot, the way he slouched away, told me not to follow. I figured he wanted to separate his personal and professional lives. I was vain enough to wonder if he had trouble concentrating when we were together at his house.

On the morning of my critique I wore the same silk camisole I'd worn to visit him at home the first time. I was imagining things might take a turn. He might cancel his critique of the other students for the day. The world was dancing in a vast cosmic circle around little me, with my faded jeans and spaghetti straps and messy hair.

I slumped in the chair before his office desk. He cleared his throat.

"Let's start with what I think are your strengths," he said. I nodded and settled in for an extensive speech. "You've got the basics down, nothing wrong with that. Your grammar, syntax, your grasp of literary conventions: not a problem."

"Well, *that's* good," I said lightheartedly. I smiled and he didn't.

"The thing about fiction," he said. "And I don't care what genre we're talking, whether it's mainstream, or sci-fi, or *porn*, to be convincing you've got to feel the urge to write it, right down in your gut."

"Uh-huh," I said. I lowered my chin. I was wearing a sly grin and probably seemed drunk.

"You have to know with every fucking fiber of your being that this is who you are and what you have to do. Otherwise, it's nothing but an exercise." He folded his hands on the desk between us.

"Okay," I said. "But isn't this an exercise? An assignment, to learn to write crime fiction?"

He sighed. He seemed to consider his words before answering.

"No, not entirely," he said. "It's an assignment to see how much you've understood about the subject, sure, and as far as that goes you deserve an A. You comprehend what I've been saying all semester, and nobody in the class puts more effort into it. You've read the equivalent of a master's program in crime fiction, Greta."

The inkling began at the base of my spine. A squiggle, a nerve-spasm, an awareness of bad news riding in from some place far away, heading right for me with a mallet in its hand.

"It's no tragedy, not being able to write fiction. Most of the people in this class can't write a story to save their lives. My aim is to demonstrate the difficulty, you see, to make students appreciate what real writers do."

"Why?" I asked.

"To create a demand, an appreciation, for the kind of book I like. But you're smarter than most of these other students, Greta. You might not have the soul to create fiction, but I think you could become a first class book reviewer someday, if you keep going." He said this in a tone of kindness rather than the admiration I craved.

At this point some people would have said thanks and left the office. Other people would have flung a book at his head. Here's what I did. I stared him in the eye and asked, with as little emotion as possible, "What the living fuck are you talking about?"

"I'm offering you an honest response, given all of my experience and expertise..."

"You're a book reviewer. And a *teacher,"* I said, trying to make it sound insulting.

"If you want more extensive notes, although I don't think they'll help…"

"Like what?"

His shoulders drooped. He licked his dry lips.

"Okay," he said. He picked up my story gingerly as though having to consider it for another minute might kill him. And I think, in some sense, maybe it did. "Okay. You've introduced sixteen named characters in twenty-two pages. The narrative can't contain all of these people. Even if it could, the premise doesn't justify it. The reader's going to need a *chart* to keep track of everybody coming and going, it's like a soap opera…"

"So I have to cut some characters. Big deal."

He sighed heavily.

"Cutting deadwood won't fix the problem in this case. Setting aside the extraneous characters, there's no central, driving force to your story. The pace isn't slack; it's non-existent. You've employed a mish-mash of styles and devices, and they don't work together. Maybe all of this could be pulled together into a commentary, or— you know, as much as I hate that kind of thing—a meta-story, if there were enough weight to it. But what you've written just doesn't have the intellectual heft. Now, if it were attempted by one of the top guys in class…"

"Top guys?"

"Brendan or Bret or that other guy, the one with the hair standing on end…?"

"It's a Mohawk and his name is Bert. Brendan, Bret, and Bert are your top guys? The Three B's?"

"Three what?" he asked.

"We call them the Three B's and they sit up front so they can suck up to you. Do you really think those future frats want to write *crime fiction*? They want a good grade, you asshole."

"There's no reason to get hot under the collar," he said.

"To borrow a cliché."

"Nothing I tell you today is going to turn you into a writer," he said. "I can only tell you what I see, based on my experience. I can't work magic."

"Go ahead, take out your frustration on me," I said. My voice began to crack. "You know what? Nothing is going to rejuvenate your talent. Or give you an idea for a novel. No matter how many times you fuck your students!"

This made him snap, ever so gently—silently yet surely. I'd done it. I'd blown up and now he could write me off as a girl. More maddening, he seemed relieved. He *was* relieved. I was a problem. He wanted me gone.

I grabbed my backpack from the floor and slung it over my shoulder. I'd never expected a high grade based on sex, or so I told myself. I had believed my talent would shine through and impress the hell out of him. Now I knew this would never happen. I knew I wasn't his best student, or even one of his 'top guys,' I was just an average girl he'd fucked for the second half of one semester.

"Greta," he began. "We can't all do what we'd like to do."

"Gretel. You might as well call me Gretel," I said before I shoved the office door open and walked out of his world.

Oddfellows Hall on 10th Ave between Pine and Pike on a cold December evening, ice puddles cracking underfoot. To the west, on Broadway, laughter and the jingle of sleigh bells on shop doors.

The stairwells in this labyrinthine building have long fascinated me. Each one is wide with blocky wooden banisters. Each seems a little off the mark. With so much square footage and so many wings—rehearsal rooms, artist studios, and performance spaces—it makes sense, a certain uneven amount of settling. But there's more to this, a mysterious desire on the part of the stairs to keep going infinitely into an unseen level, a floor between floors, a corridor between walls.

How long have *you* been sitting on the middle step, clasping yourself with both arms, feeling the reverberation of the stairs as each gallery visitor and theatergoer ascends? Deeper into the chambers above a piano thumps and an unseen musician strokes the keys. You're here to see a new dance performance but you left your friends and walked out. If they ask later you'll say you have a migraine. Masking rage with illness is your specialty. If you could murder the slender girls on stage, mar the skin glowing from exertion and joy, and escape without punishment, you would do it. Your heart is lean and cruel and hidden.

Your first recital was attended by a famous choreographer who praised your wit and admired the willowy strength of your body in motion; words you accepted as your due, swept aside with a nimble step and a shake of the head. Years later, you marvel at how often the scene has repeated in memory. Your shoulders and knees were trembling when you turned your gaze from that of your idol. You fear the repetition of the cherished moment means you've grown old and pathetic. Nothing significant has followed for decades. Slim little accolades of the past have gone threadbare like souvenir programs handled too many times. Your friends urge you to teach; the thought of it is killing you.

Your fingers and ankles ache. Your right knee is in searing pain. Your spine requires constant adjustment. Simply sitting on a flat surface is agony. You are in agony, aren't you? Waiting on the stairs while half a dozen acts of youthful creation fill the rooms above and around you.

Good. Good.

It would be selfish of me, otherwise, to take your chin in my hand, as I do, and force your gaze down to the mottled back of your hand. It would be unkind to whisper in your ear, as I do, a suggestion for you to follow later, at home, alone.

You envision the straight-backed chair and white silk rope. They conjure a deadly Butoh performance you witnessed in Pioneer Square, the plummeting dancer colliding with brick and earth, followed by the screams of onlookers. You tilted your head back and your eyes followed the hypnotic descent of a coil of white rope cast loose.

You review the recent, broken years, your body no longer able to describe the nature of youth and longing. You've considered your options and embraced the most poetic.

I don't have to plant an idea, only its possible execution. I only confirm what you already know—no one will miss you. And then I must move on. It's been a brief collaboration but a satisfying one.

Chapter Five

I moved to Seattle in 1991. In keeping with most of my brief life, it was an act of spite.

After I climbed into the aforementioned rank-smelling Gremlin I inherited from my mom's brother, I zoomed away from my last meeting with Lee Todd Butcher. I imagined him chasing me to the parking lot, calling out as the Gremlin spit gravel at his feet, but he never appeared in the rearview mirror. I drove eighty mph in a residential zone, ran a red light, swerved into a McDonald's drive-thru line, bought three milkshakes, drank them, and threw up on some shrubbery in the parking lot.

When I got home I shredded and burned the story I'd written for Lee Todd's class. I donated to Goodwill the crime novels I'd collected. In the subsequent days of misery and boredom, I dropped out of community college and applied for a job at a photocopy center. I wasn't qualified for anything; Copy-Z paid employees from the first day of training; I put on a nametag and went to work.

The job turned out to be limbo except with no chance at redemption. A fluorescent buzz filled the shop, 800 square feet lined with 50-sorter-bin copiers running 24 hours a day, 7 days a week. My starting pay was $4.25 an hour, 32 hours a week (no medical, dental, vacation, or retirement). My boss was named Mary Patty. I never knew if that was her first and middle name or first and last. I didn't care.

Mary Patty wore a neck brace on the days when she was having her period. A co-worker and I figured out the synchronicity by comparing notes on Mary Patty's tampon disposal habits. She was thirty-two, skinny enough to be anorexic, and obsessed with her fiancé, a snide creep named Trevor who wasn't above borrowing money from Mary Patty in front of staff. Trevor had roaming fingers and everybody hated him. He had an undertone too, a thin layer of witch hazel and oil.

The first weeks at Copy-Z were tolerable because I was busy. I learned to run the big machines, standard easy stuff like clearing paper jams, flipping stacks of paper back and forth accordion-style to allow air between the sheets before loading, checking and adding dry toner which was as fine and black as soot. Then I moved on to a few light maintenance maneuvers like replacing filters and readjusting the photoreceptor belt.

After all of these lessons were learned, and as boredom came silently creeping back into my bones, I made a point of memorizing the individual quirks of every machine in the shop. Tiny tricks to keep a job running without placing a service call; stacking books on the midsection to keep the top door snug and prevent the paper backing up, or standing next to the sorter bins to reach in, snatch the first page of the first set and straighten it as it dropped.

At the end of every shift I took a bathroom break. When I blew my nose, the snot came out with black streaks from all the toner in the air. I read in some magazine that the toner was carcinogenic and we should wear a mask at all times but nobody did. Three or four months in, I didn't notice it any more. The pitch cloud was like the dark ivy crawling up the walls outside. After a while it seemed natural.

I told my parents I was saving money to rent my own place. They repeated the news to their friends. Eight months later I was still living at home, rising at seven a.m. and slugging down enough coffee to carry me until break time, eating lunch (usually a donut and more coffee) with people from work, then driving home and crashing facedown in bed. Wearing the same clothes for two or three days because nobody told me not to.

When people say their job is a grind, most of them have no idea what it's like to be the handmaiden to a machine cranking out the exact same thing, hour after hour, day after day. They mean they're bored or they hope to move on to a more challenging or interesting position, in time. The only chance for advancement at Copy-Z was to become an assistant manager at $5.00 an hour and fill in for Mary Patty when she went on vacation. This was a fate to be avoided at any cost, in my estimation. In the short time I earned a non-living at Copy-Z, we had four assistant managers.

Ronan was an obsequious rat. He often followed Mary Patty to the threshold of the women's toilet to remind her he was 'at her disposal,' like a tampon. She fired him and he actually cried. Tears ran down his face and he drooled and whimpered. He was like a character in a movie whose dog has been killed in front of him. Everyone in the shop had to accompany Ronan to his car and sort of tuck him in and fasten his seat belt. After we walked away he sat there alone, weeping, with his forehead against the steering wheel.

Xavier never answered photocopy questions without also mentioning his work as a serious painter. He was kicked out for making posters and chapbooks without paying.

Polly was a glazier who wore Japanese silk robes draped over her 4' 9" frame. Polly brought her cats to work and baked Mary Patty a pan of vegan zucchini brownies with tufts of fur clinging to the corners.

Harmon was a speed freak. He popped black beauties, white crosses, whatever was available in quantity. He could operate six machines full-time, over half a million copies on one shift. He was given a raise and offered management training.

The only perk to my job was being able to call out, "Break!" any time we needed a smoke or a coffee or a walk in the alley to breathe—not fresh air but different air, full of auto exhaust instead of dry toner.

The day Lee Todd Butcher strolled into the shop I yelled, "Break!" Then I headed right out the back door.

As I was rounding the corner of the building I saw him standing on the sidewalk waiting for me. This time I wasn't going to run. I stomped over in my chubby Doc Martens and said, "You look like shit."

He really did. His face was waxy with a faint yellow tint. His jeans and jacket hung like a display on a clothing rack.

"You look good," he said. "Are you taking care of yourself?"

"Who cares?" I asked. I felt childish and banal, exactly the way I'd felt the day I stormed out of his office.

"Listen, Greta," he said. "It's important to me to know you're okay."

This was a statement my dad would have called 'rich.' Suddenly I was more pissed off than I had been in months.

"Thanks so much, teacher," I told him.

"I'm not joking," he said. "I hate to see you squandering your life in a place like this." He jerked a thumb over his shoulder in the direction of the copy shop.

I took a step toward him and put my hands on my hips. I'd never been more aware of the difference in our ages. He was as insubstantial as a scarecrow. I could have knocked him down with one punch.

"This is nothing," I said. "I'm saving money to leave this dump."

He let up on the scowl. "That's good," he said. "Where will you go?"

"Any place I want," I told him. "New York, Chicago…"

"No, come on," he said. "Don't go dive into some monster city where you'll get swallowed up like all the other girls your age…"

"And maybe get fucked over by a famous writer?"

"You know that's not what happened," he said.

"Because you're not famous," I said.

"No one took advantage," he said. "If anything, it was the other way around."

"What?" I exploded. I punched his shoulder and he winced. "Why the fuck are you here?"

"I'm not here to start anything," he said. "I happened to see you the other day, working in this place, and I wanted to make sure you were all right."

"Great, thanks!" I shouted. I wanted to hit him in the face. I really felt the urge. "Great! Don't come back because I won't be here. I've saved enough money. Screw it. I'm moving away."

"Where?"

"Seattle." It popped into my head and the word popped out of my mouth.

"Seattle?" His smile was weird and crooked.

"Is your hearing going now?" I asked. "Seattle. It's on the coast, about 300 miles west of here."

"There's nothing there but junkies and shitty music," he said. "And serial killers."

"Exactly! I'm thinking about taking the Ted Bundy Tour. Sounds like fun!" In fact, the day before, I'd spoken with a co-worker about morbid, unofficial attractions offered by the soggy city. We joked about renting a yellow Volkswagen and trekking from one body dumpsite to another. Then we laughed at the idea, at all of our ideas, the shapelessness of our destination, and the sheer nastiness of how we felt. We made photocopies for a living, so our attitude was 'Fuck it all.'

"Don't move to Seattle," Lee Todd said. "I was there on a book tour once. There's nothing to do. Half the news stories are about sea lions. It's like Disneyland. People go there to commit suicide..."

"What I do is none of your business," I said.

"Greta, you should go to college."

"Maybe I will," I told him. I turned away and headed back to work—to finish my shift and hand in my notice. "Maybe I'll go for a degree in forensic science. Or how about this? I'll turn the story you hated so much into a novel and sell it. Or maybe I'll hook up with a dirty, old writing teacher, okay, even better than a serial killer, a has-been in sweat pants!"

"Greta!" he called from somewhere behind me, a voice fading into the past. "Greta!"

"Fuck off!" I yelled without looking back.

What a long, miserable bus ride across Washington State. Long stretches of emptiness except for railroad tracks and freeway signs. Ranches with paint peeling off the barns and houses, apple orchards, a few scattered towns where boarded up hotels stared out, ruined and vacant. The nauseating combination of gasoline fumes and the egg salad sandwich eaten by a grizzled hag next to me, the chattering tourists, the hiss and sigh of pistons.

Coming into view at last, the city was a series of muddy streaks, blue ones and gray ones, Elliott Bay providing a cold backdrop to a handful of skyscrapers and a cluster of historical buildings. Old and new sat on top of one another in no particular order. The rat-tat-tat of jackhammers provided a cruel rhythm.

Outlying in all directions were brick three- and four-story apartments. The morning air buffeted seagulls and pigeons. Sleepy artists with day jobs and hung-over receptionists, crazed bicycle couriers and shabby law interns crowded the downtown corridor, all slurping coffee and wandering through their workday, when I arrived by Greyhound.

The flutter in my chest didn't stop with the tired grunt of farewell from the bus driver. I figured he must have delivered a couple of generations of young women like me. Gazing up and down, taking in the homeless men and seedy street musicians, I had no doubt I'd made a terrible mistake. After all the hype, the place was a dump. It was every bit as gray as my hometown, only bigger and more disappointing.

What was I thinking? Thousands had come before me and thousands had been wrong about their destiny. Writers, singers, painters, dancers must have come here every year to try to leave a footprint on this town's ass. They probably ended up working at the Dog House Bar and Grill, or the Elephant Car Wash with its revolving pink sign. What the hell made me any different?

I would have driven to Seattle but the Gremlin was already in need of repair and I knew I'd have to count every penny to live on. So I'd sold the car for parts, trusting my dad's assurance that everything in the metro area would be accessible by bus.

As a measure of how secretly and mysteriously precarious my life had been up to this point, a month after I moved my parents split up. I wasn't one of those girls who pined for the long-lost days of golden childhood when mummy and daddy held hands and sang songs to each other in a meadow filled with butterflies, but it would have been reassuring to have a place to return to, if things didn't turn out well.

I don't know if my parents ever loved each other. At best I'd say they got along because they liked the same food and music and they were frugal. They didn't argue much. Nor did they seem happy. They cooperated in the daily business of working, eating, sleeping. They shared duties. They weathered the long, deadening days required to raise a child. And once that child was finally thrust out into the larger world, their work together was done. My absence set them free.

My father took a job transfer and moved to Michigan, which sounded so far away it occurred to me, briefly, I might never see him again. My mom sold the house in the suburbs and moved to a one-bedroom apartment she said she liked much better because it was easy to clean.

Is there any more efficient way to prevent a child returning home than to relocate to a place with no guest room? Our simultaneous departures made me laugh. I realized with a chill that none of us had ever liked the suburbs.

So this was it, my new adventure—a hint of drizzle in the air; a few sunken-faced teenagers with lumberjack shirts slung around their waists like kilts over ass-revealing, ruined jeans; the crackling odor of street food; tattoo artists smoking cigars on the pavement in front of their shops; the transvestite Sisters of Perpetual Indulgence striding uphill, nearly seven feet tall in their boots, arms linked, wimples tart, veils and habits billowing in swan-like black waves behind them; teenage boys in undershirts kissing in alcoves; teeming newsstands; band posters peeling off telephone poles and kiosks; "Monkey Gone to Heaven" bellowing from the open window of a second floor apartment rife with philodendron vines and curls of black ivy.

This was not my parents' hippie, New Age 'vibe' shit and it wasn't Lee Todd's 1980s delusion of coke-driven mega-success. I was here and it made a stupid kind of sense because nothing made sense and nothing had to make sense and there was no pretense about it anymore. The rundown, burnt-out former lumber town fit my state of mind perfectly.

"Fucking hell," I said out loud on that first day, and began to drag my suitcase up the sharp incline of Denny Way, across the freeway overpass, toward Capitol Hill.

There's a rough, peeling pine bench near the entrance outside Woodland Park Zoo. From the parking lot the cries of caged animals with no visual reference carry a note of despair. They often call me to this spot.

Given a chance *you* would blossom, wouldn't you? From a nefarious creature skulking behind a row of lockers in the bathroom and hobbling home to masturbate on your futon, you would grow and spread your limbs and become a full-blown rapist. Deny all you like. Throughout your childhood your sweaty joy was leafing through library books of classical art. Your pudgy fingers soiled the corners of those glossy, oversized tomes.

What do you love? What do you seek? Impassioned scenes of sexual frenzy, especially those ivory-skinned nymphs rutted by earthy satyrs; the soldiers of Odysseus enslaving the women of Troy; Leda subjugated, half conscious, enraptured, penetrated by Zeus—absolved in your eyes by his fine cloak of feathers. Whatever is hidden is made magical in your mind. It becomes inhuman and therefore natural and allowed.

There's nothing magical about you, a seventeen-year-old boy who can't keep his hands out of his trousers. Wherever you turn, you find fragrant, nubile pubescence 'pretending' not to notice or want you. The pounding hooves of the centaur on the forest floor, hands spreading the robes of your conquest and prying open her thighs, while a dull genderless teacher of no consequence drones about civil liberties and the Constitution, you imagine all of the American Revolution as a band of men on horseback chasing busty maidens across fields of gold.

Your lewdness is transformed into love, in that fervent attic of a mind. In there, your chubby face takes on the weathered contours of a handsome man. Your weekend job soliciting magazine subscribers by telephone gives you a daily glimpse into the auditory world of women you imagine hurling to the floor and fucking senseless.

Oh, you virile ravager of bitches! Here you go, lumbering across the parking lot with your booty, your camera full of the tiny hands and faces of precocious children.

It's a quick, bright, satanic joy to track you, to watch you huff and puff as you approach the bus stop, to lurch forward and catch your ankle as you run to board the afternoon bus. So eager to get home and pet your dick with all the images you've stored up today.

Your pear-shaped body tumbles end over end, somersaulting into the street, landing with a loud plop in front of the tires a split second before they roll forward, printing the lower half of your buttocks with a zigzag tattoo. Poor you.

Chapter Six

"Nobody likes a dead narrator these days. Not in books, and not in movies. If you think you can do better than *Sunset Boulevard*, you're wrong. Besides, readers won't care what happens to your protagonist after he dies. They only want to know how he's going to get out of a bad situation, not what he does with his spare time in the fucking afterlife. Which doesn't exist." – Lee Todd Butcher, RIP

How did I get from my bitchy first ascent toward the concrete mecca of Capitol Hill, to the scene of my demise on the floor of my shitty apartment? The way we all travel from mild yearning to keen desperation, from frail, unspoken hope to cynicism—one lousy step at a time.

Relocating was an act of defiance but I was never sure what or whom I was defying. If I'd had the kind of ambition Lee Todd respected I would have designed a better plan. I would have moved to New York or Chicago, cities with credentials. Unfortunately those places presented a challenge I wasn't equipped to face. They were too expensive, too sophisticated, too crowded, and too grownup. Despite what I told Lee Todd, in the end I chose Seattle for the same reason I chose community college; it was cheap and it was nearby, relatively speaking.

"You won't get a good job," my father told me the day he dropped me off at the bus station on the fringes of my hometown. "Not without a degree."

"Thanks, Dad," I replied. "I appreciate the encouragement."

"Maybe you should apply to the University of Washington," he said without much conviction.

"Mary Patty said her niece couldn't get in, and she graduated number one in her high school class. They have a waiting list. Also, I can't afford the tuition."

"Well," he said. "You're taking the hard road. As usual."

Months later my dad's words came back to me as I sat on the sofa in my apartment—my first and, as it turned out, my only apartment—dressed in flannel pajamas, my face lined with sleep and boredom. This was the unofficial uniform for my first job in Seattle.

For the impressive sum of $5.25 an hour I had finagled a temporary position with a sex chat line. By 'finagled' I mean I asked a woman for a job and she said yes while we were both drunk at a party.

The owner ran the business as a franchise out of California, where it was legal. In Seattle the courts had yet to decide whether or not a local manager could hire women to talk dirty to lonely men on the phone. While the managers waited for a final ruling they were allowed to maintain the business, so long as it didn't involve sex.

There was only one glitch to this plan. Before being reduced to friendly conversation the service had openly catered to men seeking pleasure. With the same company name, same phone book logo of a sexy silhouette, and same phone number in effect, you can't blame the guys who just didn't get it.

"What I want to do is get behind you…"

"Roy?"

"So you can feel how hard I am…"

"Roy?"

"Huh?"

"Roy, we can talk about your day at work, if you like."

Pause. I could hear dead air on the line.

"Roy?"

"Yeah, uh, Sean?"

Yes. My chat name was Sean.

"Yeah?"

"Uh, Sean, can you just keep talking? I mean, can you explain this to me again? Just talk."

Yes, I could. Explaining the temporary change of service was 99% of my job.

"We can chat about anything you like as long as we stick to friendly subjects rather than intimate ones," I said. Besides flannel pajamas I wore a headset with cushy ear pads, a food-stained robe and fuzzy animal slippers. My hands were busy drying dishes and trying not to make splashing noises that might give me away.

"Right, oh man," said Roy (maybe his name and maybe not). "Could you remind me what's, uh, intimate?"

"Touching," I said.

"Right..."

"Touching yourself."

"Right..."

"Describing sensations of a sexual nature."

"Oh, right..."

"Roy?"

"Oh baby..."

"Roy? You're going to need to stop now."

"Yeah, I just need a second..."

"Listen, if you keep doing what you're doing..." I tried but it was always a pretty tricky thing to tell a man in the throes of chat that his pleasure was going to get me fired from my job.

About this time I could hear the telltale silence—strange but it's true, in the blank depth of the telephone line it was just barely possible to distinguish between real emptiness and the silence indicating a manager had tuned in to eavesdrop and evaluate. This was their idea of quality control.

"Roy?" I said.

"Oh yeah! Oh yeah!"

"Sean?" Kitty's voice piped up.

"Oh, Jesus, have mercy!" Roy went on.

"Sean, I have to interrupt this call," said Kitty.

The silence that followed cut me off from Roy's finishing moment. I knew there would be a reprimand phone call from Kitty in a minute, and a warning, and I was right.

"Look, Greta, I'm helping you out here. I hired you even though you have no experience in the industry."

"I know," I said. "I appreciate it, Kitty."

"Well, you don't act like it. If the police catch one call on tape, I'm screwed."

"I get it."

"The whole business is screwed."

"I get it."

"If you can't steer the guys into neutral territory, and keep them there, I'll have to let you go."

"I know. It's just really tough to know for sure. I mean, they could be masturbating the whole time and I wouldn't know it," I said. Which we both knew was sort of true and sort of a lie, like everything else about the job.

"You're the one in charge," Kitty said. This was another one of those true-and-not-true things. "Ask questions to lure them into an ordinary conversation."

"Right," I said.

"What?" Kitty wheezed and I heard her take a puff of her inhaler followed by a puff of a Marlboro.

"Nothing."

"What do you want to ask me?"

"Kitty, they just don't have a good reason to pay by the minute to hear me talk about movies and food. You know?"

Blank silence would always follow my inane confessions. Ten seconds of deep, blank silence.

"Greta, you're a good kid," she said. "But this is a real profession. I take it seriously. I'm making a living but I'm also offering an important social service."

I'd heard this speech before. Kitty had spent her adult life stripping, pole dancing, managing strip clubs, and talking lonely men through sex. She believed she was bringing contentment to men without understanding partners, men who would only do harm if left unattended in a cold, mean world.

"In a few months, any day now, the court will rule in our favor and we'll open the lines up to full service again. When this happens there will be girls I keep, based on how much of our clientele they've helped to maintain. The girls I keep will get a pay increase and a bonus for sticking with us. The girls who can't handle simple conversation, who can't give these guys what they need without being obvious about it, are the ones I'll have to let go. Do you hear what I'm saying?"

"Yes," I said.

"Do you?" she asked.

"Yes," I said because I understood. There were more experienced women, like Kitty and her best operator, Nina, who could get a man off while describing a trip to the aquarium. They did it so smoothly no one could accuse them of even trying. Their regulars knew what to expect. These guys kept their actions quiet and returned for 'chat' several times a week.

"The sea jellies are translucent and shaped like soft, bulbous bells... Oh, the moon jellies have such long, long tentacles..."

I was doomed. Most of my guys never called a second time and none of them could touch themselves without shrieking. I could see my future career in phone sex dying before it started, thanks to something both Kitty and I knew without admitting it. I might have been able to learn the clumsy art of jacking men off long distance by talking dirty but I was shit on a stick when it came to ordinary conversation.

The worst parts of the day were the extended periods when no one called. As an operator I was required to remain available throughout the shift to be sure I didn't miss any clients. But a caller wasn't announced and forwarded. Rather, he wandered into the void and we had to lure him and persuade him to remain, by talking. This was how he knew for sure someone was there. He could check by calling out but most guys wouldn't do this; presumably it made them feel awkward in what was already an awkward situation. They usually dialed up, heard the silence followed immediately by a friendly voice, answered that voice and let it bring them home. This was why we were told to keep talking even if no one replied. Which sounds easy until you try it for a four-hour shift.

"What a beautiful night," I might say, for example. And when no one answered, I'd go on. "Nice breeze outside. I think I'll open a window and put on some music." Still nothing. "Who likes the Pixies?" Silence. "Well, I sure do!" Dead silence.

This went on for six weeks. For the last three days of my employment no clients would talk to me. If a repeat client checked in looking for Nina or Kitty or another competent gal, and found me on the line, he would hang up. Finally Kitty called to say her husband Fred was on his way to my apartment to pick up the headset and hand over my last paycheck. Thus ended my career as a professional phone friend.

The dregs of summer have ruined the yards up and down this street in Lake City. Here's a two-bedroom house, the lawn strewn with junk—a punctured inflatable pool; two T-shirts ripped off the back clothesline and torn to ribbons by a neighbor's dog; a rake; a few CD covers; and a sofa with its stuffing spilling out the back.

You remind me of someone. Family resemblance to an endangered owl, I think. Not only the girth, although you've got it, and not the patchy whiskers dangling in loose strands decorated with bread crumbs and bits of boiled egg. Whom do you resemble? Someone I used to work with? Maybe.

You're disgruntled. No matter where you go these days, you find stray evidence of Californians and New Yorkers sneaking in. Prices are edging up, not much right now but pretty soon everything will skyrocket, and you know who's to blame. There's proof in the doubling of traffic on your once-dead street, and proof in the new coats of paint on old houses.

This neighborhood used to be a paradise, you say. This was a street where dogs howled at night and rattled the chain-link fences with their paws, where the doublewide trailer homes of people you knew were robin's egg blue or pale salmon, old paint flaking onto the ground. Every third or fourth lawn, crowded with yellow weeds, featured a half-gutted sofa. Your sofa remains, defiant, and you like to sit here, ruminating in the twilight.

I find you sitting on the collapsed end with a can of Rainier beer in one hand and a garden hose in the other. Every time you take a swig you put your thumb over the hose and spray another batch of dandelions.

Overhead the clouds break; rain begins to spatter the street; there are no sidewalks to speak of. You go on spraying and drinking, spraying and drinking, and grumbling to the chubby neighbor seated next to you, another Seattleite since birth. Two sons of the city, claiming territorial rights for five generations of lumberjacks and carpenters.

"I don't mind the junkies living in a halfway house together. I don't mind what they do in their own house. What I mind is the county trying to build that house right across the street from mine."

"Uh-huh," your neighbor replies. "We should've gone to the town meeting, Hawley. Put in our two cents and said 'hell no' to a junkie house."

"I wrote two letters!" You take a slug of beer and shift your weight to pass a quiet shaft of gas. "I wrote three letters to the mayor's office. He's as crooked as the day he was born."

"Then you've also got your Isle of Lesbos over there," says your neighbor. He points diagonally to the next house over.

"Well, I don't mind them playing their music as *loud* as they want. The trouble is, we're not talking about Gruntruck or Tad…"

"Aw, jeez, you and Steve were way better than those guys, any hour of the week."

"Yeah," you say. "I don't know. We were all right."

"You should've played the Gorge that time…"

"Fuck you, Jim," you say. "I wasn't going to play just for the privilege of playing! Goddamn promoters. They paid Soundgarden, why couldn't they pay us? Like we ought to be happy for the fucking honor of opening for Eddie Vedder!"

"You and Steve're better than Pearl Jam any goddamn day."

"Fuck yeah," you say. "We played the Comet before those losers ever picked up a guitar!"

"Changed their name from Mookie Blaylock to Pearl Jam because Epic said so."

"Sell-outs."

"Sell-outs. I bet the gals across the road don't even know Green River," your neighbor says, changing the subject and nodding toward the 'Isle of Lesbos.'

"Nope. Nope. Nope. They play that luscious stuff, that girly C-note music all day, and I'm about to swing a hammer right through that fucking porcelain Buddha in their yard…"

"You should do that. You should do it. I'd pay a dollar to see that."

"You know what?" you say.

"What?"

"I think I've got a bottle rocket left in the house from last New Year's."

"No! Oh, man! Oh, boy! That would be, that would be..."

"Yeah. Let me get that sucker out here and we'll watch Mr. Buddha do a little dance!"

"Oh shit, man! Do it! Do it!"

You drop the garden hose and it goes on dribbling. The rain has stopped. You don't notice.

You tiptoe for no reason other than excitement, then shamble indoors and rummage through the hall closet, returning five minutes later with the rocket. You set it up right there on the grass, aim it at the yard across the street, and set it off with a chuckle. Your neighbor chuckles too. He's holding the hose now. In his excitement he throws his hands up in the air. A splash from the hose knocks the rocket off course and sends it whizzing toward your couch, where it plunges between the cushions and catches fire.

You might be okay if you don't try to dig the rocket out with your bare hands... But you do.

You burn a thumb to the bone, scorch the cornea of both eyes, and set your pants on fire tossing the rocket from hand to hand while doing a mincing dance step that prompts your neighbor to fall on the ground clutching his gut, laughing. It's a dance he'll forever remember and refer to as 'Buddha Fucked Up.'

Chapter Seven

I leaned against the work counter on the service side, my awful hair yanked into a crooked topknot, my sweat- and food-stained T-shirt stenciled with one tiny word, dead center—'no.'

"May I see the goldenrod again?" the potato-shaped man asked for the fourth time. And when I say potato-shaped I mean every part of him—his torso, his head, his limbs—all could have grown out of the ground, cultivated by a farmer with blue-ribbon ambitions.

Instead of answering, I reached under the counter for the color sample catalog and slapped it down in front of him. The violence of the movement didn't faze the guy. He gathered the samples and cradled them in his hands, his blackened fingernails wandering their surface as if they held a secret he needed to decipher blindly.

"Um…"

"Yeah?"

"Um," he murmured again. "This is goldenrod?"

"Yes," I said. Pointing a badly manicured finger at every sample as I spoke. "This is goldenrod. This is canary. This is saffron."

"I see. Hm."

Beyond the glass storefront night had fallen. I hadn't noticed. The shoppers, homeless, velvet-caped vampires, and teenagers on Broadway drifted by. I liked to think of the window as an aquarium glass. Mollies and betas and goldfish stuck in a common bowl by mistake. The hour meant nothing to me. The Capitol Hill Copy-Z was open 24 hours a day and I was on the evening shift.

My life had come full circle. The outer setting had changed but it made no difference. For all intents and purposes I might as well have been minding the counter at my first job in my hometown.

"Wait," said the lumpy potato man. His features quivered in all directions and finally settled on a smile. His hair was golden-brown. "What is this one called?"

I didn't have to look.

"That one is beige," I said.

"Is it?"

"Yes. Beige."

"This is beige," he said. "It looks yellow." He raised his eyebrows as if this might urge me to change my mind.

"Maybe it seems yellow but it isn't."

"Well," he said, and began to turn the pages again.

I was leaning against the counter partly to remain upright, to not collapse from boredom and the hangover I'd been nursing all afternoon and evening. It took a lot of energy, babysitting customers who couldn't tell the difference between yellow and pale brown. There were times when it took an equal amount of energy to control the desire to throw my head back and scream. This was how I earned rent and food. Handholding and listening was half of the job. The other half consisted of running photocopies on those 50-sorter-bin Xerox machines. On a good night I ran between 150,000 and 200,000 copies.

"What color is this?"

"Oatmeal."

"Oh. No, that won't do…"

I stared out the window. A girl my age in a black leather jacket and boots walked past. Her hair was thrashed into what could have been the prototype for my hairstyle. On her it was chic and wild. On me it was a quiet mess, an outer expression of the tangled misery in my head.

"Well," said the potato man with a gentle sigh. He handed the sample pages back to me and pointed. "I guess this is the one, then."

"The beige?"

"No," he said. "This one." He pointed to a sheet of blue paper.

"Cornflower? You want all 1,500 flyers to be cornflower?"

He blinked. His uncertainty, his quavering inability to make a simple decision, had returned. All I had to do was ask him a question and he was lost.

"It's a good choice," I lied. If we were ever going to move on, I had to take him by the leash and pull him to the curb. "Eye-catching."

I said this over the deafening clatter of metal hinges as rows of collated pages fell into sorter bins all over the room.

"Do you think so?"

"Oh yeah." I nodded and grinned as though nobody had ever chosen a better color.

"Well," he said decisively, like a man buying a new car and not a stack of flyers advertising a sale on used textbooks. "Let's do it, then."

To pay rent, I had taken the only job I could find. Walking up Broadway on a Sunday morning, dodging theater people handing out flyers for a show, and the homeless begging for change I didn't have, I'd spotted a Help Wanted sign in the window of a Copy-Z. At the prospect of applying for a job with another franchise of the same photocopy chain where I'd worked in my hometown, I felt a queasy combination of relief and despair. This particular shop occupied one section of a rambling brick warehouse. The place had long since been gutted and repurposed by an entrepreneur who went bankrupt and sold the property to a Microsoft millionaire. The guy refurbished the whole block (keeping anything still viable as it was), and leased it as retail space.

Here's something odd I first noticed as I shambled through my stupid job. My face, plain but not ugly, and my demeanor, intelligent but not clever, made a certain number of strangers trust me automatically. I don't mean trust in a general or theoretical sense, or in a deep, personal sense. I mean people gave me access to stuff. The Copy-Z manager, Desiree, hired me on the spot and handed over a set of company keys and the combination to the safe.

If she had spied on me as Kitty had done, Desiree would have known I wasn't reliable. I was lazy and disloyal but my face said otherwise and nobody bothered getting to know me. Of course I couldn't bluff my way into a good job, but I had no trouble getting hired for a lousy one. I knew I could take advantage of the situation but I had to do it carefully, without leaving any traces.

During my third week of employment, a co-worker, Tam, who shared the shift with me and a couple of imbeciles named Lisa and Alisa, complained about not being able to pay her utility bill at the end of the week. Without missing a beat I suggested stealing from the register.

Tam gave me a snorting laugh. When I didn't smile she got quiet. She gave Lisa and Alisa a glance over her shoulder and then lowered her voice.

"I'd get caught," she said. "We'd come up short and you know Desiree would blame me right away. She's dying to be manager of the year. Ignorant slut. She'd go straight to the police and tell them to arrest 'the Asian girl,' I guarantee it."

"What if we didn't come up short?" I asked, not only because I had a dollar and forty-seven cents to my name and no food in my refrigerator but also because I was bored and I already hated Desiree with her ten-year CD accounts, her investment in a two-bedroom cottage on Eastlake, and her Midwest memories of the grandmother who taught her how to crochet. The woman never stopped talking about her own practical nature and how it was responsible for everything she had.

"Okay, criminal," said Tam. "How do we do this?"

"The order form Desiree makes us fill out and attach," I explained. "This is her ingenious double-check system. She makes us set these forms aside after the order is picked up. We ring up the order at the register where it's recorded on the receipt roll, and we collect payment and put it in the drawer."

"Yeah. That's about it."

We wandered outside to the alley behind the shop for a smoke while our co-workers Lisa and Alisa ran copies inside. Tam wore a butcher's apron over her jeans and T-shirt, more of a protective barrier against 'the shitty mojo' of our customers than a safeguard for her clothes.

"Well, let's say a customer pays cash and we don't ring it up. Okay, so, the order form with their name on it is the only record of a transaction because there's no receipt. And if we give the customer the order form, unless they're really paying attention they'll accept it as a receipt."

Tam had figured out where I was going before I got there. She exhaled a mighty cloud of smoke and laughed.

"You *are* a criminal," she told me. "That's... Fuck. That's embezzling. Do you have a record?"

"Only for indecent exposure," I said and pulled my T-shirt aside to flash my right breast.

"Jesus. If I thought it would work..."

"Let's test it out," I said. "Every time you get a customer who offers cash and seems distracted enough not to notice, try substituting the order form for a real receipt, and don't ring it up at the register. Let's see how much we have at the end of the shift."

"What if somebody does notice? What if they insist on a receipt from the register?"

"Then act stupid, apologize, and ring it up. They'll think it was an honest mistake because you're a girl and you're trying to do more than one thing at a time."

"Wait," she said and dropped the cigarette butt to the ground. "What do we say to Lisa and Alisa?"

"Don't say anything. They're idiots."

"But what if they notice?" The question was perfunctory. Tam didn't look especially worried.

"Lisa spends most of her time proving she can run two machines at the same time. Alisa's afraid of the customers. They won't care if we handle the counter all night. They'll both be relieved."

"Yeah, maybe," said Tam. "Okay, I can see this happening. I can visualize us getting away with this, as long as we're not greedy. And, listen, if I get caught, for real, I'm blaming you."

"Sure," I said.

"Not kidding. I'll say I'm an exchange student and you took advantage of me. You're the fucking fall guy. You punched me and made me help you…"

"Okay, I get it!" We laughed so hard Alisa heard us inside the shop and waved through the back window.

Thus began our habit of setting aside what we needed. It worked that night and every time we tried it. We couldn't take much at once, only a couple of dollars here and there, but it added up and I never missed a rent payment.

I often thought about how and why we got away with our crime. Success depended on a number of things but there was one overriding factor. To put it bluntly, Tam and I were not that hot. If we had been prettier our method would have failed. Customer scrutiny would have nailed us. In reality we were two nondescript twenty-something girls behind a counter.

Nobody ever cares about waitresses, cashiers, ushers, car washers, pool cleaners, dog groomers, valets, babysitters, gardeners, housekeepers, salesgirls—all expendable, a blur of bodies carrying out mundane business while more significant people go to important places and do exciting things.

We couldn't afford to go anywhere. A couple of times a week we got drunk at the Comet but the beer was cheap. 'Pukin' ale,' as Tam used to say. No guilt if it came back up.

On my days off I walked—downtown, or south to Beacon Hill; the bustling U-District to the forest of Ravenna; or the top of Queen Anne and over the bridge to Fremont. Or I wandered up Broadway, past the funeral home and on to the park. Not Volunteer Park but the crummy little patch of weeds and concrete next to the reservoir, where homeless people slept and the grass was littered with needles. Where stoned white people played hacky sack in their rastacaps and blond dreadlocks.

The long days rolled by. Tam and I filched money from the register every week, almost every night. Not huge sums, but they added up and kept me from starving.

Greenlake on a slow day, midweek, dappled with sunlight. The path encircling the water is dotted with shallow puddles beginning to evaporate. Quaint bungalows line the narrow streets leading to and from the lake. A scent of pizza wafts from a corner shop to the two-bedroom house with a wooden sign in the window.

Judging by the description of Reiki healing on the sign, I would expect a quiet, slender master of technique waiting beside a table with a background of gurgling water flowing over a rock sculpture and the reedy notes of a flute in the air.

I didn't expect *you*. A middle-aged woman of one hundred and sixty pounds, your hair over-saturated with fox-red dye and spiked with hints of magenta, your feet bare and sort of broad with unimaginably short, square toes. Your face is lined with a sadness you try unsuccessfully to overcome with each new client. Your last love stripped you down and left you bare, and now here you stand, welcoming anyone who wanders in.

Five years ago, you had given up hoping to be swept away. Love was crap, and you didn't want to talk about it anymore. Then you fell hard, in one night, watching Rudy shred a bass guitar on stage at the Crocodile. You saw her again waiting in line for the bathroom. She smiled. You ducked your head. She cupped your chin in her hand and kissed you, giving your lower lip a tug with her delicious mouth.

Rudy followed you to another, older club after her set, this one infested with roaches and bad music. She offered a joint, took you by the hand and hauled you outside to the alley, pressed you against a cinderblock wall, pressed her mouth between your lips, made you come with her fingers inside you.

How you longed to fall headlong, crazy. "Feel this," Rudy told you. "It's going to happen."

For a long time it seemed right, this traipsing around together without wanting more. Then you wanted more.

You earned a license in Swedish massage and made decent money for the first time. With your leather-clad Rudy grumbling all the way, you bought a house and decorated it with purple lounge chairs, silver paint, tiny spaceships, and sex toys from all over the world.

You let your stay-at-home girlfriend Rudy bathe you, gliding the soap across the slippery curves of your flesh. She said this was 'it,' this was complete; she said you were the lady she had been looking for, the woman of her most splendid lucid dreaming. You let her hands convince you.

Rudy liked to play music and 'have fun.' She didn't like 'jobs and boring shit.' You bought two cars together, a Volkswagen for the city and an SUV for navigating country roads. You hiked and made out and rented a cabin.

"Live in the moment," said your lover Rudy. "Fly as high as you can!"

You co-signed a second mortgage and opened this massage studio in Greenlake, six blocks from home. You took on as many clients as you could manage, so many you blistered your hands washing their skin and their smells away. At night you imagined epidermal flakes gathering all over your body, encasing you, sealing your eyes and mouth shut, suffocating you.

Your bones ached, your back hurt constantly. So you quit massage and studied Reiki—your tremulous hands, still shiny from over-cleansing, wavering in the air, never touching the client's skin, locating energy fields, auras, sites where psychic pain accumulated. You told your clients you were changing focus, offering Reiki instead of massage. They left you in droves.

"All I want is a massage. I want you to get in there and get that kink out of my lower back..." one of your regulars told you, the day she left for another masseuse.

When the bills and hateful calls from the bank became overwhelming, you put on your French sunglasses and went shopping. You bought a burgundy sectional for nine hundred dollars and ripped a hole in it. You cried yourself to sleep and wondered where your beloved Rudy was sleeping.

You felt too many emotions. You knew what it was to let loose and scream and cry. The day Rudy announced she was leaving you for a postal worker named Gwyneth you didn't die. You thought it was a prank. You didn't know you'd stopped being the woman of Rudy's 'most splendid lucid dreaming.'

No amount of arguing made a difference. Your ex- Rudy packed your bags and put a For Sale sign on the lawn. She drove you to your studio in the SUV, backed out of the short driveway, tires crackling over the gravel, and sped away to her new life on a houseboat with Gwyneth and a sheepdog.

You live in your studio now. You keep your smock and clothing clean. You greet every client—two or three a week—with a smile so brave it only elicits pity. You have favorite sayings printed on cards.

'Today's struggle is tomorrow's strength.'

'When we are at peace inside, the outside will change naturally.'

You stand at attention beside the table. Your hands are quivering, uncertain about all those auras and energy fields, and afraid you've already seen the only passion you'll ever know.

"Hey," I say. "What are you waiting for? Your car is parked nearby. See the lake across the street, the smoothness of the green surface? Isn't it inviting? Wouldn't you like to slip into the water?"

Once you clear the road and then the dirt path, you barrel right into the lake. A splash denotes contact followed by a sort of whoosh, and you glide. Round and bright white, your Volkswagen settles and floats naturally. Not a swan but a pleasant duck.

You have time, now, to view the dainty gingerbread houses lined up on all sides of the water. You think of how many lies are told inside those pretty homes. You have time to watch a small crowd gathering. Baby strollers come to a gradual stop. Joggers and roller skaters skid, pull over, and stare.

I'm telling you, your heart is too big for this town, too big and caring and stupid. I almost know your name, it trips at the edges of my awareness, and I almost stop myself.

Then I stop myself from stopping, and a thin stream of water shoots through a leak in the floor, bubbles between your stubby toes, and tugs you down, down, down while the neighbors and skaters look on in shock.

Chapter Eight

By this time I had a sort of friend in my apartment building. Vaughn managed a wine shop on 15th Avenue. He was square-faced, short, and built like a boxer. His hair stood on end, no matter how he combed it.

Vaughn's great love was classical theater. We met the day he came into the shop to run a stack of fifty flyers.

"Hello, there," he said when I rang up his order. "Not to alarm you but I think we share living quarters, in a manner of speaking."

I must have looked blank.

"I'm your upstairs neighbor," he went on. "Vaughn Roberts. Vaughn Evans is my nom de plume. How do you do?"

"I'm Greta," I replied.

"Please, have a flyer. It's an invitation. I'm presenting a staged reading this Sunday."

"Oh," I said. "I don't go to the theater much…"

"This is informal. We gather in my living room."

"Fifty people?" I asked.

Vaughn laughed, a boisterous, generous, theatrical laugh.

"Oh no," he assured me. "I'll hand out these flyers to people I know and maybe eight or ten will show up. Free wine and cheese, a quiche if I'm feeling ambitious. Please, join us, if you have time."

Offering wine and cheese to a person who is five pounds underweight because she has to decide between rent and food one week out of every month? The money Tam and I filched could only cover so much. And we didn't dare put a larger dent in the profits. When I got home after my shift, I taped the flyer to my refrigerator and started counting the hours until Vaughn's get-together.

On Sunday I put on a skirt and my least worn-out T-shirt and sweater. I even brushed my hair before finding my way upstairs to Vaughn's apartment at two p.m.

Including me, there were five guests. One was a tall, obsequious man who applauded after every scene. Another was a tall, cheerful woman who made use of the ninety-minute reading to finish a sleeve of the sweater she was knitting. The other two divided their time between rolling their eyes at the obsequious man's applause and shaking their heads over the knitting woman, who hummed quietly while she worked.

The play was a Jacobean pastiche. There were thirty-seven roles read by five actors employing eleven wigs and more British accents than I could count. Four actors (including Vaughn) played multiple roles while the fifth performer—a stunning, dark-haired young man— played the female lead and romantic interest, Susanna, to Vaughn's primary role, that of the dashing and promiscuous Fletcher. Only the female lead appeared in full costume, equipped with long sleeves ending in wide cuffs and an impressively cinched bodice. The four multiple players indicated changes of character with an astonishing number of feathered hats and varying sizes of ruff.

The story centered on Susanna, a lady who had fallen on hard times and had to make her way in the world by masquerading as a boy performing tragedies for the king's pleasure. Susanna's real secret, revealed in the third act, was that she was a boy of nineteen masquerading as a lady who had fallen on hard times. This part of the plot was never explained. By the time of Susanna's final unveiling, Fletcher has fallen madly in love, having come close to losing his mind in a confused state of arousal while admiring Susanna from the wings.

The script was in rhyming couplets. These were occasionally delivered with devilish winks, and received nods and murmurs of appreciation from the audience. Twice the action was interrupted by spontaneous outbursts of applause.

In the final act Susanna is compelled to disrobe for a second time, Fletcher ravishes the male Susanna, and the play skitters close to a happy ending. But of course Susanna discovers an inherited estate from a previously unidentified father and gives up the stage forever, leaving poor Fletcher to collapse, his passion wasted, his great love vanished to another continent, and his theatrical ambitions ruined.

When the actors stepped forward for their bow I felt like I'd taken a tumultuous cruise. I applauded along with the others, and jumped to my feet in anticipation of more Gouda and merlot. I pocketed a miniature baguette and a couple of croissants for later.

An occasional trip to see Vaughn's friends in a slightly overwrought but entertaining performance of one classic or another was the price I paid to never run out of wine and cheese. And every other month I was enlisted to serve fancy snacks at one of Vaughn's play readings in his apartment. The same friends gathered to hear these scripts, each of them written 'in the manner of' a famous playwright.

When I told Vaughn about my parents he dubbed me his 'little orphan' and took me under his wing. He checked my refrigerator once a week and added a few items surreptitiously—butter, eggs, milk, bread, a head of romaine lettuce, a bunch of carrots, a bottle of olive oil. One time he sent me to his dentist and paid the bill when I needed a filling. He introduced me to other neighbors in the building and filled me in on each one's history.

"Fiona Jarrett, she's a publicist at the opera. Works like mad, poor darling, and they don't appreciate her. A nasty little ambitious thug is trying to push her out of the way. I've asked around and I have his contact information. If anything happens, he will definitely hear from me…

"Ivy Traeger and Bunny Campbell are the sexiest couple alive but I don't expect things to last. Bunny's so young she doesn't have a clue. She's a pixie with a mean streak. Here she is, in the romance of a lifetime, and she's running around telling people she might be bi, which is news to Ivy. And Ivy is delicious! A bit taciturn but wonderful when you get to know her. She's a costume designer for the Empty Space and a couple of smaller fringe companies. What a gorgeous, talented, dark-eyed beauty. She'll need all the friends she can get when our young Bunny breaks her heart…

"If you have any plumbing problems, and you will, we all do, call Ted or Stacy, not Druida, who thinks she's a handyman. She's broken half the toilets in the building…

"Are you sure you're straight, sweetheart, because Ivy's going to need a friend soon and I hate to see classic beauty like hers go to waste…"

Whatever I might find frivolous about the Jacobean and Elizabethan five-act plays he loved, and the pastiches he wrote, Vaughn believed in himself. He earned an excellent living managing the wine shop but he would say he was an artist, first and always. He was certain of his talent, and sure of the genius of each of his friends. He believed any dismissal of his writing was based on ignorance or envy. He had banded together with a composer to create a theater company called Wicked Pursuits.

For a long time they had put on shows in Vaughn's living room, charging a dollar a ticket. Then they stumbled onto the deal of a lifetime.

The composer knew a retired couple dabbling in real estate. For a few thousand dollars the couple had purchased a two-story brick building in Belltown back in 1982, and did nothing with it for years. The top floor had superficial fire damage along the southwest corner and the plumbing was noisy. Otherwise the dump was structurally sound.

This couple, the Jensens, had been locked in a zoning battle for several years with an acquaintance who owned the property next door. The guy, Alan Cutler, was forever trying to sell apartment units as condos. Nobody was buying, Vaughn said, because poor and single people lived in apartments while families bought houses. Condos in Seattle were unheard of. Nevertheless, Cutler persisted. His modern homes were 'the wave of the future,' he said. His sales pitch promised 'security and serenity in a refined urban setting.'

The Jensens told a couple of weekly papers Cutler was gentrifying the neighborhood and driving artists out. They also said he used his personal fortune to fund questionable programs, hinting at fascist youth camps and survivalist compounds in Idaho.

Cutler responded to the criticism by closing down a studio where three generations of musicians had rehearsed for two dollars an hour. The Jensens retaliated by dividing their Belltown property into studios, rehearsal rooms, and performance spaces they rented for three dollars an hour, attracting a continuous line of shambling artists, musicians, and homeless people. They painted the new name of the building—RatLand—vertically next to the street-level entrance.

Vaughn and his friends leased an upstairs room at RatLand. The space seated forty. With a few strategically placed floor cushions, they could have squeezed in another six or eight. But they never needed the extra space. There wasn't enough demand for tickets.

The company painted the walls and the original fixtures black, connected an illegal lighting grid, tacked up a couple of fire exit signs, and tempted fate with staged readings of Vaughn's plays and productions of adapted classics. *Three Sisters* in drag as a one-act didn't thrill me any more than the dusty, three-hour original. But their hearts were in the right place and their work kept edging toward something good.

Opening nights generally packed the house but the rest of the time attendance was sparse. The general theater rule was to cancel a performance if fewer than ten ticket buyers turned up. Vaughn and Wicked Pursuits considered the traditional command—'the show must go on'—to be sacred. They would arrive at the theater early, prepare physically and vocally, put on their makeup and costumes and tread the boards with the gusto of European opera stars even if only five people were watching.

Inevitably a night came when I found myself in the center row of the center section with only three other patrons in the room. For two and a half hours, every speech and every song in Vaughn's musical version of *The Tempest* was directed at the four of us. After the first intermission, they were directed at the remaining two of us and after the second intermission, at me. I sat alone, dead center. Every actor in the cast of eight made a point of making eye contact with me, as though I were an integral part of the show. It was the most exhausting night of my life.

I was the usher at a fundraising event featuring excerpts from three of Vaughn's scripts. The suggested donation was five dollars. Vaughn invited everyone he knew and a surprising number of people showed up. Dressed in $500 leather jackets and Armani slacks, the men sporting Van Dykes and stringy hair, they slouched into the cramped space reeking of weed. Almost every one of them tried to slip past me without paying.

"It's five dollars," I said to a silver ponytailed man who wore a Rolex.

"Oh, hey, yeah, I know the author," he said.

"It's a fundraiser."

The man snickered and waved to his wife, who had ducked her head to sneak by and was now occupying a seat in the second row. She glanced at me, laughed, and kicked off her Italian loafers.

About half of the crowd ignored me when I asked them to pay. During intermission, while the rich deadbeats milled about in the alley downstairs, sharing joints, I complained to Vaughn about his so-called friends.

"Never mind," he told me. "They're rolling in Microsoft money."

"Then they should pay."

"No, no, no. We want their support. We're building goodwill for the company, for the future."

"What purpose does it serve," I said, "if they won't pay for anything?"

"They might pay someday, or they might serve on the board and bring in wealthy patrons."

"Will *they* pay?" I asked.

"Maybe."

Following the performance several of the deadbeats left without congratulating Vaughn. The silver ponytailed guy made eye contact with me and tossed a dollar into the collection box. He stepped away and traipsed after his wife, who was clutching the handrail and picking her way carefully down the stairs. I assumed her Italian loafers had reduced her feet to giant blisters.

"Saving up for a Porsche?"

I wish the shouted insult had come from me but the young woman who said it was standing there, full lips smirking, deep-set gray eyes sparkling with contempt, nostrils flared. She pulled a fifty-dollar bill from her bag and dropped it into the box.

"Fucking nouveau riche," she said.

"Thanks!" I smiled, an actual smile, without forcing it.

"Thank *you*," she said and shook my hand. "This was good. My name's Daisy Parrish, by the way."

"I'm Greta. Garver."

"So, what do you do, Greta Garver?" she asked. "Are you an actress?"

"No, uh," I fumbled. "I'm kind of a writer." I didn't know why I said it.

"I thought so!" She looked me up and down. "I can always spot a fellow fucking scribe. Well, see you around, Greta." Even then she surrounded me with warmth and I couldn't take my eyes off of her as she walked away.

After that fundraiser, Vaughn became a full-fledged mentor. He told me where to buy curtains and chairs. He told me which novels to read and where to find them used. Most were available at a rambling bookstore near Broadway, run by a woman who read everything in print and didn't mind adding an extra title or two if I bought something. She also shared her therapist's latest diagnosis with customers, as well as detailed coverage of changes to her prescription medication and an ongoing report on the family that caused her mental illness. No matter how obscure the book, she could locate a copy in the metro area.

On Sunday mornings Vaughn stayed home with his latest crush. I walked up Broadway to a café where I could read a newspaper and enjoy a giant biscuit-like scone with black, rich coffee for two dollars. The front window was a good place to wait for the Sisters of Perpetual Indulgence to come sashaying along arm-in-arm in full regalia.

Reading became my solace, an entry point to a universe where I didn't have to explain the difference between beige and yellow paper. Where poverty was glamorous because it was temporary.

Bit by bit I began to write sketches, brief descriptions at first, scribbled over coffee on Sunday mornings. From there I moved on to one-page stories, then longer pieces. At some point I made the mistake of showing one of these to Vaughn.

"You know, you could write reviews and short articles for the *Weekly*," he suggested.

True to my nature I had no desire to put my skills to use. The idea of having to research a subject of no particular interest to me, for pay, seemed like a death sentence. The fiction I read was an escape from the things I had to do every day to survive. I tried not to connect my love of reading with the real world.

Daily I walked the few blocks to work and back with no fear. Rundown as it was, my neighborhood was among the busiest in the city most hours. In trouble I could have screamed and attracted the attention of Vaughn and his friends within seconds.

On these walks I made a point of moving faster when I passed alleys. The wet cobblestones gleamed and shadows sprouted from behind trash dumpsters. Another layer seemed to ooze and spread just below the shadows. Whenever I sensed the heavy darkness rising across the brick walls and trying to climb out onto the street, I tucked my chin and kept my eyes on the ground ahead of me all the way home.

Despite the tedious nature of my job, the time passed quickly. The two-year anniversary of my arrival in Seattle signaled an acceptance of adult life although I didn't feel grown up. On bad nights I wondered what the hell I was doing. This is when Lee Todd's voice would come to me.

"Nobody wants to know the boring little details of a person's life, Gretchen. Think about it. When you read a book, you want to know who gets killed and why, and where the money's buried. You don't care where the hero shops for cuticle scissors. This is the difference between the gritty fiction grownups want to read and the soft soap of ladies' magazines."

I hadn't read crime fiction since I walked out of Lee Todd's office and quit community college. Every time I spied one of those lurid covers at a bookstore—blond dame cowering in a torn slip with the shadow of a man rising against the wall—I cringed. The blowhards who wrote those books could only conceive of the kind of woman they wanted to fuck, a dame, a broad, a manicured pet they could toss around.

The whole point of those stories was to underscore how men were the center of the universe. On the rare occasion when a detective novel sported a girl protagonist she was bright, plucky, and fuckable, and she had to suffer in unspeakable ways before she got her revenge. If an actual heroine was featured on the cover she was naked, resting on her knees and lifting her head like an alert terrier.

Everyone I met at readings and bookstores confirmed what I wanted to believe. Crime fiction was for hacks. To be a writer was to aspire to the literary world of traditional book awards and fellowships and retreats.

Gradually I began to write complete short stories. When I thought they were good enough to be published, I started mailing them to magazines.

The more I heard Lee Todd's voice in my head, the harder I tried to prove what a hack and a loser he was. He could cling to his meager accomplishments in crime fiction, I told myself. I was aiming for the real thing.

I think of my second year in Seattle as the season of rejection slips. Working at Copy-Z, the one advantage was free copies of manuscripts. I could never have afforded to pay for all of those copies.

The more stories I mailed out, the more rejections I collected, dozens of them, and then hundreds. As soon as I had five negative replies to a submission I would revise the story and send it out to another five venues. Slick fashion magazines that only published twelve stories per year, highbrow small press magazines all the university students were trying to get into, and everything in between. The answers drifted back from all corners of the country. No, no, no, no, and no.

I was discouraged but not destroyed. In my heart I still felt an odd, niggling sense that I was going to do *something*. I was going to be recognized for *something*. All I had to do was find the right editor at the right magazine and a bright, flickering, secret world would open up to me. Sure it would.

Chapter Nine

"If you introduce a plot twist it has to be as impressive to the reader as it is to the central character, or you risk earning the reader's contempt. Don't let your protagonist's fate hinge on some obscure little event. It's got to be big, or you're wasting your time." – Lee Todd Butcher, RIP

Eve Wallace. To save my life, I couldn't remember half the dickheads I met during my first two years in Seattle. But I would remember Eve Wallace. The discouragement I came to associate with her name finally killed my writing ambition. Like I said, I'd written plenty of stories and received plenty of rejections. Hers was the *coup de grâce*.

Who knows what made me think I had a chance, let alone convinced me I was going to win a competition against real writers. It was pure, stupid ego striking out one last time. It was a manic phase, a fit of hubris.

"Writers are assholes, all of us," Lee Todd once explained to his less than rapt crime fiction appreciation class. "No matter what we say about ourselves. No matter how shy or humble we pretend to be. Writers want to be published and win all the prizes and make all the money, and screw all the beautiful women, and everybody else can go to hell.

"Writers think they're entitled to success because talent as grand and undeniable as theirs ought to be recognized and rewarded. All of that strutting and posing, it comes from fear. It comes from having to explain, every day, why they're wasting so much time basically typing without pay."

If Lee Todd was right, this is the true nature of every writer: a rampaging megalomaniac in a one-bedroom apartment; a shambling alcoholic in an outdated T-shirt; a god in his own mind. It takes a lot of misery to kill a writer's ambition because, in a way, ambition feeds on misery. Hunger, loneliness, ignorance you can actually feel in your soul no matter how many books you read, all of it demands counterbalance. After so much failure a little success ought to come naturally. It took a few years working a shitty job, and the dawning knowledge that I'd probably never have any other kind, plus a truckload of rejection slips—and a crucial, failed, final attempt at glory—to kill off my ambition.

Lee Todd drilled a hole in each of his students and called us on our bullshit. Being young, we didn't listen. When he said our work was crap and we would starve and it wasn't worth it, some secretly believed, *Oh, but I'm the exception.* Okay, I secretly believed it. His assurance that I didn't have the talent to write fiction only convinced me he didn't know what he was talking about. I stubbornly looked forward to a special destiny for those few years after I landed in Seattle, getting up to write before my shift at the copy center and wasting my weekends revising, revising. I believed in my uniqueness every time I mailed out a manuscript.

My publication credits never materialized. Yet I clung to the ultimately mortifying conviction that, someday, I might be singled out for recognition. All I had to do was stick with it. All I had to do was get a story published. All I had to do was win an award of some kind. Then everyone would notice my writing and invite me to join a workshop in some bucolic corner of upstate New York where I would become the most promising young author in the world, overnight. Editors would toast my success. Agents would fistfight one another to sign me. Lee Todd would hear of my success and cry himself to sleep. A personal assistant would take my manuscripts to a photocopy center where some starved young woman would snarl and try to cheat the cash register while copying my masterpieces.

The last time I ever felt this way, the final season of my grand self-delusion, ended courtesy of Eve Wallace. The occasion was a contest. The prize was a thousand dollars, enough to pay my rent for three months.

After so much grunt work, my days haunted by people who couldn't fill out a two-line request form without help, I was beyond hunger. Apart from my insane writing ambition, in private I was becoming desperate in a sad and sweaty way, and anybody who glanced at me could see it.

I started to see every random event as a sign. When the contest appeared out of nowhere, I was foolish enough to think even the judge's gender was fortuitous. I allowed myself to hope. I ignored Lee Todd's wisdom, again.

"Hope is a dangerous thing in a cynical person," he said the second time we drank together. After we had started seeing each other and before I decided to dazzle him with a story he would wish he'd written. The fading middle-aged lumberjacks and cowboys at the bar, the sunburned and painted women with crow's feet, the sawdust on the floor and the nauseating aroma of cheap beer underscored his words.

"What's your name, again? Gretel?" He chuckled and winked at me.

"Ass-bag," I said.

"Don't believe in things, Gretel. You'll only hate yourself in the morning. Take it from an ass-bag who knows." He drained his glass and when I kissed him he almost slid off the barstool.

To accompany my submission to the big contest, I wrote a groveling, insincere cover letter. I praised the city whose grant writers raised the money for a literary award. I paid tribute to council members and art patrons for adding to the 'vibrant atmosphere' of contemporary Seattle. Worst of all, I expressed my deep admiration for the judge, a woman I'd never heard of before. This was the first time I heard of Eve Wallace, and we wouldn't meet for some time to come.

According to her bio note, Eve attended the Iowa Writing Workshop and Bread Loaf Writer's Conference. She claimed to be the recipient of an undergraduate award I didn't recognize, and the former editor of a small press magazine I thought I might have seen (but couldn't afford) on the shelves at Elliott Bay Bookstore. She offered no specific publication credits, only a standard statement about her writing appearing in 'numerous magazines.'

The minute I read the call for submissions I knew this was it, the moment I'd been waiting for. I started working that minute, making notes, sketching out the action and characters.

My story was about a dog groomer, a divorcee with emotional scars, set up by her employer on a blind date. Her companion for the evening turned out to be a man with an inexplicably large head who tried to force a gift on her. His offering was a scrap of fur stolen from a lab at the zoo where he worked. Their date consisted of driving around town looking at houses over-decorated for Christmas. The night ended with the woman alone in her bedroom, clutching the scrap of fur to her heart.

During the weeks it took to hammer this story into shape, I was almost fired from my job at the copy center. For months I'd been writing before my shift at work, and on the weekend. The rejection letters continued to pile up in my living room like wallpaper samples, pages on every surface drifting in various directions. The pressure to prove myself in my own mind was making me testy and belligerent. A regular customer complained to Desiree, who told me to check my attitude. When you're stealing money from someone it's hard to keep a straight face through her ignorant demands that you shape up, but I needed the job.

Tam and I continued to split what we referred to as 'overspill.' She read the second draft of the story I wrote for the contest and said it had too many characters. I took her advice and killed five of them.

"Keep the Filipino chick who runs the dog grooming salon and kill the dad who buys lottery tickets, he's stupid," she told me.

"The dad's a lot like my dad," I admitted.

"Oh, sorry," she said. "But see, I think you've got a blind spot there, an autobiographical blind spot. You want to win this thing, ditch the dad."

I wanted to win. This contest had become a big deal. I ditched the dad.

Then I did a foolish thing. In my head I made a bargain. Of course I thought I would win. Of course I would, and then my real life would start. So I made a deal with Lee Todd because I didn't believe in the devil. I promised, if I didn't win this thing, I'd say fuck it all. I would admit Lee Todd had been right about me all along. I didn't have talent. I was just another loser who wanted to feel special and had latched onto fiction writing because it looked easy.

"Know what's really easy, Glenda? Being a writer. Know what's hard? *Writing*. It sucks. You have to give up your playtime. You can't party anymore because you have to write. You can't get laid because you have to write. Believe me, it's a lot more fun *being* a writer. Because you don't have to do a goddamn thing." The guy could talk about this stuff all day.

I worked every comma and semi-colon of my story to the brink of collapse. I slaughtered my darlings again and again, cutting and pasting together each new draft from my crummy banged-up Webster. Revising, rearranging, editing, polishing.

The day finally came when I thought my story was ready. Not only ready but golden and brimming with a beauty that could not fail to be recognized. I revised my ass-kissing cover letter to include more asses and I kissed them all.

I decided not to risk the postal service. (I'd once had sex with a guy who claimed to know two major drug dealers who did their best business at the post office.) I placed my story in an envelope and took the #7 from Capitol Hill west to lower Queen Anne.

The office housing the arts department was halfway up Queen Anne Hill, in a renovated school building. A person could turn gray and die waiting for a bus up the hill, so I walked. By the time I reached the office door I was sweaty and sticky, also ravenous. My stomach gave a husky growl as I walked in, loud enough to elicit a glare from the overgrown, dimpled child behind the front desk.

His nameplate identified him as Mervin. His new pullover and immaculate corduroy trousers identified him as a mama's boy.

"May I help you?" he asked.

"I'm here to turn in my story, for the literary prize," I said. I looked around because Mervin was staring at me.

"You could have mailed it," he said with an underlying *harrumph*.

"I'm on my way to lunch nearby," I told him. "With my agent."

All of this was clearly bullshit and he must have known it, of course. For one thing, there were no literary agents in Seattle. My writing had been rejected by fifteen agencies in New York and L.A. One secretary asked me not to contact her company again after I bombarded the office with five samples and a series of ever-more elaborate introductory letters.

Mervin's face widened until it achieved a tight grin. He made a vague motion with his right hand toward the wall behind me and to my left.

"Feel free to toss your submission on the pile," he said merrily.

As I turned it took all of my self-control not to let Mervin see the reaction that shot through me. I realized he was waiting for it, twiddling thumbs and planning how he would recount the story of the uppity girl writer.

I held myself in check and walked to the wall where four two-foot-tall stacks of manuscripts, some in envelopes and some not, occupied wire baskets. The height of the stacks would have toppled them if they hadn't tilted toward one another, braced just as though a spiteful office manager had shoved them into place rather than sorting them into smaller stacks.

With reluctance I lay my manuscript on top of the left-hand pile. I felt a stabbing sense of abandonment. I was suddenly afraid Mervin would discard my story as soon as I left. With as little fuss as I could manage, I picked it up and stuffed it between the other submissions. Since Mervin didn't know my name and most of the envelopes were identical, I decided this would pose enough of a challenge to put him off.

Without looking at Mervin I returned to the front door. On my way out I heard him offer what sounded like a snarky farewell.

By the time I reached Queen Anne Avenue and started my descent—that jerky downhill stomp people acquire on the streets here, an involuntary, embarrassing imitation of the old hippie Keep on Truckin' walk—my stomach was yowling and tears were rolling down my face.

I went back to work. One hundred and fifty thousand copies a night, cigarettes with Tam, robbing the cash register, taking shit from customers named Summerly and Montana.

Three months later, rejection dropped through the mail slot onto the floor of my apartment with a sound like someone saying, "Fuck you." Not simply rejection. The type that stings worse than any other, a clinically polite form letter without personal notes or any indication of how close I'd come. Signed not by Eve Wallace, the judge of the competition, but by that squirrel of an office boy, Mervin.

I stood in my apartment in ripped underpants and a perspiration-stained tank top. I heard the traffic in the street—that beep-beep-beep of passive-aggressive drivers—and I screamed. I let loose and *screamed* with my head tilted back and my vocal chords humming like violin strings. I heard a crash upstairs and felt a spasm of pain in my throat.

A minute later my doorbell rang. I knew it would be Vaughn.

"My God!" he exclaimed. He held in one hand a bottle of Pinot noir and in the other a corkscrew. "What's wrong, darling? Here, have a glass of this and tell me what happened."

I hadn't even felt like crying until I heard the velvet tenderness of that well-trained theatrical voice. In a minute I was a sobbing mess on the couch, with Vaughn's muscle-man arms wrapped around me.

"Who did it?" he asked. "Who hurt you? Tell me and I'll tear out the son of a bitch's spleen."

"No!" I hiccupped. "No!"

"Okay, I'll just break his collarbone. What did he do to you?"

"Nothing!" I took a breath. "I lost! I lost the story contest!"

"Oh no. Those bastards. Those blind, stupid bastards!"

"This is the end," I said, ashamed of my morbidity yet unable to stop.

"What do you mean?"

"I quit!"

"No!" Vaughn held me by both shoulders and gave me a gentle shake. "Now, stop talking like that. You have real talent. And you're so young! You're only a child! You have years and years of great writing ahead of you, sweetheart."

When he said these things, I felt a quick flash of shame at the times I'd casually trashed Vaughn's work in conversation with Tam. For a while I'd tried to drag her and her friends along to see Wicked Pursuits productions. One by one they had stopped showing up, and Tam's friends had stopped answering my calls. Whenever I raised the subject at the copy center, Tam rolled her eyes and said, "No more theater, man. Never again."

"Obviously, the judges don't know good writing when they see it," said Vaughn. "Which does not surprise me, in this backwoods, barefoot lumber town."

I slurped wine and nodded. "God, I've met so many assholes in this town!"

"Tell me about it!"

"Remember that arts administrator who lost her shit with me because I wrote the organization's name on my grant application? Jesus! I was only applying for a hundred dollars."

"Insane bitch," Vaughn said. "She was menopausal."

"'We are *not* the applying agency!' she kept screaming at me. 'We are the *supporting, umbrella* agency, under whose 501(c) 3 status you're applying!' She was screaming so hard I thought her vagina would fly out from between her legs onto the floor."

"What the hell was she so upset about?" Vaughn said. "Her *supporting* agency was going to take ten percent of the grant. They stood to make money, and they didn't have to do a thing."

"They even made me pay for a copy of the application! Fifty cents!"

"Cheap bastards," said Vaughn.

"It didn't matter because they turned me down. 'Insufficient evidence of ability to accomplish stated artistic goals.' I guess that says it all." I hiccupped and Vaughn poured more wine.

"Go on, sweetheart," he said. "Get it off your chest."

"Remember that English Department chairman, the jerk-off who answered my phone query about entry-level jobs? The guy invited me to his office for a chat. Two hours of ingratiating bullshit later the guy said, 'Well, we don't actually have any jobs at the moment. We haven't had an opening in three years. Most of our people stay until they retire. But it's nice to get a look at you. I like to see what's out there in your age group.'"

"Fucker," said Vaughn.

"Yeah. I left a wad of purple gum on the glass-paneled door on my way out."

Vaughn laughed.

"Then there was the literary maven, Cecile, who inherited 'a million and a mansion.' Did I tell you about her?"

"You did," said Vaughn. "Wasn't a condition of the inheritance that she could never sell the house? That big, old, draughty 1920s thing on 17th?"

"Right. She couldn't stop talking about how she 'simply didn't have enough money' for the upkeep or the overhead, or some other thing poor people never worry about.

"So Cecile inherited this monster house, and she turned the ground floor into a 'writing center' and claimed it as a tax shelter. But the zoning laws baffled her so she never knew for sure if her 'writing center' was legal."

"Poor thing!" He laughed again.

"She was always catching cold from standing outside in the damp garden, ushering writers in through the side door and whispering instructions. They had to remove their shoes indoors and promise not to tell anyone where they had been that day…"

Vaughn roared with laughter. "Oh, yes," he managed to say. "Cecile."

"And later on when people started donating stuff to the 'writing center,' the IRS complications drove her into therapy," I said.

"What the hell did people donate? Pencils?"

"All kinds of junk," I said. "Six scratched-up computer terminals with mainframe, delivered to her doorstep. She goes, 'Oh no! Does anybody know how to hook these up?' Pacing in her kimono robe and a necklace made of candy, dusting a framed poster of Stevie Nicks and clutching a brass Ganesha idol. 'Do they connect to one another? Or do they just *sense* one another, electronically? Does anybody know what a mainframe *is*?'"

"We're going to need another bottle," said Vaughn. While he went upstairs and returned with *two* bottles, my mind went on racing.

There were the open mic readings at Squid Row Tavern, where writers signed up to enthrall the half-tanked crowd with hot-off-the-typewriter poetry and prose. All the times when I stood at the mic and read a paragraph of my work, and got a boozy smattering of applause. Only to be upstaged by some guy like Ord, of San Francisco, draped in burlap robes, reeking of ejaculate, clopping around on handmade wooden platform sandals, attended by three softly moaning, longhaired women who wore crowns made of leaves, and who explained to anyone who would listen that Ord was a genius *and* a fertility god.

The times I saw Jesse Bernstein read his poetry to the same crowd. The way the audience smirked and raised their glasses, and if you asked what they thought of the poetry, they would shake their heads and say, "That's Jesse, all right. Never changes." Following his suicide most of the published tributes centered on his body odor, addiction, and madness.

"This place *eats artists alive*," Vaughn said when he sat down and popped the cork on our next bottle. "If you do anything well and you're serious about it, nobody cares. Now, if you wrote a zany musical about housewives battling mildew and the high cost of suburban living and you called it *My Latte or My Life* you could make some money."

I was finally laughing. Thank goodness for Vaughn, I thought. I liked him. I really did.

"Let's drink, and then let's dance, and then you sleep on it, and don't make any hasty decisions," he said. "I'm not letting you give up on your destiny."

I burrowed against his shoulder. He smelled so good, so warm and real.

"Drink," he said. And we drank.

We toasted to the necessity of following your dream. We talked about fate and artistry, and what a cesspool Seattle was. We laughed and cried. I promised to keep writing stories but I was lying and I knew it.

This time, with this competition, something had broken. Or something had been confirmed one too many times. Maybe losing had convinced me that the incessant, tin voice echoing in the back chambers of my imagination, saying, "You're a fraud, you're a girl, you're full of shit, you don't have any stories worth telling," was my true voice, my legitimate voice.

I was born to make photocopies, the voice reminded me, to live and die serving the most trivial needs of other people. I was nothing. I was nobody. I had nothing to lose. On that day—ground up, wounded, and aching with disappointment—I had no idea how dangerous a defeated person could be.

Part Two

"Never introduce new information or a change of direction by having a character walk through a door and announce it. Because, let me tell you, that is some lazy-ass construction. Give the reader some goddamn credit." – Lee Todd Butcher, RIP

Chapter Ten

Over the summer my girlfriends traded in scruffy oxfords for boots, steel-toed if we could afford it. Buckled for damage, or laced up and tied in double knots. We wore them with flannel shirts and threadbare jeans falling off our hips. We wore them with flower-print dresses slipping sideways over a black bra and tattooed thighs. We wore them to coffee shops and grocery stores, to work and to weddings. We wore them to bed.

All day and night, into the vaporous hours before dawn, our boots could be heard stomping up and down the hills of Seattle. Pounding the pavement of Denny and Broadway. The sound was our anthem. Girls proclaimed, over and over, "We will not be killed by your hands, motherfuckers! We will go where we want and we will not hesitate to kick your ass to death on the sidewalk if you cross us!" Where did we find the words? From what corner of our souls did we summon the rage?

Mia Zapata was dead: a bright, flickering storm cloud, a beauty shouting victory in the dank green vomit-stained taverns and clubs. Strangled. Raped in the goddamn street at three a.m. and left there on the ground.

When we first heard the news we didn't stomp. We couldn't move our limbs. Shock numbs the nervous system. We stopped where we stood. Grief shot down and the impact flattened us all, boys and girls, anyone.

Chorus, in our youth and ignorance we chimed in on those itchy, lightning-rhythm songs. We pounded the floor in droves, sweating, screaming. So much green beauty on stage, we looked away. We took it all for granted. Remind me someday, when I'm old, how we took all of this for granted.

Every girl is calling out, listening for an echo, a voice assuring her she is her own captain and her destiny, a soul rising to be seen, unashamed, unabashed, unafraid to walk home in the pitch dark between busted streetlights. And then.

Despair like pins drove into our flesh, rusting, festering. The knowledge of death was a new communion, bitter ashes to our tongues.

And here came a deadly orchid, a black heart with a pale certainty. We had always known the violence men could do. Had seen it skirting the room at drunken parties on the Hill. Spent our youth folding it into a box with tissue paper, placing it on a shelf, telling ourselves it wasn't part of us. It was a gown we had grown out of. It was another generation, our mother's fear, fringed with ruffles and rotten lace, nothing to do with us. Because we were young and we went everywhere. We had no taste of mortality. And then.

The orchid took hold. We nurtured it with nods and glances. We held secret conversations about it. We nursed it with resentment every time we hesitated before stepping out the door. Shame flared in every spinal cord each time we glanced over our shoulders. And shame fed the rage until one day we stepped out the door wearing god-awful boots and a new determination not to cower but to kill any man who tried to stop us. Alone or together, in a vicious, unmerciful pack drawn from the shadows, we would kick and punch and crush those who wanted to stop us.

"I pity the fucking fool who comes at me in a dark alley!" a girl of no more than twenty shouted beneath my window one night, as she stomped up the shoulder of Summit. She would have slammed an attacker to the cement and smashed his throat in. I would have run out to the curb to join her, in less than a heartbeat.

Mia Zapata sang our song. The man who crushed her body was alive. He was free, anonymous, masquerading as every man, and now He would pay.

We knew good men, kind and compassionate men and boys. We knew them but we rated them as exceptions to the rule after Mia died. We knew them as friends and allies but no longer part of 'us.'

In the aftermath of that July night, we began to train ourselves for something we had never expected to face. We prepared for combat. We set our minds on survival. Utility posts and shop windows were soon plastered with the call to duty. Train your body and your soul. Take the streets by force because—as the days droned on and police failed to find and arrest Mia's killer—the truth hit us hard: We were on our own in a *dangerous world. We had to be ready, and strong enough for the coming years. If we didn't want to sit quietly, burning down to nothing indoors, we had to kick ass and save ourselves by any means necessary.*

Rage fueled our conversations, over coffee, on the bus, under store awnings, and in the rain. Wherever I went, I heard young women talking.

"He thought that joke was funny?"

"Tell you what was funny. When I cracked his jaw with that tiny reading lamp his mom gave him. Fucker. Eat a lamp, fucker!"

So our days went. We stomped and screamed and promised vengeance. We searched every alley and public bathroom, determined to draw Him out. If one of us could be a target, we would all become targets to draw from the shadows the piece of garbage that killed Mia. And then? And then? God help the shit-eating bastard.

I let Daisy's words fade in the room between us. I knew her deep gray eyes were fixed on my expression.

"It's *good*..." I told her, allowing a note of skepticism on the second word.

"Are you sure?"

"*Yeah*," I said. "I'd cut the dialogue but the rest is good."

"Can you feel the mood, the climate, the atmosphere?"

"Yeah, sure. Your tone, your language, it's powerful..." Then I nodded and turned to the window. Maybe I lit a cigarette. Yeah. Maybe I was such a bitch I lit a cigarette and stared out the window until she couldn't stand it anymore and started to twitch.

"What's missing?" she asked. "What is it?"

"I'm not sure."

"Come on, Greta, I ask you to read my shit so you can give me notes. What the fuck?" She trumped me by lighting a cigarette — one of mine — with her Godzilla Zippo.

Daisy Parrish was twenty-four, lithe, golden, and sure of her feelings about the universe. She was 'born to write,' as she explained the second time we met, in an overstuffed booth at a joint on Capitol Hill. She felt alive in the world; everywhere she went she was a living part of the stories there.

I told myself my life was okay; things had calmed down and I'd fallen into the routine of going to work at the copy center, drinking at loud bars where the music made it impossible to think, sleeping; I wasn't tormenting myself with the fantasy of being a writer. I was in sync with what I was meant to be. But when I listened to Daisy, I tried not to acknowledge the envy writhing in my gut like a worm.

"I don't understand how you could give up like that," she said the night we ran into one another at Ileen's. "Not if it's who you are, you know. Not if it's in your fucking soul!" We drank some Belgian ale she loved, a fruity concoction I puked up later in the alley.

Writing really was in Daisy's fucking soul. Her mother was a photojournalist who had worked for *Rolling Stone*. Her dad stayed home and raised six children on fifty acres of farm and forestland in Northern Oregon. His areas of expertise included mycology, fermentation (home-brewed beer and bread-baking), and raising goats. All of Daisy's siblings were prodigies including a cellist, an oceanographer, two poets, and a physicist.

Daisy considered herself to be the least accomplished product of her wild and woolly family, still trying to 'make her mark' after having stories published in five major newspapers on the west coast. She was ambitious but not driven, a basically happy creature engaged in the work she loved. Compared to my fretful, alien attempts at writing fiction, her gonzo-infused reporting was a natural, joyous extension of who she was.

Of course I couldn't admit how much I wanted to walk in her boots; stay up all night dancing in a stranger's kitchen wearing only body paint and a navel ring; drive a truck to Wyoming in a thunderstorm; wake up in a field of wheat and cavort with beautiful men and women; or interview one of America's last great literary lions at his ranch in Idaho, and then call him an asshole in print.

"I can't believe that fucker," Daisy had proclaimed, the day she got back. "He has three ex-wives and four daughters waiting on him all day, washing his clothes, cooking his favorite meals, feeding his fat ass, hanging on his words. And he makes all of this money writing novels about men who treat women like shit!"

She sold the profile piece to *SF Weekly*. It was one of a handful of articles and interviews with which she acquired a small, fiercely devoted following in L.A., San Francisco, Portland, and Seattle. But she still thought of herself as a writer struggling to get published, to find her voice and pay the fucking rent, as she liked to remind me. The words felt like a knife between my ribs.

I poured two more glasses of Bordeaux. We lit new cigarettes off our half-smoked ones. She collapsed onto the couch and let out the yelp she always used to describe its lack of springs.

"No shocks," she would say. "You should stuff this goddamn thing with down. Or pot."

"I enjoyed the essay," I repeated. "Mia Zapata, the city, you're getting close to nailing this moment, the way young women feel…"

"Did *you* feel it?" she asked. Her eyes trained on me, not missing an inflection.

"I'm not a club kind of girl," I said. The word 'girl' clogged my throat. I was living in dread of the day I called myself a woman and someone laughed.

"But?" She stretched sideways on the couch, extending her left leg and leaning on her right elbow. "Tell me if it's garbage!"

It wasn't garbage. I wished I'd written it, or lived the life that would allow me to write it. Instead of the ratty, time-wasted, half-drunk biography I owned.

"Are you covering familiar territory?" I asked. I let the words hang, chill and echoing, while I slugged a mouthful of wine and hoped she wouldn't throw her glass at me. I never knew. There was the time I criticized her "Santa Steals from Soup Kitchens" piece for being maudlin. That time she stopped mid-stride on the sidewalk, whirled at me, and screamed, full-throttle, "People need to know what the fuck is up with Santa!" Then she laughed so hard she had to hold her ribs.

"Familiar?" she said and took a long draw on her American Spirit. She let the exhaled smoke fall to her lap. She stared at me. "To whom?" Her lips formed a frosted pink bud, in the wake of her words.

"You," I said. "I mean, you've written two tributes to Zapata, and you sold one to *The Stranger*, right?"

"That was just a quote. They quoted me."

"But the article was about Mia, right?"

"You're serious?"

"I don't know," I said. "I wouldn't know. You decide."

She stared at me for a second. Then she was on her feet, pacing.

"Fuck!" she said. "Fuck! I blew it. I waited until I could write with a little more perspective. Now it's too late. Fuck!"

She would have gone on like this for a while. Then I would have reassured her and she would have submitted the essay to the *Weekly* and maybe she would have won an award or maybe they would have hired her to write a weekly column.

But there was a knock at the door.

"I'm gone," Daisy said. She left her essay on the coffee table, a forgotten, mangled draft with one corner of the pages soaking up a wine stain. "I need a boy tonight! A *beautiful, hot boy* who can kiss, and who can play bass like a motherfucker!"

"I'll see you around, then," I said.

"You going to meet me at the OK Hotel tomorrow night, baby?"

"Nope. 7 Year Bitch at RKCNDY," I lied. I didn't visit clubs for the music, only the noise, the buzz of drunken voices, and the boys. Occasionally I let Daisy drag me out of my apartment to be part of her entourage.

"RKCNDY? Never mind. Fuck you, baby."

"Fuck you, too."

She wrapped me in a fierce embrace and kissed me on the lips. She tasted like honey and wildflowers. Every goodbye with Daisy felt like the last farewell before a 19th century ocean voyage. She pulled her leather jacket from the coat rack. She gave a little grin and an elbow-squeeze to Vaughn when she sidestepped him at the front door.

"Call me this weekend," she said and disappeared.

"Interrupting?" Vaughn asked. Wearing his 'tell me something scandalous' expression.

"No. We're done," I said. "Come on in."

I poured Vaughn a glass of wine and we parked on the dilapidated couch to watch dusk settle over the street. If you were seated you couldn't see the ATM or the homeless people who slept in the alcove, only the deepening gray and purple shadows of clouds. From down the hill came the familiar beep-beep-beep of a driver stuck too long in traffic.

"God, this place is Purgatory," Vaughn said. "No. It's an alley off a closed market square in a condemned neighborhood of Purgatory."

"You love it," I said.

"I love Port Townsend, but Seattle? Okay, maybe two blocks in Wallingford, and a couple of bars on Capitol Hill. Listen…"

"I know. Some little jerk is losing his mind out there but he's afraid to really honk the horn…"

"No, listen." Vaughn pulled a piece of paper out of his vest pocket and handed it to me. "This is *perfect* for you. It's a way in, a way to get started."

The ad was clipped from the back page of a newspaper.

Theater Reviewer Wanted
Experienced candidates only
206-328-6200
Boom City

"This can't pay much," I said. "And what do I know about theater?"

I knew a little more than I let on. I'd spent half of one miserable summer stage-managing a repertory company of teenagers but I wasn't about to confess my humiliating secret to Vaughn. He would have enlisted me for more than collecting donations and serving hors d'oeuvres.

"Jesus save us," Vaughn said. "What does it matter these days, in this town, how little experience a theater reviewer has? Do you think these people the weeklies send out to cover shows have any idea what they're talking about? At least you have a brain, my dear, and you have good taste, and a college education…"

Intimidated by Vaughn's cultural savvy, I had exaggerated my accomplishments in community college. I lied. I lied like a motherfucker, and ever since Vaughn had been urging me to aim higher and get a better job.

"Your credentials are superior to those of the sad creatures we get. Remember Demeter, the *P-I* critic who ran from her seat before the curtain came down, dashed out to the lobby, and loaded her purse with opening night pastries?"

"Yes. What ever happened to her?"

"She married a Norwegian boat builder and she's trying to have a baby. Every woman's right, of course, none of my business. Although, my god, she's forty-seven, forty-eight...? The point is, Demeter did not write a review. She absconded with fifteen dollars' worth of crème puffs and never mentioned the show."

"Don't you want to kill people like that?" I asked.

"Uh, no," he said. "Throttle, yes, murder, no. Did I tell you about the giant man the *Weekly* assigned to review us last time? Poor, lumbering, morose, old thing with a scrap of wig stuck on his giant head? We had to open both of the doors to get him into the theater. He wouldn't fit in a regular seat so we hauled in a divan."

"Well, I guess competence is more important than anything else..."

"Yes, it is. He lacked competence as well. It's all because of Jane Bash, the performance editor at the *Weekly*, who absolutely hates me."

"Aren't you just being paranoid?"

"No," he said. "This is true, this really happened. Did I tell you she auditioned for one of our productions? Beatrice. She wanted to play Beatrice to my Benedick. Jane is six feet tall! She has arms like a male nurse, she would have towered over me."

"Who played Beatrice?"

"I cast Henry-James Moody because he had the chops and he's equally adept at verbal and physical comedy, none of which I would say about Jane."

"You cast your ex- as Beatrice?" I asked.

"I made a purely aesthetic decision for the sake of the production. Henry-James Moody is an incredibly underrated actor."

"Okay," I said.

"Well, this was a few years ago when Jane was auditioning all over town and nobody would cast her. She had large teeth, gigantic man arms, and the most awful voice. It was both adenoidal and gruff, like a high-pitched bark, because her vocal chords would seize when she was nervous and she didn't know how to loosen up. Oh, and she brought a wig along to the audition, and asked whether I imagined her character as a blond or a brunette."

"A little presumptuous," I said.

"Obnoxious, absolutely convinced she was getting the lead. When I broke the news, you could read the devastation in her eyes. Of course she put on a brave smile and stumbled out the door. Couldn't be helped, though, she was atrocious."

"Not your fault," I said.

"Maybe not but she gave up acting soon after, enrolled at UW, and earned a PhD with a dissertation on some deadly branch of Semiotics."

"Oh, great," I smiled. "What the world needs."

"But I thought, oh well, theater's loss is academia's gain, right? They can keep her! Then I read that the *Weekly* hired Jane right out of grad school, big teeth, man arms, grudges and all."

"Oh."

"She did not want to review my new show. But she's so passive aggressive. Instead of saying no, she sent us this giant, sad man to sit on a sofa to one side of the stage, pulling focus and making the audience cry. And you know what he wrote?"

"I haven't read the issue…"

Vaughn reached into another pocket of his vest and pulled out a second piece of paper. "'Bursting with clichés and festooned with what appear to be the trappings of a children's party, this unintentionally comedic production makes one pine for Ibsen.'"

"What does that mean?" I asked.

"Exactly!" Vaughn folded the scrap of paper and put it away. "It's all about *him*! The poor, giant man is depressed by parties and pining for Ibsen! He's probably off his medication. Oh yes, Jane, please send your Man of Misery to review my show! Listen, Greta, if you don't apply for this job I'm taking your name off the opening night and reading list. I mean it. Don't test me."

"Fine, I give in! Please don't cut me off!" I'm sure he thought I was joking but it really was about the wine and cheese. I couldn't risk losing this one scrap of civilization in my crummy life. Vaughn's congenial readings and his gifts were my only claim to luxury. Without them I would be impoverished and pathetic again, as downcast as the Man of Misery. "I'll apply. But I am not qualified, so don't expect anything."

I slept badly. I slept badly most nights. Perched on an incline between Bellevue Avenue and Olive Way, my apartment building made settling noises, groans and gurgles. They probably occurred during the day, too, drowned out by sounds of life. In the dark these ordinary utterances of frame, floorboards, and plumbing were magnified. At times it felt as if the entire structure were alive and shifting on its haunches, trying to get comfortable.

I'd been on the day shift at the copy center for months and it was slowly driving me insane, but it was a form of insanity I knew and believed I could handle. Another job, a real job, would be a trial. Even a brief plunge into the world of people who gave a shit about art and current events would only underscore my status as an outsider and a loser.

"In fiction and particularly in crime fiction everybody identifies with an outsider," Lee Todd used to say. "Especially conformists, they idolize mavericks. But then, who doesn't? We all want to be the guy who comes to town, proves everybody wrong and stupid, and leaves no forwarding address. That guy doesn't give a shit what we think of him.

"Listen. In life nobody has the guts to be that guy. Because you know where he's going when he climbs into his car and leaves those other people in the dust? He's going home to a cockroach-infested apartment with carpet nails coming loose and a stained mattress for a bed..."

I had become that guy, the loser who goes home to nothing every day. I didn't know how I'd accomplished it but this was my life. The thing is, I didn't want to think about it.

The next morning a brief phone conversation got me an interview. This should have been a tip-off to how desperate they were but I was distracted by other concerns. One, the interview was scheduled for noon the same day, a Friday. I had to call in sick or beg Tam to cover for me. Two, they asked me to bring my resume (no problem) and a non-fiction writing sample (big problem).

This might sound like a shitty excuse. In fact, there is no excuse for what I did.

If I'd been serious about getting a job at a newspaper I would have kept a portfolio or tear sheets for such occasions. I hadn't been serious about getting a real job, a grownup job, in my life. I'd always wandered along vaguely expecting a brilliant accident to make me rich and famous. My talent would emerge and an admiring agent would be standing by to see it. A relative so distant I'd never heard of him would die and leave me a fortune because he'd met me once as a child and thought I showed promise.

When none of these events occurred I began, mildly at first but more overtly with each passing month, directing my irritation at anyone whose hard work resulted in success. Ever so briefly and acutely, I wished that person a small disaster, a private catastrophe to wake her up and make her realize all of the events of her life were random. I could be her or she could be me. She wasn't special or talented, only lucky.

As far as the reviewing job was concerned, I couldn't imagine traipsing from one theater production to another, taking it all seriously instead of merely providing a warm body in a seat in exchange for treats. How in the world would anyone sit down and write an honest and thorough critical analysis of performances she didn't want to see in the first place? I thought of the runaway critic Vaughn mentioned, scraping an armful of pastries into her bag and bolting for the door. I imagined her boat builder waiting outside in a canoe, ready to ferry her away from the ugly memories.

I hung up the phone and lit a cigarette. I'm not blaming the cigarette. I take responsibility for the following chain of events.

When I tapped the ashtray I noticed Daisy's essay about Mia Zapata. Heartfelt, earned, unsentimental, and passionate, Daisy's tribute was exactly the kind of non-fiction piece I needed. It was well written but it wasn't exactly journalistic. (Daisy knew this; she only asked my opinion to confirm her own, to narrow down the market for the piece.) It was personal, with no attempt at being objective. Not the aim of an honest reviewer, I thought. (I knew nothing.) Surely such emotion and poetic language couldn't be the aim of any reviewer with a shred of integrity. The essay was well written, guaranteed to get me the wink of respect I craved before I was booted right out the door.

I decided to use it. I wouldn't get the job but I wouldn't have to feel like a loser. I could tell Vaughn I'd tried, really tried, and that would be the end of it. I could go back to my pointless, easy job at the copy center. Wine and cheese nights would still be mine, for a minimal effort.

To be absolutely sure of failure I wore a sheer black smock, with a print of tiny scarlet roses, over leggings and a black bra. I didn't shave my legs and I chose a scuffed pair of Doc Martens with busted, repaired red laces. Looking as unprofessional as I could imagine, I power-walked all six blocks, to build up a sweat-sheen. I took the front stairs two at a time instead of using the cavernous service elevator.

Boom City nested on the second floor of a former grain storage warehouse. In the 1970s the space had been split up into six units and leased to small businesses, including a theater company. The company had moved on and the other units had changed hands dozens of times. By autumn of 1993, they were occupied by an independent film distributor, a yoga studio, a rainwear designer, an architect, a massage therapist, and *Boom City*.

The poverty of the newspaper announced itself with a half-painted logo on the glass door, a silhouette of a large head, the top open to reveal a cityscape with the Space Needle in the foreground and fireworks flaring overhead. The logo suggested a custom job abandoned for lack of payment. Rejection was looking more likely by the minute.

Not that I liked my shitty job at the copy center. If anything I'd learned to hate it more every day. Yet aside from the boredom, lousy pay, and being talked down to by half the customers, I didn't mind it so much after I'd given up writing. Thirty-two hours a week at a photocopy center was its own kind of hell. Yet when I moved on, if I ever moved on, I wanted it to be for money and security, or a windfall I could live on. Not spending my nights watching bad acting in garages and basements, getting paid by the word to tell playwrights and directors what their high school drama teacher should have said, years ago. "You suck. Get out."

The second I walked through the door of the *Boom City* office I took a deep breath and sighed with relief. I was in no danger of being hired. If these people had money, I reasoned, they would have spent some of it on real desks instead of horizontal doors with two-by-fours nailed on for legs. And carpeting instead of remnants tossed at random angles over a peeling wood floor. Lamps rather than clip lights attached to open windows. Or a phone system to transfer calls instead of relying on staff to shout at one another over cubicle panels with surface fabric roughly the color and texture of congealed oatmeal. (Except one panel with a foot-wide collection of what appeared to be nose pickings. As someone would later explain, this was 'the Snot Wall, a thing and a tribute to a thing.')

In the center of the open reception area a solitary green metal desk served as nothing more than a caddy to a single-line telephone. One side of the desk was dented. Beyond the desk a tangerine sofa propped up a young woman with skin as pale as any I'd ever seen. If I had to guess her profession I would have said 'Dust Fairy.' Her frilled skirt was tossed up over silk panties, and one arm was crooked over her eyes.

"Shelly!" someone yelled from deep within the labyrinth of cubicles. "Shelly! Wake the fuck up!"

A head wearing 3D glasses popped up over a partition. A round cushion came hurtling out of the cubicles. It hit the prone young woman on the sofa and bounced to the floor.

"No, no! Fuck this!" the young woman groaned. Standing, she wobbled on ridiculous wedge heels. She took a few steps and collapsed into a chair behind the metal desk. She gazed at me, her upswept hair askew. "Who are *you*?"

"Greta Garver," I said. "I have an appointment but if you're too busy…"

"Ha ha," she intoned without mirth. She turned to her left and shouted while holding her abdomen, "Who has an appointment with Greta Carver?"

"Garver," I said. "No big deal."

"Answer me!" she screamed. "Who the fuck is seeing this woman? Greta! Carver!"

I felt like a lost kid at the mall. Waiting to be remembered by an errant dad.

"Send her to the coffee shop!" somebody yelled.

"What?" she yelled back.

"The interviewees are going to Rosebud. Send her there. Can you hear me?"

"Yes!" She turned to me. She took a breath. "You know where Rosebud is?"

"Yeah. West. The other side of Broadway."

"Go and talk to the editor. She'll be sitting in the corner. She always sits in the corner, in the dark. Freak." She shook her head. "I didn't say that." When I turned away she called after me, half-heartedly, "Good luck!"

Outside, the autumn temperature finally registered. The sweat-sheen I'd acquired felt like underwear made of ice. My sheer, sleeveless smock practically whistled through the air as I walked. I clenched my teeth and tried not to shiver.

I had a brief impulse to head for the nearest tavern to get shit-faced. Lie to Vaughn, say I aced the interview but they had twenty other candidates who were more qualified.

Of course, as I said earlier, this would have been a lie. I was qualified enough to review theater, at least the amateur variety. I'd spent the worst summer of my teenage life stage-managing a series of high school productions. I had expected my one and only theater gig to be an easy Performing Arts credit. I learned there was a reason why the job came with a bullhorn and a first aid kit.

A person with any self-respect would have quit. Someone whose family didn't make a religion out of white-knuckled stoicism would have walked away. I gritted my teeth through ten weeks of Shakespeare-quoting, fatuous sixteen-year-olds in smelly costumes and gray wigs; drunk kids who had signed on as crew members before they'd seen the monolithic set pieces they had to move every night; and a middle-aged director who cried at rehearsals and threatened to kill himself when actors forgot their lines.

My job was to break bad news, patch up minor injuries, say no whenever the director ran overtime, and take responsibility for anything odd or filthy—like the loaded diaper we found behind the risers on opening night. ("Ah, we need you over here, Greta, *posthaste!*") That was the summer I learned to hate Shakespeare, the sound of snapping fingers, the odor of musk aftershave on decrepit costumes, parents, children, electrical equipment, paint, and men named Cyril.

The cold drizzle of Pike Street gave way to the hobbity interior of the Rosebud. The fake-antique sled on the wall fit the café's name but still managed to clash with the floral mauve décor. Sauntering through the door was like stepping inside a quilted tea cozy.

When my eyes adjusted, and after I secured a loose bra strap, I spotted the editor in the shadows. She occupied a corner table between a fern and a philodendron, a mousy woman with horn-rimmed glasses, a brown pageboy, three intertwined scarves, and a dour expression, picking through a stack of pages with the disdain of a lifelong curmudgeon.

"Hello," I said. "I'm Greta Garver. I was told to meet you here for my interview."

I imagined she was checking the air between us for my scent, so she could decide whether or not to bite me. Then her lips parted drily. She frowned and said in a voice a woman can only achieve with two decades of whiskey and cigarettes, "All right. Let's see your resume and writing sample."

"Sure." On the way over I'd stopped by a copy center (not the one where I worked), for a fresh edition of the essay. I couldn't present her with the wine-stained original.

"Your resume says you have experience stage managing."

"Right," I explained. "Just a summer in high school. One summer."

"Do you like theater?"

"Sure."

"Why?" she asked.

"Uh. Well, the intensity of live performance," I began. "The intensity is unique..." Pomposity bubbled from every word and drifted upward to pop against the ceiling. "The physicality of the encounter and the performer's vulnerability call for a higher commitment than TV or film actors—and audiences—are willing to make." Absolutely treading water. If Lee Todd could have seen me he would have laughed until his sweatpants fell off. "Because we invest more, we expect more, or we have a right to expect more from a theatrical experience..."

"Okay," the editor said in the middle of my speech.

"Well," I said, reaching for the pages of the writing sample she'd been perusing between slurps of coffee. "Thanks for seeing me. It was good to meet you."

She shook my hand, held onto the pages and said, "You're hired. You understand this is a staff position, not freelance. I hoped the ad would provide a filter. The weekly pay is lousy but you're young so you can probably put it together with the two-cents-a-word you'll get for the copy you write and scrape by somehow. You'll be required to submit at least three reviews every week, no less than five hundred words each, and you'll be on probation for the first three months. If you can write and meet deadlines you should be fine. Judging by this essay I'd say you don't have to worry about the first requirement. If you're not a junkie you have an advantage over the last person who held the job."

My give-me-a-fucking-break expression must have appeared to be pleasant shock because she began congratulating me. Somewhere between the fumbled thanks and the muttered information about pay scale and schedules, she blurted out an introduction for the first time.

"You report to the arts and entertainment editor, Steve Billings, who reports to me. Under better circumstances Billings would have been here for the interviews but he's the one who hired a junkie. So. He's on probation now as well. Nevertheless, you'll turn in all of your copy to him for approval. And I will decide who stays and who goes. I'm the editor-in-chief at *Boom City*. Eve Wallace."

Chapter Eleven

In my lazy fashion I used to thumb through the *Stranger* almost every week and the *Seattle Times* on the weekend, plus a couple of arty magazines. The *Weekly*—or *Weakly,* as some spelled it—was the journal of choice for baby boomers, the real estate-invested, art-loving, politically correct readers in their 40s and 50s who kept crystals in meditation nooks and flap-jacked around town in Birkenstock sandals and winter socks, reminding people to conserve water and dispose of outdated electronics responsibly. You could spot their ramshackle mansions along 10th Avenue, where the street shed its Broadway moniker, at the point where the rent doubled and occupancy decreased to two adults half of the year.

You could identify the local boomers by a stone Buddha or a painted Ganesha peeking through their weedy gardens, and by the tinkling of wind chimes on hand-carved porticos. Often inside the brick fences surrounding their property you could hear them chuckling at Garrison Keillor broadcasts, or you might glimpse them awkwardly dancing to reggae music in the drizzle. You could detect them when you entered a bathroom after they left, a mild and not unpleasant pastoral aroma of green tea and wheat grass that reminded me of cow pastures in springtime.

The *Weekly* was for stoners who were deciding to smoke less, cash in some of their Microsoft money to buy Adobe stock, and adopt babies from Romania. The *Weekly* told them where the next jazz festival would take place, and offered discounts on tours of the winery at Chateau St. Michelle, which was only a picturesque train ride away.

The *Stranger* was designed as an antidote and an addiction. Raunchy yet smart, loaded with comics, snarky reviews, insults aimed at politicians and middle aged parents and anyone else who seemed target-worthy, coupons for sex toys, massages, and bathhouses, personal ads, and of course the letters column, 'Savage Love.' It was the shit, to people who liked to call things 'the shit,' and it was growing exponentially, from a four-page inside joke to a business on the verge of rendering both of the city's venerable music reporters, the *Rocket* and the *Weekly*, obsolete.

Before the *Stranger* arrived, no one threatened the authority of those patchouli-scented papers. In its wake a dozen tiny publications sprang up. Most were DIY newspapers and art journals put out by heiresses and heroin dabblers. Kids deciding, "If someone else can do this, so can we!" Naïve pretending to be cynical, earnestly ignoring the fact that a trust fund child who can't balance a checkbook probably can't keep a business going.

As far as I could tell *Boom City* was one of these doomed, shitty little papers. They had nothing special to offer. They even lacked the rowdy charisma of the *Urban Spelunker*. The *Weekly* tried to cash in on said charisma by hiring away the *Spelunker*'s main attraction, a columnist who wrote under the pseudonym Babs Babylon. None of the columnists or reviewers for *Boom City* had become such a household name. Every aspect of the paper was mediocre, Eve Fucking Wallace was its editor, and she was my boss.

If I'd only had a brain I would have run screaming from Rosebud and never looked back. Instead, I shook Eve's hand and promised to report for duty the following Monday. I told her I was between jobs and didn't need to give two weeks' notice. Knowing I could call Desiree and simply tell her to fuck off was the one giant bonus to my situation.

All along I'd treated the interview as a lark, a joke, knowing they would never hire me. Then I actually met Eve. Suddenly I couldn't resist the chance to get a closer look at the bitch that snuffed out my writing ambition. I had no idea what I would do next but I found her ignorance of our secret relationship thrilling. I was enraptured by the thought of knowing what she didn't know, staring at her weasel face during our conversations and realizing if

I stabbed her with a pen, just took one out of my bag and thrust it through her windpipe, she would have no idea why. I couldn't walk away.

I avoided telling Vaughn about the new job. All weekend he kept stopping by, pestering me for details. I told him there were dozens of applicants, hot young wannabes lined up around the block. I told him it might be weeks before I heard back. I said I'd let him know if anything happened.

Here's what happened.

On Monday I met the narcoleptic receptionist again. She said her name was Shelly and not to ask her last name. She said she had to take medication to stay awake. She was draped from neck to ankles in plastic when I arrived, and a taut, sunburned teenager was cutting her hair. Shelly told me to go and wait in the production room, where I found a guy crawling on the floor connecting cables and checking outlets.

Sly gray eyes, black hair to his shoulders, slender, androgynous, both gawky and graceful, he dusted off his jeans and faded Soundgarden T-shirt. Then he sat next to me and began to sketch in a notebook.

"I'm Charlie," he said without looking at me. "I'm not an extrovert and I'm not coming on to you. No one here has good manners, so I have to introduce myself."

"Greta. I'm the new…"

"Grunt," he said.

"Reviewer."

"Not to hurt your feelings. Theater reviewing's a back alley. You know that, right? Nobody cares about it. You plan to write features, later on, right, like a grownup? Sure you do, it's okay to admit it. Anybody can review theater. That's the opinion around here. If you make a wrong move they'll replace you the same day just to prove how easy it is."

His words crackled in the air between us like static, like a remote radio broadcast. He stood, crossed his arms loosely, and rubbed the center of his back against the corner of a filing cabinet.

"Okay," I said. "Good to know."

"Please don't be sad." He stopped scratching his back and managed to pull a sad face without pissing me off. "I'm not messing with your head. These people can be assholes, some of them. Most of the time they're assholes. It isn't their fault. They're overcompensating little shits."

"Meaning...?"

"I'm being snotty. *Boom City*'s a nest of adventurous babies all trying to outdo their parents' success so they can say, 'See, mommy? I did good.'"

"You *are* snotty."

"Shut up," he said lightly. "You should know this. The publisher only hires two types. There are the people who can afford to work without pay, if it ever comes to that; and the ones who are broke but too vain or proud to admit how much they need the lousy paycheck. He hates to pay people. And he hates to say no. It makes him nervous."

"Which category are you? The type who can afford not to work, or the type who's too proud to beg for your paycheck?"

"Guess!" Charlie's grin had its own style, insouciant as an unexpected kiss. He held his dark hair back with one hand, inviting me to study his angular face.

"You come from money but your dad's cheap," I said. Taking a stab was a habit I learned from my mom. "He won't cut you in on the family inheritance until you prove you can make it on your own. He wants you to be a man."

His eyelids fluttered almost imperceptibly. He laughed at the melodrama.

"And you're broke," he said, quietly evening the score. "Your parents are paying off a third mortgage, or they've divorced and left no forwarding address."

It was my turn to wince. I smiled to cover my embarrassment.

"Anybody can see that," I told him. "I win."

"Why do you want to write reviews for a subhuman weekly salary plus two cents a word?"

"Who says I want to? How do you know how much I make?"

"You took the job," he said, maybe annoyed, maybe teasing. "I know everything about this dump." He lit a cigarette. I waited for him to head for the stairwell, the designated smoking area. He stayed where he was, leaning against the file cabinet with one leg propped against a plastic chair. "What are you doing at *Boom City*?"

"Fine. You're right. I want be a journalist. Might as well start here," I said. "Eve says I have the right background..."

"Okay. Whatever you want to tell people, or yourself, it's all right with me. Watch your back, though," he said. "Your spot was filled by three other people in the past year and a half."

"Eve told me to focus on..."

"Ignore what Eve tells you. She's an okay lady but she's out of her depth. Just between you and me, if the publisher ever finds the kind of editor he wants, he'll fire Eve over the phone."

"What are you, stalking everybody?" I wondered briefly how I could ever study Eve while this guy studied both of us.

"Listen. Your fellow reviewers, the music and film people, are douchebags and dummies. I'm the only person you need to listen to if you want to keep your stupid job. Okay?"

"What about Steve Billings?" I asked. "You know, the arts and entertainment editor, the guy I report to?"

"He's the biggest dummy in a store window full of dummies. Eve doesn't let him hire people any more. She's taken over part of his job. It's humiliating but he hasn't said a word. By the way, if you want his job you can probably steal it as soon as your probation's up. The guy hates being an editor."

"I see," I said. "Why do you think the publisher wants to replace Eve?"

Charlie sighed. "Last year he wanted the paper to be more professional. Eve got the layout, the cut and paste, off the floor of the reception area. She made the publisher hire Shelly—well, not Shelly per se, just a person to answer the phone, type personal ads, and sort mail. Not exaggerating. This year, he's more ambitious. He wants better features, bigger targets, more news."

"What kind of editor does he want?" I asked.

"My guess? He'll know the beast when he sees it. But I'll be surprised if it isn't a guy, a kid, a hotshot like the ones he reads in *Harper's* and *The New Republic*. He's always talking about these post-gonzo little jerks he admires. Anyway, here's a workflow chart." He handed me the page on which he'd been sketching. "Because no one else will tell you when or how your reviews get published in the paper. I've included the standard word count for your section. But that can change with any issue. If I say you're over the limit, I'll tell you by how much."

"Then what happens?"

"You cut," he said. A strand of dark hair slipped over his shoulder and he flipped it back. "However many times I say you're over, you cut. Then I go back to work."

"Doing what?"

"Stuffing ten pounds of shit into a five-pound bag," he said. "I'm the Production Manager."

Both double doors to the room shot open. The guy who strode through them was no more than twenty-five, built like a surfer under a hoodie and black jeans, with a shock of wheat blond hair that rode slightly ahead of him, like a bank of rolling sea foam.

"Chuck, Chuck, what the fuck?" he shouted at Charlie and clapped him on the shoulder. When he noticed me he laughed, sheepishly but loudly like he was performing sheepishness. "Sorry," he said to me. "You're the new, you're the new, you're— wait a minute." He sprinted out of the room. Through the open double doors we heard him talking to Shelly in the reception area.

"Who's the new, what's the new reviewer's name?"

"Gerta," she answered without hesitation.

"What are you, what's the, what are you *doing*?" he asked Shelly.

"Martin is giving me a trim," she replied.

After a few seconds of silence he said, "Shelly, how can you keep, why do you keep, look, you've got to be *ready* for things."

"I'm ready."

"More ready than that," he said. "Ready for something."

"Like what?"

"Things that happen. Somebody could walk in. The phone might ring. You have to be, you need to be ready."

"I'm ready," she said again.

"But you've got a plastic sheet around your neck and you, it's like you wandered in from a salon, or, or maybe *this* is a salon. Christ!"

"Yeah?"

"Shelly, this is a business. It's, this is a place of—you know—business."

"I get it," she said. "I get it." Followed by the rustling of plastic. "Martin, I'll meet you downstairs on my lunch break." Kissing sounds, the fake *mwah* kind.

The blond guy barreled into the production room again. He raised his eyebrows at Charlie and me. Then he held up one hand, covered his mouth, hiding his laughter. "You heard that, right? Sorry! Welcome aboard, Gerta." He stuck out his hand.

"Greta," I said and shook it.

"Jesus, sorry," he said. "Shelly's an idiot. I wish I could remember to fire her. Okay, Chuckie D. Whatcha got for me?"

Charlie had returned to work at his desk. On the PC screen before him he was moving blocks of text, resizing ads and comic strips, and making a soft thumping sound with his tongue. When the publisher clapped him on the back, Charlie looked at me and said, "By the way, this asshole is Carl Stitch, the publisher. Don't make fun of his name or he'll have your whole family killed. Carl, this is Greta Garver and she's a genius."

"Ha!" Carl said. I didn't know what he meant by that.

"Maybe an exaggeration," I said.

"No," Charlie insisted. "I read your writing sample, the piece about Mia Zapata." He turned to Carl again. "Eve finally hired a reviewer who can write."

My sample, the essay I stole from Daisy, made the rounds of the *Boom City* office before I arrived. By Tuesday most of the staff had praised me for my guts, my voice, my talent, and my youth. Oh yeah. I also lied about my age, said I was a year younger just for the hell of it. The only person in the office who appeared to be over thirty-five was Eve.

"You know what? You're a prodigy," said Fucky-Face the moment I met her. I can never remember what her real name was, although she introduced herself. She was a round-eyed buxom girl with wispy hair, wearing a Girl Scout beret and listening to Seven Year Bitch on a boom box that occupied three quarters of her desk. She was friendly and solicitous. Outside the office she was popular, sought out by friends for compassionate advice. Every time I saw Fucky-Face she was on the phone lending quiet comfort or simpering advice, or she was out lunching with a pal. I never addressed her by name because all I could recall was the moniker slapped on her by a couple of hamsters working part-time for Charlie. They said her typical expression—furrowed brow, lips parted in a soft O—prompted the nickname, and I believed them.

"Oh, that piece," I said to her. "First draft, kind of embarrassing. You know. I dashed it off for the interview."

"Wow," said Fucky-Face. "I think that proves my point, don't you?"

"No. No. It was nothing."

"I loved it! I made a copy and showed it to some of my friends, I hope you don't mind. A lot of people wrote tributes to Mia but you did so much more than that."

Shaking my head and trying to step away didn't kill the compliments. Fucky-Face kept coming.

"Someday," she said. She gathered my hands in hers, dry and warm and a bit chubby. "All of this—the city, the country, the world the way it is today, all of us—won't matter to anybody anymore. We're going to leave so little trace we might as well not exist. But you know what?"

I didn't dare breathe. It was mortifying being trapped at the entrance to her cubicle with people eavesdropping all around us. I kept staring into her beaming, flushed, girlish face framed by the winged kittens and pastel ponies decorating the wall above her desk. I stood there like an idiot, half-smiling, waiting for more praise.

"We'll be gone. But those words you wrote about Mia and what she meant to all of us, those are going to live on. Those are immortal. You see?"

"Oh, well…"

"I mean it! That piece is book-award material. You should have an agent."

Technically speaking, Fucky-Face was a volunteer, an acquaintance of Eve's with a real job editing text at Microsoft. She came to the office one day a week to fact-check anything Eve deemed questionable. In a pinch, if the intern of the moment was out sick, Fucky-Face was also a meticulous proofreader.

Ed John Maynard was a nineteen-year-old who hitched a ride from a farm in Idaho to follow his destiny in the city. He was paid three dollars an hour and he would do anything. Distribution. Reception desk when Shelly wasn't available. Pizza run. Ad collection. Cleaning the production room. Taking out the trash. He also wrote letters to the editor on slow weeks, and penned short reviews in music and film under a vast number of pseudonyms.

"Uh-huh," he said when he met me. "You smoke?"

"Yeah."

"Can I bum?" He had the large eyes of a feral animal coupled with a human affectation, the cocked eyebrow of a film noir gangster. In all other respects he was nothing but a gangly kid.

I gave him a cigarette and told him to fuck off. He laughed.

"Read your story," he said. "The Mia thing. Not bad. Not bad at all." Then he pinched the cigarette between his lips and headed to the stairwell for a private smoke.

"Moo," said the blonde with the pixie haircut. Her eyes were sapphire and she had the twinkle of a Disney heroine when she smiled.

I didn't know if she was speaking office code, so I said nothing.

"Ginny Moo," she said. "Ad sales. Marketing. Special events. We do brunch at my place every other Sunday. You're invited."

"That's nice."

"No. What you wrote was nice. Better than nice. Fucking *great*." She tapped me lightly on the shoulder and strode away. Baggy shorts cut for an old man, for the beach. Muscle shirt. Bare feet. Silver toe rings in the shapes of stars and moons. Moo.

Ginny turned out to be the only granddaughter of a Dallas oil tycoon who married and started a family in his 50s. He had two sons who ran the business and one of them was Ginny's dad. All of this information came from Charlie because Ginny didn't like people to know she was slated to inherit millions.

"So, how do you know?" I asked Charlie.

"We were kind of back and forth, for a couple of months last year," he said.

"And she told you her family history?"

"What can I say? Some girls cry when they make love. Ginny blurts out financial stuff about her mom and dad."

"What else do you know?" I asked Charlie, on my third day.

"I know you're going to have a hundred enemies, right off the proverbial bat," he told me. "They will loathe you." He pantomimed hurling a knife at my forehead.

"Why? Nobody knows me. How can they hate me?"

"Take my word for it, Greta. Some people would kill for a job at the *Stranger*, and if they can get some experience at this dump first, they can apply for a job there."

"Wouldn't they make more money at the *Weekly*?"

"Yes, but the *Weekly* is uncool, so, so uncool. Uncle Jim the groping dinosaur and his girlfriend in the tent dress work there. Everybody wants to be *cool*. Don't you, Daddy-o?" He winked and walked away.

Steve Billings didn't show up until Wednesday. His reddish brown hair had the texture of a raccoon pelt run through a washing machine and toweled dry. His pants and flannel shirt were a few sizes too big and his oversized hiking boots made a series of clunking and whooshing noises when he walked.

I introduced myself. Steve stared at me with his mouth ajar and his arms hanging slack. He made a sweeping gesture toward his cubicle. I entered and sat in the only extra chair. When he took a seat next to me our knees almost touched. He went on staring and I decided to take the lead.

"I guess I'll be working with you," I said.

"Yeah. Right," he said.

"How long have you been with *Boom City*?" I asked.

He shrugged. And said nothing.

"This is my first reviewing gig," I said. "I moved here a couple of years ago from eastern Washington. Pretty boring. Where are you from?"

His eyes were as dead as the bottom of the ocean when he said, "Seattle. Been here all my life."

"Wow," I said. "You hardly ever meet a native here."

"Yeah," he told me. "People keep moving in. More every year."

There was a peculiar smell to Steve. Not quite oily or dirty but not quite clean. I wondered when he had last showered.

"Does your whole family come from Seattle?" I tried but I couldn't think of another topic. Not with his dead eyes fixed on me.

"Yeah," he said in the same flat tone. "Four generations. Watch the newbies come, and watch 'em go."

"Wow," I said again. If I could have slapped myself without appearing to be insane I would have. "Well, nice to meet you, Steve." I stood up and started backing out of the grubby cubicle, by far the messiest one I'd seen. "Let me know if you want to talk about anything. Or anything. You know?"

He was peering at me with shark eyes gone dark and hands folded together in a massive tangle in his lap when I left. For all I know he sat there all day staring after me.

Vaughn was ecstatic when he heard the news. He insisted on bringing me a bottle of Veuve Clicquot. We toasted the future. We toasted art. We toasted new beginnings.

"Holy shit," said Daisy when she stopped by and I opened the door with a half-empty crystal glass in my hand. "What are we celebrating?"

"Our Greta is a newspaperwoman now!" Vaughn announced. He poured champagne all around and we toasted ourselves, our future selves, our life in the city, and everyone we ever knew. The noise attracted our neighbors and Vaughn invited them in for another round.

By nine o'clock we sprawled across my sofa, chairs, and carpet telling stories and laughing like maniacs. Daisy leaned her head on my shoulder and drew long, decadent clouds of cigarette smoke. Ivy reclined against a large cushion like a gorgeous Russian aristocrat, puffing a joint and passing it to Ted and Stacy.

By that time Vaughn's prediction had come true. Bunny had run away with a guy who played drums in a band from L.A., leaving Ivy brokenhearted and all the more beautiful in her dark-eyed sorrow.

"Read it again, Vaughn," she said. She waved a slender hand in the air.

Vaughn cleared his throat and spoke in his sweet baritone.

"I loved you first: but afterwards your love

Outsoaring mine, sang such a loftier song

As drowned the friendly cooings of my dove.

Which owes the other most? My love was long,

And yours one moment seemed to wax more strong…"

Ivy raised her hand again, a signal to stop. Her eyelids fluttered but she didn't cry. She lifted her glass and Vaughn filled it, an unspoken bond of lost love dancing in the air between them.

I woke the next morning with gray dawn light sneaking through the bedroom blinds. My tongue was coated in moss and my legs refused to move. I spied Daisy on the other side of the bed, sleeping deeply with a faint childish grin curling her lips. She had stripped down to an undershirt and panties to crash beside me. I wondered what amazing adventures she had been pursuing since the previous week. I had a fleeting impulse to wake her and confess but I couldn't put the words together.

"I stole your story." Or…

"I'm a fraud." Or…

"I got a job using your work." Or…

"I'll never write the way you do. So I plagiarized your essay."

Nothing would make sense out of what I'd done. And nothing could explain why I'd accepted the job, or why I was staying despite the lousy deception I'd pulled to get it. How could I admit the real reason I was at *Boom City*?

"You see, I think it might be fun to try and ruin a woman's life..."

At night the towers of the Pacific Science Center resemble waiting monsters, their arched backs struck by teal and violet light, silent, brooding, animals of great height pausing near water to listen.

You stop here three times a week, to sit on the bench and recall those heady, happy years when your children loved this place and the nearby carnival, the carousel with its heroic, pretty horses. Your wife was alive then; every visit meant something new, no matter how often you returned. You know every inch of the science center, from the mechanical demonstrations of backhoe and tractor, to the mad charms of the insect room.

Tonight your house is full of angry teenagers, smelly former friends who won't give you the time of day anymore. With their loud entourage your kids have broken into the liquor cabinet and stolen the good scotch, replaced it with tea. To safeguard your stash of weed you've begun wrapping it in cellophane and carrying it with you.

Before children your life was quiet. Then your wife insisted on a family, and you went along for the ride.

When they were little they were noisy, bright, hilarious. Where has their sense of humor gone? Why do they ignore your anecdotes and roll their eyes at your jokes? There must have been a first time but you missed it. You lagged behind, a man lost in nostalgia.

If you linger too long a guard will stop by on his rounds and ask you to move along. You have no reason to move along. You feel so tired sometimes, weariness settled in your bones. Go on and lie down. Watch the burbling water in the fountain. Take off your coat and roll it up as a pillow. You won't need it. The night is losing its edge. You won't feel the bitter cold until it's too late.

Chapter Twelve

"Apparently you know your way around the office," Eve said on Friday.

I didn't know what she meant. Was I showing off too much? Did she hear me quizzing Charlie about Carl's dissatisfaction?

"So let's get you started," she said. "Vanessa is the music reviewer. Music is the big section of arts and entertainment. Including the club calendar for the week, music brings in half of the paper's ad revenue. Vanessa writes five or six reviews a week, her freelancers write the rest. She's the best person to explain what you need to know. I want you to shadow her."

"Shadow," I said. "Don't you want me to write theater reviews for the next issue? Won't there be a gap, if I don't...?"

"It doesn't matter," she said. "Whatever's opening now you can catch on the second or third week. I don't care."

I thought of Vaughn. He was constantly complaining about papers running a review the same week a show was scheduled to close.

"But won't it affect my—you know—"

"Your what?" Eve's thin, pinched lips reminded me of a leather clutch I gave my mom for Mother's Day when I was seven.

"Readers," I said. "I mean, readership. My, you know, my audience?"

Eve studied my expression and shook her head. "Don't overthink this, Greta. Most of the regular readers never look at your section. They read the personal ads, the columns, the film and music reviews, and the comics."

"But isn't the idea to increase readership?" I tried not to let this sound pathetic.

"A worthy objective," she said. "I wouldn't attach too much significance to the numbers, if I were you. At this point what I want is better prose. Theater doesn't make money but that's no excuse for sloppy writing."

"The section might make more money if the writing is better."

"Hypothetically, yes," she said. "Just don't get your hopes up. Maybe a few hundred people in the entire city go to see live theater without being affiliated with it. By that I mean a few hundred people who are not actors or directors or board members. Theater companies and theater actors comprise most of your 'readership.' They buy cheap ads and expect miracles in return. We offer them a handful of reviews every week, and they're never pleased. These are the people who will be courting your favor, sending you press kits and little bribes, which they call 'gifts of appreciation.' They're not your friends. They'll try to be, but you can't give in to it or the writing will suffer. You cannot lose your objectivity. This is why I want you to shadow Vanessa. She's experienced, she's detail oriented, and she keeps the right distance from the musicians she has to review every week."

Eve put on her glasses and turned her attention to the piles of unopened manuscripts on her desk. She smirked at me. "Unless you'd rather read the slush pile?"

The office was strangely quiet. I surmised this was the typical shame and lull of a hard morning-after, following a party at somebody's house. I had my own hangover to nurse.

"Where do I find Vanessa?" I asked Shelly.

"Nobody finds Vanessa," she said. Her eyes were crusted together by sleep and yesterday's mascara. She was sorting back issues into small stacks for storage. "Go have a smoke and she'll find you."

I was sitting on the top step of the stairwell a couple of cigarettes later—the aroma of tobacco thoroughly mixed with the odor of sweat and sandalwood drifting up from the yoga studio on the ground floor—when the door banged open next to me. I flinched and felt vaguely nauseated. I stifled the queasiness with a gulp of coffee from my to-go cup.

The woman who walked in and sat on the step next to me was already smoking. Not American Spirits. A Marlboro hung from the corner of her lips, ash curling in a mad, gravity-defying spiral. She reminded me of fashion models I'd seen in the 1960s magazines stored in my mother's closet. Her dark hair hung in long, messy strands, with blunt bangs and several 'frosted' white streaks. Her boots climbed to mid-thigh. She wore a fox fur stole over one shoulder, draped elegantly against a purple silk blouse and a black mini skirt. A gigantic black silk purse hung from her crooked elbow.

"I'm Vanessa," she said and raised a gloved hand in my direction. "What's your story?"

Her attempt at hunkering down with lowbrow little me couldn't disguise her accent, New England Old Money with a dash of European *joie de vivre*. She enunciated as though her front teeth were too large.

"I'm here to write theater reviews," I replied.

"I'm told by the higher-ups you're supposed to shadow me for a week. Why? Don't you know what you're doing?"

"Yes," I lied. "I have a little experience. But the editor thought..."

"Eve," she said. "God, she's an imbecile. Have you ever heard of a competent American fiction editor who hasn't read Melville? My granny read Melville to me when I was a toddler, for god's sake. Eve's knowledge of pre-World War II literature would fit in a thimble with room left over for a tea party."

"When was Eve a fiction editor?" By now I realized being the new girl was a good means to ferret out information.

"1983, allegedly," said Vanessa. "When Minimalism ruled Manhattan. The woman's education is absolutely shocking. What are you reading?"

"Oh," I said. "These days...?" I took a drag on my cigarette, to buy time. "Cortázar, Calvino. Latin American and European writers, mainly."

"And romance?"

"What?"

"Tell me your guilty pleasure fiction," she said.

"Oh. I don't know. I used to read crime fiction."

"Crime? What kind of crime? Hardboiled? Domestic? *Noir?* Psychological suspense…?"

I took another drag. I let it out.

"All of the above," I said. "Hey, where is everybody today?"

Vanessa raised her hand and flicked her cigarette butt down the stairwell to the concrete landing below.

"Let's go," she said.

Forty minutes later—because Vanessa would only take a taxi and would only climb inside the taxi if the driver responded favorably to the fake smile she offered as a down payment—we were sharing a table at the Weathered Wall. The throb of indistinct sound on all sides made me queasy.

Vanessa emptied her purse onto the table and combed through the mass of lipsticks, brushes, compacts, art gallery postcards, handwritten invitations, three pieces of Italian candy, a baggie half full of weed, a pillbox containing five black beauties, one of which she popped into her mouth and washed down with a dry martini she'd talked the bartender into mixing on the sly, a red dildo, a monogrammed handkerchief (*VV*), a gold and white dildo, a press pass with a picture of her wearing a push-up bra and zebra-striped Capri pants, eleven dollars in ones and change, a paper fan from Uwajimaya, a rubber stamp of Kali, individually wrapped condoms in two sizes, a cocktail napkin from a sleazy bar called Charlie's, a tampon, a bottle of purple nail polish, and what appeared to be an expensive emerald ring (which she tossed back into the purse with a shake of her head and a chuckle).

"You like crime fiction," she said, voice pitched only slightly above the band playing across the room. "But you haven't named a subgenre or which authors you admire. You have to give me more to go on or I can't figure out who you are."

I scanned the crowd, a broad tangle of people my age, most of them skinny and most wearing some variation on the ripped flannel grunge costume of the moment. Only a few had anything approaching Vanessa's sense of style.

"Atrocious," she said suddenly.

"What's atrocious?" I asked.

"This band," she said. "They call themselves Atrocious, and they're terrible. What is this, funk and slam poetry fusion? They have no idea what they're doing. Let's go." She up-ended her martini glass, raked the pile of her belongings back into her bag, and before I knew she was standing up, she went striding through the crowd. She didn't bother to push people out of the way. They moved aside as she walked or she trod on their feet.

On the sidewalk, the music was muted but still throbbing in the background. Vanessa slung her bag over one shoulder and I followed her up the street.

"Tell me your influences," she said. "Give me something to go on. Who are your mentors?"

"Have you heard of Lee Todd Butcher?" I asked.

"Oh, god," she said. She was putting another cigarette between her lips when a handsome boy sidled up next to her and offered a light. She ducked her head, ran the tip of her cigarette through the flame, and kept walking without breaking her stride. The boy watched her go with an expression of irreparable sadness. "Butcher. You like *Butcher*?"

"Well, he isn't my favorite author but I've studied his books." I scrambled for something more to say. "He's no Chandler or Hammett."

"He's no Leonard," she said. "He's no Ellroy. He's no Willeford. He's a hack."

"Of course," I agreed, wondering how to disown my implied endorsement. "I only mentioned Butcher because I know him..."

"Uh-oh," said Vanessa. "A friend of yours?"

"No, nothing like that. I took a class he taught, a long time ago."

"You didn't fuck him?" she asked.

"No, no," I said. "Why would I...?"

"Well, I did," she said. "I thought he fucked every woman he ever met under the age of twenty-five."

I was already out of breath trying to keep up with her long-legged stride. I tried not to sound shocked when I said, "Oh. Where did you meet him?"

"Cocktail party in Manhattan," she said. "A book release. Not his. He was washed up, making the rounds for free drinks. One of my girls pointed him out and dared me to fuck him, so I did. I heard he left the city before I moved out here. God knows why I came to this place. The west coast is over."

"I guess you met him before he decided to start teaching," was all I could come up with.

"Must have been," she said. "I wouldn't know. Butcher wasn't writing, anyway, he was beginning 'the slow descent,' as my granny used to call it. He just died recently, didn't he?"

There are moments when you forget where you are. A gut-punch renders you blind and speechless. When the surrounding space comes into focus again it is with clarity so stunning you will never forget the smallest details. This is how Lee Todd's death, his absence from the earth, came to be associated with the smoky trail of a Marlboro, the cool click of heels on uneven pavement, the ice-tinged night air, and the blue-black sky spiraling above and away, into infinity.

"Are you coming?" Vanessa asked. She was up ahead, waiting with her bag slung over her shoulder. "We have to catch a taxi. I have five bands to see tonight."

The rest of the evening spun on an enormous wheel around us—loud music, bad beer, and sad-faced lanky boys trying to impress Vanessa with lame jokes and bravado—and overhead a silence as deep and merciless as the sky itself. It was after four o'clock when I finally stumbled up the stairs to my shitty apartment, lurched from the front door to the bathroom, and threw up all over the tiles.

This fringe theater on Capitol Hill is wedged between a long-ago-gutted mechanic's garage and a pizza joint where they serve by the slice. These drafty, partially underground buildings all have their legends. One story describes a fire in which three auto mechanics were killed. They're said to haunt all of the businesses on this block, turning on lights employees swear they left off, cracking windows and mirrors, tripping customers on the stairs. All lies, of course, as far as I can tell.

My eyes don't have to adjust to the darkness backstage. I can see all I want to see. *You* clutching your linen handkerchief, dabbing your nose with it, mildly allergic to the dust embedded in the velvet drapes and the chairs, even in the shabby gold carpet lining the lobby.

For some reason I feel more than the usual awareness when I see you here. Call the sensation *déjà vu*. Dreamlike yet vivid, I have a vague memory of the dainty chin and round blue eyes. Nostalgia brings to our encounter a piquant intimacy. Do you feel it?

I watch you observing the performance from the wings. Longing suffuses your body, desire hums within your delicate bones. The actress on stage is playing the role you were born to play. You know this character by heart, you know her so well—Masha—she fills your nights with raw suffering and endless desire. By sheer will you've drawn her toward you, merging with her soul and separating, merging and separating, sailing across pale skies.

"I am in mourning for my life..." How many times have you recalled the line and murmured it to yourself? In a park in the moonlight, under a canopy of oak leaves, in your chair at the box office, or backstage setting props in place, you catch your breath and say the words. This is your line, your meaning, your Masha, and no one has ever cast you in the role.

You've spent eight years teaching scruffy kids how to stand and deliver the words of Chekhov, your god. You teach them to ask why they speak these words and not those, why they ought to care about the characters they mangle in poorly rehearsed classroom scenes.

You volunteer to handle the box office at one production after another. You spend sleepless nights preparing bake sales. You donate books to the theater company library. You run errands for the artistic director and compliment him on his children, his condo, his knowledge of the classics, and his taste in furniture. You alienate friends by begging them for odds and ends for the annual auction.

You study French and renew your passport in hopes of being invited to Marseilles for a month-long workshop where you will be nothing more than the housekeeper picking up after ungrateful students. At the last minute you discover you're not invited.

Younger, prettier, more fuckable ingénues are given scholarships and recommendations, while you work and struggle to be noticed. This season, the artistic director's favorite niece is cast in the role of a lifetime, the character that has lived in your broken heart for twenty years.

Hungry girl standing in the wings, waiting, watching one more Masha weeping on stage, I put my hands on your shoulders, feel the loneliness raging inside you, and the murmur of something yet unknown metastasizing in your heart and lungs. I know there's nothing more I can do here, no more damage I can cause that hasn't been inflicted by life itself, and I leave you watching, waiting, longing.

Chapter Thirteen

Daisy dropped a textbook on the table. *News Reporting and Writing*.

"I'm supposed to read this," she said, pouting. "It's like going back to high school."

"Are you reading it?" I asked.

"Fuck no!" She sat down opposite me and glanced out the café window. I was drinking one cup of coffee after another to master my hangover while Daisy smoked and studied my face. "Want to read it and tell me what I need to know, in a page or two?"

"You're kidding, right?"

"Maybe," she whined, one corner of her lips curling.

"Your editor gave you a reading assignment?"

"I know. It sucks," she said. "I've got, like, my own style and I know the rules. I do. I've paid my dues, Greta. In classes and workshops, and internships, all of that shit, you name it."

"A weekly paper in Portland hires you to write features and the editor gives you a textbook?"

"He gives the same book to everyone he hires. It's like an in-house style guide. I guess it isn't such a big deal. I can read it tonight. I just…" Her gaze followed a boy and girl, maybe fifteen years old, making out while walking down the street. Beside them a crew had begun to break up the sidewalk with jackhammers.

"What's wrong?"

"I don't know," she said and exhaled a stream of smoke. "I like it when people trust me. I've gone to all these places—Peru, Tibet, New Zealand—I've interviewed Exene Cervenka and Lydia Lunch and Janet Fucking Reno."

"I know."

"This isn't a thing I'm doing for fun until I get married and have a baby. Shit!" She stubbed out her cigarette in a saucer. "Fuck it. Tell me what you did last night."

For the first time I wondered where Vanessa had ended up after our excursion. Too many images clipped through my head at once. Vanessa dancing to Big Chief with a drummer who kept begging her to come see his band; a girl in a baby doll dress offering a flask; a guy with jeans ripped across his ass leaning into Vanessa and calling her a cunt; the flash of a smile in a crowd, wheat blond hair and blue eyes; a couple sitting on a sidewalk holding their hands over their ears while the music thrummed away indoors; an outer wall covered in Home Alive posters.

It occurred to me Vanessa's last trip to the women's toilet for a line of whatever she was snorting might have been followed by a swift exit through the alley and a speedy change of venue, without me. I had no idea how I got home.

"The bitch dumped you," Daisy said and laughed, after I recounted my night out. I hated to talk or even think about it. Every route I attempted was bound to lead me back to Lee Todd.

"Are you going to read the textbook?" I asked. The blood pulsed hard in my temples and it was all I could do not to lay my head down on the table.

"Are you listening to me? I said I would. Man, you had a crazy one," she said and laughed again. "I love this gig in Portland. But I'll fucking miss you."

"When will you have time to miss anybody?" I asked.

"Listen to you. We're both working writers now. We have no lives."

"Features? Shit," I said. "You're on your way."

"To Portland," she said with a grin. "It's a real start. This is exactly what I want. It's all coming true!"

"Are you moving there?"

"Well, yeah," she said. "But I'll drive up to Seattle every couple of months."

"We'll hang out, then."

"We better!" She slapped my arm. "Don't shit me, you bitch. You better make time to hang out with me!"

We finished our coffee and Daisy dragged me up Broadway to the Deluxe for a round of rejuvenating Bloody Marys. It was Saturday and this would be the last time we were both free of deadlines for several months.

We walked back down Broadway, wandered into a vintage shop to buy silk scarves. We followed a lanky young guy with beautiful hands until he met a tattooed girl with maroon hair in the reservoir park.

"Gross," said Daisy. "I'm not going in there. My friend Gigi stepped on a needle in the grass."

"Yeah, fuck that," I said. "Dog Shit Reservoir."

We walked arm in arm past Bonney-Watson Funeral Directors and on to Pike. Next door to the Army-Navy Store we stumbled into Ballet, a Vietnamese restaurant where I used to hang out with Tam when she and I worked together.

Daisy and I ate lunch at one of the little Formica tables and added hot sauce to our pad thai. Fortified, well fed, we spent the day shopping bookstores and thrift shops, lost and contented in the quiet pockets of the lazy city on a Saturday afternoon.

Chapter Fourteen

I never told anyone about my relationship with Lee Todd. Vanessa didn't ask me for details about him and I decided to let her think he was nothing to me, a teacher I barely remembered. In reality I only thought about him more as time went on. Whenever the blues took hold of me or I stopped to consider what the hell I was doing with my life, Lee Todd came sauntering back to my consciousness with his droopy eyelids and his words of wisdom in cadences that implied exhaustion beyond comprehension.

"If anyone in this classroom decides to ignore my advice by becoming a writer, for fuck's sake don't try to offer the world a *message*. These hulking novels full of allusions to this classic book or that philosophy, they're bullshit. Nothing you have to say is going to make the slightest difference to society, or humanity, or even the handful of readers who buy your work. If books had the power to change the world, we'd all be sitting around laughing our asses off in Utopia by now. The world is still the same shithole it was the first time some prick put ink to paper with 'the best idea anybody ever dreamed up.'

"The same ten stories get written a thousand times every year. Some drunken critic randomly hails one of them as the greatest story ever written and people get wound up about how it *changes everything*. Let me tell you, stories don't change a goddamn thing. People still kill other people, and rape other people, and beat up animals and kids and old folks. People are people. People are shit. You'll never change that. Nothing you write will change it. All you can do is entertain yourself and maybe if you're talented earn some money. So forget crusading and saving the world. The best story you'll ever imagine won't make any goddamn difference."

The only story in my head at the moment was Lee Todd wandering around Manhattan in a shabby suit, crashing book release parties for booze and snacks. Fucking snide young women like Vanessa and maybe thinking, while he was inside her and she was making the right noises, *Hey, this could be my ticket…*

I knew how he thought because I'd observed him closely, if briefly. I watched him lean in when he spoke to a woman, not threatening but listening with his whole body, listening at a championship level. He didn't take women's books seriously but he knew what young straight women wanted—to be listened to by an older man. If a guy can pull it off, the expression that says, 'I'm all ears and I'm all yours,' he never has to sleep alone.

All the loner mythology, it was all crap. I finally knew in my bones how ignorant I'd been to think he only did this now and then, and with women he really liked. Lee Todd was an open bar with no waiting. Then he was dead.

What bothered me was not knowing and not feeling the slightest instinct about his death. For months I'd walked through the deadening routine of my life and every time I thought of him I gritted my teeth and vowed I wouldn't contact him because I had nothing to show for all of my time in Seattle. I had no proof of my significance, I couldn't laugh in his face. I just kept going day after day, and I imagined his words taunting me. The idea that he might be dead had never crossed my mind.

I found the obituary, realized he had spent his last weeks at Harborview, only a few miles from my apartment. He died in a hospital bed and there was no memorial service. His most popular novel was *Whiskey Fever*, now long out of print. He left a sister, two ex-wives, and a thirty-year-old son named Granger.

I stopped to marvel at a man who would let his son be named Granger Butcher, and then realized Butcher wasn't his real name. His son's name was Granger Davis Jr., meaning the man who pretended to listen to me, and then slept with me, and told me not to write fiction, was named Granger Davis. Jesus Christ.

Staff meetings were held on Monday mornings. The two hamsters who named Fucky-Face showed up together, smiling and chattering about hard work and bonuses for Thanksgiving. Moo brought her notebooks and silently made notations, adding stickers (stars, rockets) for emphasis. Once all the staff members were gathered in the reception area on cushions or in folding chairs or crammed onto the sofa, Charlie whispered in my ear, "This is going to suck." Shelly slipped in, late, and wedged between the occupants of the sofa.

Before Carl barreled up the front stairs three at a time and announced the latest 'cool, super cool' idea he had, and before Eve dragged herself in with a thermos full of coffee and a disgusting pastry slathered with frosting, the rest of us sat around the reception area making small talk, a cacophony of snarky opinions people probably should have kept to themselves.

"My feature about the dog leash law got cut. Eve hates it."

"Well. What did you expect?"

"I know. But it's neighborhood stuff. This is what Carl keeps telling us to go for. What the hell is she thinking?"

"Eve hates news. Did I tell you, she rejected my article on postering laws, for crying out loud. I mean, for anybody who plays clubs downtown or on Capitol Hill, this is important shit."

"Important shit!"

"Shut up."

"She doesn't care about Capitol Hill. She lives in Fremont, last frontier of the conscientious objector. Granola Town."

"Oh, is *that* why she's late every day? I thought it was the midnight screwdrivers."

"I thought it was menopause."

"She's not *that* old."

"She's over 35! What is this, a retirement home for senior editors? This is why we can't catch up. If Carl would let me recommend an editor…"

"I liked that piece Eve commissioned from Natalie What's-her-name, the *Village Voice* writer?"

"Yeah. We need more stuff like that. Tone down the highbrow poetry junk."

"I hear Carl's working on it. He's fed up, you guys."

"Good luck. You know he fucked Natalie What's-her-name, right?"

"Is that why she won't write for us anymore?"

"Ha and ha. You're such a dick."

"No, really, you guys, Carl mentioned a couple of hotshot writers, one of them is, like, twenty and he's already published in *Harper's*."

"Isn't Eve supposed to recruit hotshot feature writers? Isn't it part of her *job*?"

"Like I said. Good luck."

"Where is Eve, anyway?"

"Late, aren't you listening?"

"Probably holding court at Rosebud. I hear she's setting up an office down there."

"You know what? I don't give a shit about outside reporters. Why doesn't she give *us* a chance at features?"

"Promote from within?"

"Yeah!"

"Aw, poor baby want to be a real journalist...?"

"Fuck off."

This is when Carl burst into the room followed by a draught of cold air. It was a measure of how quickly he moved, the way he drew the chill from the icy street below all the way up the stairwell and into the office. By comparison, Eve, when she shuffled in behind him in her coat and scarves, resembled a babushka bundled up against a record-breaking Russian winter.

"Moy tovareesh!" Ed John Maynard shouted when she arrived.

Eve grinned but I don't think she knew why the greeting made us titter. Facing the group she remained taciturn, answering Carl's questions with no enthusiasm. Carl paced and Eve stood behind him. When she forgot to create an expression her face tended to go blank, her eyes dead.

"What have we got this week? Who's on the cover?" Carl asked.

"Call him Ismail…" Steve Billings offered with a furtive glance at Eve.

"Um…"

"He's a brilliant literary…" Eve began, rousing herself for a second.

"Not another Albanian poet?" Carl shook his head. "Jesus. We've got, I mean, okay, I'm not asking for Al Gore, you know, but can we get the fucking un-translated Albanian poets off the cover?"

Ed was the only person in the room who couldn't stifle a guffaw. I admit the ensuing silence was exquisitely awkward.

"Yes," said Eve, at last. "We can."

"Okay, good," said Carl. "Good. Okay. Right. Let's start this week. Because—I wasn't going to say this with the holidays coming, but you might as well hear it now—our circulation numbers are down."

This caused a buzz. People shifted in their seats. Only Steve spoke up.

"By how much?" he asked.

Now Carl shifted his weight. "I understand it's about, I don't have the specific numbers but, I hear from the distribution crew and the printer, all together it's about one percent."

No one laughed, not even Ed John Maynard. As I would learn in subsequent weeks, no one ever laughed at Carl's announcements, however absurd, far-fetched, or maudlin.

Eve kept her head down. Moo let out a sigh.

"So," Carl went on. "We've got our, you know, work cut out." He pointed at the half-finished logo painted on the door. "It's *Boom City*, people. This is the city and this is—it's about to explode. We have to be ready when it happens. We're going to be on the cusp, on the edge, on the cutting edge of all this—stuff."

I expected the meeting would return to the subject of the week's content. Instead it degenerated into gossip about what the *Stranger* and the *Urban Spelunker* were running for the holidays.

Standing before the entire staff, Eve seemed catatonic. In private conversation she was bolder. She did, in fact, like to schedule one-on-one meetings in the same back corner of Rosebud where she interviewed and hired me. There she sat for a couple of hours each day surrounded by manuscripts and paperback editions of poetry and short fiction. She built a comfortable palace of paper, and nested in it. I could only guess she found this public place more private than the office with its crummy open cubicles, constant traffic, and Shelly screaming phone messages from her desk.

Following the staff meeting that morning Eve told me to join her. We walked to the coffee shop together, making uncomfortable small talk about weather and Thanksgiving plans. I had none. Vaughn was visiting a friend in Vancouver. Eve alluded to vague commitments with friends. We reached Rosebud before she could offer more specific details.

Once we settled in at her favorite table with cups of espresso and croissants, she launched the subject of our conversation. "Vanessa says you didn't get together with her for a debriefing over the weekend."

"Um, I wasn't sure how long I was supposed to shadow her," I said, trying not to sound defensive.

"More than one night would have been good," she said.

"Okay. I guess I could track her down today…"

"On Monday?" Eve raised an eyebrow and laughed. "You won't see Vanessa at the office until she hands in her text for the week. Then she'll disappear again, crawling around in clubs for a few nights."

"Aren't the staff meetings mandatory?" I asked, realizing for the first time she was the only absent employee.

"Not for Vanderbilts," she said, and moved on before my jaw could drop. "Vanessa turns in flawless copy and she knows what she's doing. I expect to lose her to *Rolling Stone* one of these days. Well, never mind. We might as well get you started on your own, if you're so confident."

She slapped a stack of manila envelopes on the table in front of me. A quick fan through them revealed they were press kits from theaters. Each envelope contained a press release and an invitation to call for complimentary tickets. Some also contained a couple of black and white production photos.

For the first time, the reality of what I'd signed on to do took hideous shape in my mind. I recognized Vaughn's company logo and flinched at the accompanying photo of two men wearing tight suits and an excess of makeup, pretending to laugh uproariously. One of the men held the strings to a batch of party balloons. I remembered what the Man of Misery wrote about the show, "...festooned with what appear to be the trappings of a children's party..." and noticed the phrase, "Back by popular demand, just in time for Xmas!" I hadn't seen a single show yet and I was dreading it like a U2 concert.

I trudged back to the office hugging my stack of press kits to my chest. Charlie spotted me when I dragged ass through the door.

"Here comes our critic of doom," he announced with a grin.

"Please," I said. "Where is everybody?"

"Excuse me!" Shelly growled from the sofa. "I am here, at my station, being professional. If anybody gives a shit."

We tiptoed away from the reception area. I followed Charlie into the production room.

"After the staff meeting most of the drones go out to breakfast," he explained. "I thought you joined them."

"I'm not worthy," I said. "No one invited me."

"Ah, you're a newbie. You are too slow and feeble. Don't worry. Things will change. In another week they'll take you for granted." He sat at his desk and slurped coffee from a large mug shaped like a coiled snake.

"So, where did you sneak off to?" he asked. He took a seat at his lopsided desk and began to move text around on his computer screen.

"Rosebud."

"Eek! You really have to book, get your ass downstairs the second the meeting ends, if you don't want Eve to get her claws into you."

"She clawed me pretty good," I said. "Turns out, I was supposed to follow Vanessa all fucking weekend."

"Eek, Part Two. Here's a tip. If you lose track of Vanessa, follow the trail of needles..."

"Really?" I had to reconcile this with the poise and fashion sense I'd associated with our music reviewer. "She seems pretty, you know, together, for a junkie."

"I didn't say 'junkie,' did I? For a user she's a hell of a control freak. Just the right amount, at just the right time."

"Yeah, right!" I scoffed.

"You scoff?"

"Yeah," I said. "That was me, scoffing."

"Hacks aren't allowed to scoff," Charlie said, wagging a finger. He hit a button and a page of formatted text rolled out of the printer next to his computer.

"Sorry. I forgot I'm a hack. In a few days I'll turn in the worst reviews you've ever read. Then Eve will fire me and my hack career will be over."

"Aw, poor baby!"

"Shut up," I said.

"You're overestimating this dump. *Boom City* is garbage. We're sixteen pages on a good week, and we never pull in enough advertising to get bigger. We never will."

"How do you know that?" I asked. "Carl's out there all day, drumming up business. Moo and her sidekick—what's that guy's name again?"

"Pfefferle."

"Is that his first name?"

"No," said Charlie. "I don't think he has a first name." He rolled the page of formatted text into a ball and tossed it into the trash.

"Moo and Pfefferle are on the phone all week, making deals," I said. "Trying to lure advertisers from other papers."

"Yeah. But. Most of the time they fail. You know what the *Stranger* does? They undercut the *Weekly* rates and throw in free ad design. You buy an ad with those guys, they make you part of the cool kids' club. You want your business to look young and sexy? No problem. They resize images or replace them altogether, to fit their dimensions. Trust me, one day soon they'll redesign the paper so it's the same dimensions as the *Weekly*, and then it is game on, suckers!"

"Why doesn't Carl do that?" I asked. It seemed simple enough. But I knew little about the production process, at least the parts that didn't involve me.

"Because we don't have enough staff, dodo. I'd have to work a hundred hours a week, instead of sixty, to keep up. Production only has two part-timers and I expect to lose one. Carl's going to use the one percent drop to justify letting someone go. Merry Christmas!"

"Why does the *Stranger* have so many more people? Are they rolling in ad dollars or what?"

"Yes, yes they are. Also, if you're really cool you can get people to work for pizza until you can afford a paycheck. Maybe you haven't noticed. We're not cool." Charlie shrugged.

"Why aren't we cool?" I noticed how easily I'd slid into thinking of *Boom City* as 'us' and the bigger, better competition as 'them.'

"Want me to count the ways? We're not cool because our content sucks. Our feature writers specialize in making one point—postering utility poles is good, for example—and then beating it to death instead of building on it. Our name sucks. It sounds like a 1980s roller skating rink. Our logo sucks, it's complicated and trite, the *Stranger* logo is simple and badass. Some of the reviews are okay and the arts calendar is okay but nobody wakes up thinking they've got to read the new issue of *Boom City* before they buy movie tickets. We're not funny enough. We're not sexy enough. If there's no cool factor, you can't pull in the advertisers. Not enough ads, and pretty soon we hit the shitter like all the other tiny papers…"

"Sell more ads." Obviously, I didn't get it.

"But ads aren't cool," he said. "The kids don't like ads."

"Well, then, leave out the ads. What are you saying?"

"Okay, listen." He started scribbling numbers on a piece of paper. "If you want to break even in this business you need *at least* 51% ads against 49% editorial including the graphics. Now you can go as high as 53% ads before the readers begin to notice but if you hit 55% they're going to call the paper a sellout and stop picking it up."

"Where is *Boom City*?" I asked.

"Are you kidding? This is the reason we can't afford compatible hardware and full-time production help. The same reason we'll all be collecting unemployment next summer. On a really good week, the sales team pulls in about 47% ads."

"But it's a percentage," I said. "So why not adjust…?"

"Exactly," Charlie replied, grinning like a teacher encouraging a slow student. "When we drop this low, Carl should respond by cutting the number of pages and the word count should decrease, to adjust the percentage. Go from sixteen pages to twelve."

"Why don't we do that?"

"Because Carl is married to the idea of sixteen pages and over," he said. "Less than sixteen pages and his manhood might be challenged."

"The *Stranger* was putting out sixteen-page issues earlier this year."

"They're smarter than we are," Charlie said. "They know what the fuck they're doing. They took time to grow. They weren't afraid to go smaller when they had a lean advertising week. Even now, the publisher would put out a twelve-page issue, if he had to. It isn't the size of the paper. It's the ad-to-editorial-content ratio. Every week I tell Carl not to fill the gaps with more comics and photos. He tells me I can go back to work at Wizards of the Coast any time I want. Then we put out another issue and lose more money."

"How does he pay everybody?"

"You really don't know anything, do you, dodo?" Charlie smiled. "Multiple trust funds."

"He's making up the difference *out of his own pocket*?" I couldn't believe anyone would spend his own money keeping a shitty newspaper alive.

"Well," said Charlie. "It isn't like he earned it. His dad's filthy."

"Is this going to be a long one, Grandpa Walton?"

"Hush, child. Once upon a time Carl's ancestors owned half of Portland and Vancouver, and most of Vashon Island. A thousand real estate deals later, they live like kings in Port Townsend and support about a dozen charities. Last year they donated a small island, thirty square miles, to the Audubon Society. They're on the board of directors for half the arts organizations in Seattle. Preservation, conservation, giving back to the little people... Carl's mom is singlehandedly trying to make up for the rape of old growth forest by supporting park ranger workshops for runaways."

"And his dad?"

"He's trying to make a man out of Carl. The paper was a gift, a business to practice on, like a Suzuki violin."

"A gift? It had a past life? Carl isn't the founder?"

"Correct. *Boom City* was the *People's Journal*, back in the day, staffed by two reporters, a Socialist publisher, a columnist who also handled distribution by bicycle, and a chain-smoking Wobbly to do the cut and paste. They covered labor disputes and criticized the mayor for re-zoning and selling off parkland. They had a column on Duwamish news, a column on women's rights, and a bi-monthly humor column written by a local curmudgeon called Cascadia Joe. They barely survived on subscriptions and donations. When the guy who held it all together died of a stroke Carl's dad bought the paper from his widow."

"For Carl to run?" I asked.

"No. Carl was in high school when this happened. His dad used the *People's Journal* as one of his write-offs. He called it a public service, a tax shelter with a clear conscience. He let it drift until almost everyone aboard was lost and demoralized enough to quit. When Carl flunked out of college, his dad offered him another chance to fail. And here we are."

"Here we are," I said. "Shit."

"You got it. Ten pounds of shit in a five pound bag."

"Who stayed on?" I asked.

"Pardon?"

"You said almost everyone quit. Who didn't quit?"

Charlie smiled. "Can't you guess? Steve Billings was a kind of senior gopher, an all-around interviewer, fact-checker, and cub reporter. He tried to get a consortium of business guys together to buy the paper but Carl's dad refused to sell."

"Why does he stay?" I knew the answer but I wanted him to say it. "Why not start over at a daily, if he's got the chops?"

"Some humans are like koalas. They'll cling to the dying tree they know rather than venture to the next, confusing new tree."

"Is Eve a koala, too?" I thought I snuck this in pretty smoothly. Charlie's expression told me I was wrong.

"Eve is a blank, a veil behind a veil. Carl met her at a fundraiser for a literacy program, and a week later she showed up for work. Speaking of which..." He turned his attention to his monitor, leaving me to fade away.

With no idea what to do, and the vague notion of somehow wrecking Eve still lurking at the back of my mind, I began my new job in earnest. No one seemed to care what productions I chose. No one seemed to care how seriously I took the reviews.

My first week's selections were *Six Degrees of Separation*, *Love in a Tub* (a horribly unfunny adaptation of a Restoration comedy about a guy wearing a barrel), and a new play 'in perpetual development' called *Polly and Bluster*. John Guare wrote the first of these, apparently to shame his rich Manhattan friends into noticing that other humans are not squeaky toys. The youthful actors played middle-aged characters with an earnestness that made me grind my teeth. The Restoration thing was staged in a leaky basement where the audience sat on high stools and shivered from the cold. The title characters in the last play were two homeless teenagers who spat and swore a lot and carried skateboards they couldn't ride because the performance space was only ten feet wide.

Writing five hundred words about each of these spectacles might have been the hardest thing I'd ever done for money. My relief at accomplishing my goal turned to irritation when Charlie told me he could only fit a thousand words into the paper. A professional might have tried to edit all three to the essentials. Here's what I did. I threw out *Polly and Bluster*. The show was heading into its last week anyway, and what can you say about a script the artistic director labels 'in perpetual development'? Fuck it, I decided. Why would anybody want to watch a couple of twenty-five-year-old actors bluff their way through a grim drama about loudmouthed teenagers huffing paint and living behind a trash dumpster?

"For god's sake," Shelly said when I arrived at the office the day after the issue appeared. "Can you tell the guy who directed that *Plush and Betty Show* to stop calling?"

"Who?"

"Burton Jeffries, or Jefferson Burton, or something," she said. "He keeps calling to yell at me and I told him you weren't here, and he's crazy. Here's his phone number."

There's a first time for everything, a consequence that teaches you not to do that thing ever again. This was the one and only time I returned a call from a director. In my defense, I hadn't eaten breakfast and I was lightheaded after learning I would be paid for the number of words actually published, not the number I'd written.

"Hello, is this Mr. Burton?"

"Burton is my first name," he said, followed by a loud sigh.

"Hello, Mr. Jeffers…"

"What? My name is Burton Jersey, is this a sales call?"

"No. I'm calling from *Boom City*…"

"Oh! Are you the theater critic there?"

"I write reviews. I'm not really a…"

"Who the hell do you think you are? We gave you a complimentary ticket to a stunning production of a serious work of art, you saw the show, and you didn't write a single word about it! This is our last week! You should be ashamed of yourself!"

"I'm afraid the schedule…" I began.

"It's people like you who are killing theater!" he shouted. "Do you know that? Killing it! Stabbing it through the heart and tearing out its spleen and dragging its bloodstained carcass through the streets! You're a menace! You're a fucking menace!"

"We didn't have enough room in the paper this week…"

"Then cut the goddamn Restoration comedy! Anybody could figure out a serious play about real issues is more important than a show about a man in a tub! What's wrong with you? I'll tell you what's wrong with you, missy; you don't know what theater is about! You don't understand art! You don't have a soul! If you ever set foot in this theater again…"

Some people would have let him scream it out. Others would have apologized. Here's what I did. I hung up on the guy and went out to get a breakfast sandwich.

To say the least, Burton Jersey was not satisfied with our conversation. My hanging up on him only enraged his refined sensibility. Over the next two weeks I received a half dozen letters at the office, each building on the anger of the one before. The last letter was printed rather than typed, written in red ink, entirely in caps.

WERE I A LESS PEACEFUL AND CULTURED PERSON AND WERE IT WITHIN MY FINANCIAL MEANS (AND IT IS NOT SINCE I EARN NOTHING DOING WHAT I DO BECAUSE THEATER IS A LABOR OF LOVE YOU WOULD NEVER UNDERSTAND) I WOULD HIRE A SQUADRON OF HIT MEN TO FLAY YOU ALIVE AND FEED YOUR LIVER TO A HYENA...

He did not explain where one would go about hiring a squadron of hit men if one had the financial means. Nor did he note the scarcity of hyenas in a city in the Pacific Northwest. But after that he must have felt he had expressed all of his bile. The letters stopped.

I should say, *Burton Jersey's* letters stopped. Every week I managed to offend someone, an actor or director or playwright whose production I had attended and then failed to proclaim a masterpiece.

What I found both fascinating and disturbing was the regularity with which theater artists took exception to ordinary praise. Reviews I thought anyone would have been ecstatic to receive, they found cruel or cutting. If my opinion of their efforts didn't include a couple of superlatives in every sentence, they gathered in bars and coffee shops to discuss my shortcomings, my educational and mental deficiencies, and my sex life or lack of a sex life. I know this because each batch of complaints—most of them typed and mailed to the office, a few others emailed and sorted by Shelly—contained identical phrasing and theories.

An ingénue, whose ten-line performance I called 'a promising debut,' told me I was probably a nymphomaniac cruising for little boys. Her director said I was a nymphomaniac cruising for ingénues.

A playwright I praised for 'lyrical and poetic nuances' told me to climb into a trunk and breathe my own fumes until I died. The artistic director who had selected the play for a festival called me a trunk-dwelling moron who probably got off on my own fumes.

And so on.

In light of these responses to what I thought were pretty reasonable assessments, I began to wonder what would happen if I wrote *scathing* reviews. What if, every time I had to tuck in my elbows and pull in my knees at another dark, musty, dilapidated, unlicensed fire hazard of a performance space, and fake interest in a poorly paced rendition of a classic that should not have been revived (not only because it was racist and sexist but also because it was badly structured and boring), what if I reported *all* of the show's flaws? What if I stopped overlooking whatever was ridiculous or unprofessional and began to tell what I actually noticed, instead of striving to find the fledgling good element in everything? Since nothing I could imagine would equal the hostility flung at me by people I'd praised, I decided to give it a try.

The first experiment centered on a fringe production of a kitchen sink drama by a local playwright inexplicably named Scarf Dennis. To offset the grim aspects of the script Mr. Dennis called for all but two of the characters to be represented by puppets. This might have brightened up the whole mess if the puppets didn't occupy a domestic setting every bit as sad and ugly as the full-size set occupied by the confused full-size actors.

The best moment of the evening came during a confession speech when a puppet echoed every word spoken by one of the actors until they reached a line in which they admitted killing a child—and the entire third row of seats collapsed, the ancient spine of the worn-out row finally broken from too many years of use, too many asses to bear. Patrons sprawled in every direction on the floor, leaving some of them literally rolling in the aisles.

Making the roller-coaster-worthy screams that followed this mid-show disaster the main focus of my review accomplished three things. First, the city sent an inspector to examine the space and it was declared unsafe and shut down pending fines and repairs. Second, the anger formerly directed at me was immediately converted into seething, *silent* resentment. The hate mail slowed down. Two theater patrons wrote letters of thanks for my civic-mindedness and another used my review as eyewitness evidence in an ongoing dispute against the owner of the building. Third, Steve Billings finally smiled at me and told me I was doing 'okay.'

He also said he had spoken with Eve and I was going to get a pay hike, an extra five dollars a week plus two and a half cents a word instead of two. Why? The kerfuffle over my review made the daily papers and brought a brief, almost imperceptible boost in circulation. I had passed my first test as a reviewer, and learned a lesson. Being noticed is important. Being liked is not.

"Congratulations!" Vaughn shouted when he heard the news about my miniscule pay raise.

"Are you kidding?" I said. "Vaughn, everybody hates me."

We sat in my living room drinking Pinot noir. Outside the rain came down in gray dull torrents that seemed engineered by nature to make the days before Christmas as depressing as possible.

"No, they don't hate you," Vaughn said. "Not any more. They fear you, and that's worth its weight in gold, my dear. Besides, you have friends. You have me. I think you're a hero. Somebody should have shut those fools down ages ago. The whole place was a danger to the public. And you know, if no one from the paper had seen it happen the company would have apologized, handed out some coupons for free drinks at Mama's, and let it go. Hell, if they could duct-tape the seats back together and keep using them, they would have done that, too."

"Yeah," I said, thinking of the codes routinely violated by Vaughn's theater company. I opened a few press kits while we talked.

"If they liked their audience they would put on better shows to begin with," he said. "There's nothing out there but revivals of Broadway hits from the 1970s, campy Shakespeare, new plays that sound like they were transcribed word-for-word from the writer's life or a TV series, and people trying to put *Reservoir Dogs* on stage."

"And cross-dressing parodies of Bette Davis movies," I said.

"I don't mind those so much."

"And oh good," I said as I studied the press kits. "Now I can add *Santa Baby Booties*, *Xmas for G-men*, and *Chimney Sliders* to my list."

"Look at you, becoming a real critic," he said. "You're taking the job seriously, aren't you? Don't worry about upsetting people. Good for you. The city needs a kick in the pants."

"Sorry I didn't make it to your last reading. Things got kind of crazy."

"Honey, don't give it a thought. And I mean what I said. Forget about these people who can't handle an honest review. If you clear some of the deadwood it's only going to help the artists who know what they're doing. Sometimes I'm ashamed of theater when I see what's playing down the street."

"It's awful, isn't it?" I asked.

Lighting grid and fake fire exit signs notwithstanding, I was beginning to appreciate the dedication with which Vaughn and his friends approached their work. I'd never seen one of his actors go up on his lines. There were no scenes in which the actors searched for a pool of light in which to stand. The places where they performed were at least comfortable and clean. I'd never seen them offer what I would call a great evening but they never caused a row of patrons to hit the floor screaming.

"It's dreadful," he agreed. "A lot of it is. Just do your job. The editor said not to try and make friends, right?"

"Yeah," I said. "But she's crazy too."

"So you told me. What's wrong with her, again?"

"She just doesn't fit in," I told him.

I was about to launch into my fourth speech of the day on the subject of Eve's weirdness—how she brought smelly bacon and egg sandwiches to the office and kept them in her desk until lunch time; how she showed up one day wearing tiny butterfly clips in her hair and then took them out after Shelly burst into laughter and asked if she wanted a subscription to *Sassy* magazine; the rumors about her drinking. Suddenly I couldn't find any more words or accusations.

I hated everything about Eve yet there was nothing awful enough, day-to-day, to warrant making her miserable. In conversations at the office, in the glare of daylight, my feelings took on a grimy sheen of pettiness and spite. The gossip I repeated became distorted, maliciously inflated, until even the people who started rumors were taken aback by my version. The anecdotes I exaggerated became bitter little monsters crawling away from the light. They made me wonder what silent, shadowy corner of my soul was called forth by this woman, and why.

Plymouth Pillars Park at the base of Capitol Hill affords a panoramic view of the city. The limestone pillars are perfectly out of place overlooking downtown, the freeway directly below, and the bay beyond the city.

I stand here often at night, watching commuters change buses, watching cranes at work renewing the skyline. Periodically I toss a pebble down onto the freeway traffic. Most of these never make contact. A few hit home with a resounding crack of windshield glass. Call it a series of experiments in chance and mortality. The drivers call it an accident, a stray rock pitched by the tires of other vehicles. Bad luck. Once in a while it's fatal.

An hour might pass, and another. In the dark furrows of grass, in the tiny greenbelt I spy a multitude of insects doing battle for command of the universe. Behind the garages and sheds flanking the bus terminal I find a wide variety of fungi sprouting in the shade of the outer walls. I discover tools and discarded uniforms, thrown aside and forgotten, decorating the rotting floorboards alongside the carcasses of dead rodents. Green-black fingers of moss emerge from the concrete and cobblestones to grip one factory foundation after another. The buildings look as if they might be yanked underground at any moment.

I sometimes turn before dawn and climb the hill, over the vertical and horizontal curves, and return to my old apartment. Today I run my fingers over the keys of an upright piano in the corner. The sound awakens *you* and you lift your head from the pillow, scan the bedroom for signs of your cat, Marshall.

He's climbed out of the warm bedclothes to investigate a movement, a draught, less than a breeze, winding through the living room. He sits at my feet staring up at me, making no sound. We are simpatico. I enjoy these private moments with cats, gazing at me with absolute calmness while their owners shake their heads and tell them nothing is there. Then comes the chill, the frisson, when the cat refuses to budge, won't take its eyes off an empty chair, a vacant corner, or the ledge of an open window.

"Marshall!" you call out sleepily. "Hey, Marshall!"

Bed is his favorite place but I'm a new addition to the apartment where he spends his long, boring days. I'm here, I'm there, I place one finger over my lips and he stifles an urge to answer you with a lazy 'meow.'

I'd like to say I like what you've done with the place but fuchsia and ferns don't appeal to me, certainly not at $1,000 a month. The pink marble countertops in the kitchen are nauseating. What were you thinking when you signed the lease?

I explore the canary yellow madness of your bedroom with Marshall at my heels. You've fallen back asleep and your thoughts are dead to me. Your hair cascades in all directions around your pillow. Your arms are flung wide. You snore with abandon, and dream of clouds. There's no pipe on the nightstand, no drained wine glass. Do you have no vices?

I consider leaving the door open. Losing your cat might cause a much-needed crack in your charmed existence. Marshall looks up at me and his mouth opens and closes in a silent goodbye.

"So long, lucky boy," I say before I depart, leaving him inside your apartment, closing the door securely on my way out.

Chapter Fifteen

Charlie wasn't exaggerating Carl's cheapness. Everyone at *Boom City* had one or two unpaid duties in addition to their stated, underpaid job. I helped Shelly input the personal ads. This section of the paper—Charlie called it the 'find me and fuck me' department—was nothing compared to those of the bigger weekly papers. At best we offered readers two pages of what resembled classifieds but were really solicitations for sex in all manifestations. Girls wanting boys and vice versa; girls wanting girls; boys wanting boys; polyamorous seeking same; girls and boys wanting to play dress-up or dominatrix or role-play; bi seeking gay, straight and bi; transgender seeking boys or girls; next came the real specialty categories—boys and girls pretending to be animals or famous people or dead people; necrophiliacs seeking people who wanted to play dead; vampires seeking virgins; etc. These ads were either mailed in with a check or someone would phone in with a credit card, and Shelly took the order. Every day she also invented new ways to reject people, usually men, who got off on reading their fantasies to her. She learned to weed out most of the creeps by insisting on a credit card number first, followed by address and phone number.

Steve's secondary job was compiling a column under the pseudonym Dick Dagger. The column was called "Sick Dick" and it was supposed to be satirical. As Charlie recounted to me, for the first couple of months Steve (a failed musician and novelist) had invented his targets—fake socialites and business owners with outrageous names—and reported their embarrassing antics all over the city.

Maybe it was the pressure of having to fabricate so much fiction every week, or maybe it was Steve's natural inclination to hate anyone who wasn't born and raised in his native city. Whatever the reason, he soon decided to aim his criticism at real citizens of Seattle. To accomplish this he wooed and won over individuals who worked at the places run by or frequented by his targets.

Steve's mission was to get attention yet avoid trashing anyone who advertised with us. The only power he had was his audacity. With such a small readership *Boom City* was no threat to anyone. On the other hand, a good bit of reliable gossip might get picked up and printed by real newspapers. Casual readers were only interested in the more outrageous and salacious Sick Dick stories. A few local journalists were beginning to rely on Steve's tips, most of which came directly from his minions. What was supposed to be Steve's secondary responsibility became his ace in the hole, his guarantee of a position even if Eve fired him as arts and entertainment editor.

Steve's Minions—Charlie mocked them with the title 'Pike Street Irregulars' but I preferred the name the rest of the staff used behind their backs—loved to sneak in and out of the office by way of the smokers' stairwell. This backstreet approach added to the intrigue of their nefarious adventures. The more paranoid among them phoned in tips from home. The more spiteful used breaks at work, and company phones, to call in tidbits about their employers and superiors.

Steve courted people who were well placed to observe bad behavior but I was pretty sure some of his minions exaggerated or even fabricated stories to curry favor with him. They were paid nothing. Steve was smart enough to offer them VIP treatment when they visited, and they were said to be included in all of the Sunday brunches at Moo's house.

One by one, day after day, they emerged from the back stairs at *Boom City* and navigated the tangle of ratty cubicles to find Steve in the far corner. Along the way they helped themselves to soda, candy, and any baked treats left lying around for staff. They had the stunned arrogance of groupies, the fervent soulless stare of Manson followers. They ignored the rest of us, gliding by in a fog until they reached the final rabbit hole at the end of the row. Then they grew taller and the color came rushing to their cheeks. They greeted Steve like way-back college roomies, open-armed and conspiratorial. In return he offered them the attention and friendly demeanor he denied the rest of us. He beamed at the arrival of each minion. He set aside what he was doing and offered them a seat, a cup of coffee, a chance to vent, a place to be heard and appreciated.

Although individually they didn't make a particularly striking impression, some common element was slowly shaping my perception of them as they trudged past the slovenly workspace I shared with Ed John Maynard. Ed replaced the paper's regular film reviewer after the guy had a meltdown at the Egyptian in the middle of a Hal Hartley retrospective. ("Fuck all the goddamn quirks and kooks and fucking words!" he was heard to scream as a security guard led him outside.)

During Steve's birthday party in November I got a chance to view the minions together in one corner, and my lazy intuition came into sharp focus. I saw the tattered edges and fragile egos, in bold relief. I ran my observations by Charlie who, of course, knew the history on most of the minions. I let my imagination fill in the gaps.

Lorna had been a lingerie model at nineteen. Nagged by her parents, her boyfriend, and her agency to maintain a size two, she had binged on Dunkin' Donuts and Twinkies and then purged in the bathroom before every photo shoot. A few times she threw up so hard she burst the capillaries around her eyes and had to stop working until the mask of bright pink dots faded.

When she wasn't in front of a camera, Lorna flipped through fashion magazines while she ate. She would have been mortified to dine at a good restaurant and risk being seen by friends. She lurked outside fast food joints wearing a wig and sunglasses, and consumed greasy meals behind the wheel of her BMW. Kentucky Fried Chicken, McDonald's, Taco Bell… You name it; Lorna put it in her mouth.

Laid up with a broken leg after a ski trip in Vermont, she stopped vomiting and went on gorging. On her twenty-second birthday she could barely squeeze into a size fourteen.

Seeing her daughter's lucrative career slipping away, Lorna's mother packed her suitcase and sent her to a spa. There she was starved and lectured until her brain seized upon an attitude of self-deprivation to survive. People were so horrible, so pious and mean. They pretended to listen, but as soon as she told them how she felt— how she would quiver with the impulse to reach out and slap another woman on the street; or seeing a baby in a crib or stroller, she reached involuntarily to pinch its cheeks until they bled—her confessors invariably betrayed her.

The next conversation was invariably about professional counseling and medication, or surgery. In every scenario they dreamed up for her, Lorna was wrong, wrong, wrong. Her body was committing an act so heinous she dared not admit it, dared not glance in a mirror and accept her burgeoning self, or she might call down the hatred and vengeance of the gods.

All of these layering fears plagued her at night, and scarred her with circles under her eyes and worse—deep waves of flesh loosened by starving herself in compliance with her mother's wishes, the universal wish for her to be a size four, the universal desire for less of her.

Back home after a month at the spa, Lorna survived on rice cakes, celery sticks, and water when anyone was watching, or might be watching. In the fine, cool darkness, on the marble floor of her bathroom, she feasted on peanut butter cups, thousands of them, washed down with the pure, zesty, precious flavor of original Coca-Cola.

By age twenty-five she had given up the cruel precision of zippers and buttons on size eighteen separates. She opted for muumuus, for comfort, until an autumn breeze swept one of her favorite dresses over her head where it caught and wrapped around her ponytail. From then on, Lorna wore only a pair of man-sized long johns beneath farmer's overalls from the Army Navy Store.

"If it's sexy enough for Farmer John, it's sexy enough for me," she said to Steve every time he laughed at her outfit. In other words, every time she visited the office. She smiled broadly, dimples adding texture to her face. Her hair was always perfectly brushed and tossed and smelled of expensive product. Her makeup must have taken an hour every morning.

She would offer a petite curtsy to Steve and hold one finger under her chin, a coy gesture held over from her teen modeling days. It made Steve roar with laughter and put his arm around her shoulder. They stood together giggling for a long time, comrades in the shit factory of life.

After Lorna left the office, if there were no other minions around Steve would say, sadly, "She lost all of her modeling money. Her mother stole it." Next time she appeared they would huddle at Steve's desk and she would show him photo after photo of bygone days, every precious angle of the body she once commanded, while he stroked her hand and sighed. "Look how little you were!" he said. "I could have held you in the palm of one hand!"

Eventually Lorna starved herself down to a size ten before jumping off a balcony in Belltown at the age of forty-five. 'The age of no return,' she used to call it. Her suicide was deemed an accidental death.

Whitman was fifty in man-years. In his mind, I think he was eternally twelve. His wide-eyed reaction to almost any stimulus wore thin during Steve's birthday party. I caught a glimpse of his real face when Lorna, dancing barefoot, shimmied past and ordered him to, "Loosen up!" Whitman's wide eyes narrowed and deepened until they glinted like black ice on a country road.

It would not have surprised me if Whitman were suddenly arrested on suspicion of being a serial killer. Every time he appeared he had a new complaint about his father. He made it sound like he had taken in the old man out of pity. Charlie said Whitman lived in the attic of his father's house in Ballard, the place where he grew up. He had worked most of his life, earned a nice salary but never moved out of his father's house and never took vacations.

Whitman's usefulness stemmed from two decades of employment in the administrative office at a temp agency. He had a wizard memory and was quick to spot unhappy oddballs who had been 'tried out' and let go by various clients of the agency, clients targeted by Steve in the cartoonish guise of Dick Dagger. Whitman put the sharpest and angriest of his misfit temps in touch with Steve, to whom they confessed their former employers' secrets.

Whose software startup was bankrolled by his mom's lover's money from an embezzled pension plan? Who was screwing his children's nanny, again? Who was concealing her chemotherapy from the board of directors, to prevent a hostile takeover by a rival company? Which Buddhist entrepreneur was secretly making plans to move his manufacturing to China?

In his role as Dick Dagger, Steve was a miracle worker. He could sit down with a lonely outsider over lunch and within two hours he had enough material for a column that would scare the shit out of a successful hedge fund manager, bank executive, or city councilman. And he did this without offending Carl's family and their friends, or creating enough heat to attract a lawsuit. By naming certain individuals and keeping other identities secret or giving them fictional names and characteristics, he terrorized half of Seattle's nouveau riche.

Whitman was found naked in his father's house the day after 9/11. He sat upright on a scabby armchair, clutching the urn full of his father's ashes. Cause of death was unknown because 'sheer misery' wasn't on the coroner's list of options.

Becky Shelton was the box office manager at one of the city's grandest and most acclaimed theater companies. She had trained all of the other employees except the artistic director and had watched while they schmoozed and fucked their way to better, more creative positions. At one time or another the head of publicity, the literary manager, the associate artistic director, and the woman in charge of recruiting volunteers had all reported to Becky. She was known universally as a loyal old dog, 'Becky in the Box Office,' shortened over time to 'BBO.'

By the time her fortieth birthday rolled by without notice, Becky was repressing enough bile and rage to crush the new theater she'd helped build supervising phone call pledges in a capital campaign. Her salary had been frozen since 1988. Her half-hour lunches were spent eating homemade sandwiches in the break room.

When the A.D. accidentally left her name off the capital campaign list of 'angels' in the season brochure, Becky finally snapped. Her contribution to Sick Dick included a profile of the associate artistic director, a Southwest transplant with a wife and four children who spent late nights drunk in the parking lot at a local dive, fucking various actresses who were later cast in shows he directed.

Becky also noted how the literary manager had secured her title by giving hand-jobs to the errant A.D. plus a couple of rich patrons of the arts. As a strange bonus, Becky provided Steve with a top-secret letter confirming the A.D. was only hired after he promised to cover any extra costs in his lavish productions by 'borrowing' money from his wealthy aunt's bank account.

Sick Dick caused a purge of Becky's company unlike anything the arts community had ever witnessed. All without naming names. The only person still standing when the storm was over was Becky. Afterward she would have done anything Steve asked.

Apparently Steve didn't ask Becky to go on living. Her body was found in the trunk of her car a few years later, the circumstances too peculiar to rule out either suicide or foul play.

Dagwood (not his real name, which was known only to Steve) presented as a helpful, compulsive volunteer. Opera, dance, theater, auctions, charity events, Dagwood volunteered and received a free seat or a free meal, or both. From the week I arrived in Seattle I spotted Dagwood. He was a staple of the arts scene, tearing tickets and handing out programs all over town.

Here's what I noticed about handy, helpful Dagwood. The guy had a taciturn manner toward patrons who asked 'too many questions.' He prepared two stacks of programs, one with discount coupons inserted, and one with no extras. There was a pattern governing which pile he chose for a given ticketholder. The people he cheated in this petty and meaningless way were not randomly selected; they were people he didn't like.

Dagwood was an exquisite example of a local conceit: difficult to describe, amorphous yet instantly recognizable to anyone connected to the artistic hive of a city. Dagwood represented the spite factor, which is a constant. Wave upon wave of hopeful, talented young people land in every big city every year. Many will give up. Others will thrive. Some of the ones who give up linger in a ghost state, a Dagwood state, volunteering and handing out programs, and then mumbling to patrons to 'bring a map of the neighborhood next time' if they need directions and snarling that 'of course there's no bar in the theater since they have no liquor license as is stated on the sign in the stairwell.'

Dagwood's body was found two days before Christmas, in 1999, in the bathroom at a department store. He was on his knees with his head in a urinal, a situation the store manager described as 'unfortunate.'

As individuals the minions must have seemed innocuous to the people they met at work, at a bar, on the bus, or on the street. Yet between them, thanks to Steve, they wrecked the careers of at least a dozen employers and colleagues. And all he had to do was make them feel special for a few minutes each day.

Chapter Sixteen

I ended the year drunk with Charlie on the floor of the production room at *Boom City*. As usual my gifts were too few to justify decorating a tree in my apartment—a bottle of champagne and a basket of gourmet goodies from Vaughn, a card and fifty bucks from my mother, a book from Daisy (something by Adrienne Rich), and a cassette tape of *In Utero* with a gift certificate to Fallout Records from my dad, who overestimated my love of music and underestimated my ability to buy tapes cheap.

The rest of the staff had taken the week off and most had flown out of town to visit family and friends. Charlie hated his family and my parents didn't invite me to spend the holidays with them. So we sat on the floor and drank Vaughn's gift, smoked weed, and sang at the top of our lungs, "I wish I was like you—*easily amused!*"

We were supposed to answer the phone. Every time it rang Charlie picked up the receiver and said, in sing-song rhythm, "Have a holly jolly Christmas. It's the best time of the year. Oh by golly, have a holly jolly Christmas this year! You've reached *Boom City*. May I help you?"

By this time the caller usually hung up. No matter how many times this happened we fell all over one another laughing. Later we made out, fully intending to fuck. But we fell asleep from the wine and woke up looking like victims of a hurricane.

"Hey," I said. I tugged on Charlie's shirt and he blanched.

"I'm going down the hall now to be sick or kill myself."

"Okay," I told him.

While he was gone I slipped into the main office, went to Eve's cubicle, and rummaged through her desk. I found two drawers full of unopened manuscripts and a Thanksgiving card from somebody named Theresa who stamped a paw print next to her name.

"Pathetic," I said.

"What's pathetic?" Charlie asked. He stood in the cubicle watching me. His long, dark hair was pulled up in a crooked ponytail and the tail of his linen shirt hung outside his pants. "Who you calling pathetic?"

"Eve. She's like a fucking ghost."

"Why do you say that?" he asked.

"She barely exists. She has no friends."

"She's friends with Leslie," he said.

"Who?"

"The gerbils call her Fucky Face," he said. (Leslie! Why can't I remember this?)

"Look at this stack of manuscripts," I said. "This one's postmarked September. So is this one… I think Eve stuck these in a drawer and forgot!"

"Ooooooooooooooo," Charlie said, holding both hands up to his lips to feign surprise.

"Don't you think she's unprofessional?"

"What's your deal with Eve?" he asked.

"What do you mean?"

"You hate her, don't you?" He sat on her desk and pulled his legs up until he was cross-legged.

"Who doesn't?"

"I don't," he said. "I don't hate anybody. Even Carl, and he's a psychopath."

"He's not that bad."

"Sorry? You know where he's spending his vacation? He's hunting elk with his dad and their rich friends. They're staying at a *lodge* for rich dudes where they pretend to be rustic and grrrr and people wait on them and wash their clothes and clean their rifles and feed them Belgian waffles with whipped crème. Carl's a piece of shit, a complete, total piece of shit. Yet I do not hate him."

"Eve is worse," I said. "She's a phony. She's old. What is she even doing here?"

"You're such a dodo. You think getting older is a crime?"

"No. But you can do some things when you're young that you should get over by the time you're Eve's age."

"Like what?" he asked.

"Drinking all night…"

"Says the girl who once barfed in a trash can because she couldn't make it to the bathroom." He laughed.

"How did you know…?"

"You told me last night," he said.

"Well, I'm not middle aged. I'm, like, twenty-four. Five. Four."

"Too drunk to remember how old you are?" He slid off the desk and headed toward the production room. "I have work to do. Then I'm going home to sleep for three days. Have a holly jolly Christmas, dodo!"

I stumbled home to my apartment through eerie, almost empty streets. A taxi cruised past at ten miles an hour. The white gray sky began to shimmer. Raindrops speckled and then pelted the pavement. I tried to move faster but every muscle in my body ached.

I was half a block from my building when a movement caught my attention. Peripherally I noticed a silhouette, a flimsy form arched and clinging to the bricks beside a white window ledge. I stopped to squint at it through the rain and thought the figure moved, inching up the side of the building next to my apartment, flattening and then arching and moving again.

I held both hands up as a visor over my eyes but the rain was coming down hard. I could barely make out the corner of the roof. I couldn't say whether the shape I'd seen was three-dimensional or an optical illusion, shape or shadow, animal or human. But when I reached the arched portico to my building and heard a low whistling nearby—behind me yet strangely close to my ear—I bolted inside and raced up the stairs.

Chapter Seventeen

The year 1994 began with an announcement from Carl. Circulation had dropped by another two percent and things had to change. He looked directly at Eve when he said this at the top of the staff meeting. Afterward she disappeared for the rest of the day.

"Where's Eve?" Moo asked around three o'clock.

"Nearest bar?" I said. "The Comet?"

Moo frowned at me. "Why don't you ever come to my brunch?"

"I was planning to come to the next one," I lied.

"It's a social thing but we make plans, too, talk about projects and share ideas. You don't know what you're missing. One time, one of the editors from the *Stranger* showed up."

"Really?" These stories were legion. 'The night Courtney Love ran over my foot at SIFF.' 'The party where I told Eddie Vedder what his fans won't tell him.'

"Yeah. He was drunk and I caught him going through my underwear drawer. He called me a liar and Joey my boyfriend punched him in the face."

"Okay," I said.

"But you totally don't have to do it, if it isn't your thing. I mean it isn't required. Eve never shows up."

"No, I want to be there. I'm definitely coming to the next one," I said. If I could count on Eve not being there maybe it was a good place for some damaging gossip.

"Cool!" Moo flashed one of her bright white 'everything's okay, then' smiles and left my cubicle. I heard her say to someone in the corridor, "She said she would," and Charlie came strolling in.

"Are you acting casual?" I asked.

"Are you coming to brunch?"

"Sure."

"Why?" he asked.

"To be part of the—team, I guess."

He studied me as if I were an exotic bird behind glass. Then he crossed one foot over the other, spun 180 degrees, and walked out of my cubicle.

"I told you," I heard Moo murmur.

"Shut up," he said.

"Hey, Greta!" Shelly called out. "Eve says meet her at you-know-where. Have fun."

I wondered how many people were aware of my feelings toward Eve. It seemed unfair to be singled out as the mean-spirited one, given how much the whole staff made fun of Eve behind her back. Somehow I'd gone too far, taken a more hostile tone or otherwise tipped people to my true intentions. There were times when Charlie looked at me as though surprised by my nature.

Two strips of bacon and an egg over medium stared up at me. Ileen's, née Ernie Steele's, offered no pretentious items aimed at brunch lovers. No veggie quiche with a side salad. The menu remained simple even after the joint changed hands. The most noticeable upgrade? The new management scrubbed decades of brown grease off the white Naugahyde walls.

I'd just come from a fairly raw conversation with Eve, in which she hinted at the possibility of assigning work, selecting the shows I would see and review. Over my assertion that choosing the shows was my prerogative, she claimed I wasn't seeking out the most provocative material. We had to increase circulation and I had to shape up, she told me. Passing the heat from Carl right along to me. Her proposal would make my job a lot grimmer than before. I imagined slogging through an adaptation of *The Call of the Wild* at a children's theater, or a solo performance of *Macbeth* set at an insane asylum.

"Are you eating your food or hypnotizing it?"

There's a moment before acknowledging a stranger's intrusion when almost anything can happen. Some people would have ignored the comment. Others might have engaged in conversation and then gone on about their business. What I did is hard to explain. Chalk it up to fatigue and a three-day hangover.

"Why?" I asked. "Do you want it?"

The formerly retreating young man, slender and brown-haired, with a quick dazzling smile, climbed onto the barstool next to me. "My name's Nate," he said. "Are you inviting me to breakfast? Because..." He glanced at his watch and snatched a slice of bacon. "I'm free."

The waitress poured a splash of coffee into my half-empty cup. She stared at Nate on her way back down the bar. He popped the bacon slice in his mouth and chomped it down.

"What are you, a street urchin?" I asked. Avoiding his gaze, the flattering intensity of his attention.

"Good guess," he said. "Mime." He touched my face with a fingertip, pointed at the corner of his eye and let it fall down his cheek.

"You're the shittiest mime," I said.

Nate pointed to his eyes with both index fingers and mimed one teardrop after another, a tsunami of tears.

"Okay," I said. "You're an actor, right?"

"Bless you, milady," he said and mimed a flourish with an invisible hat. "No. Actually, I'm not an actor. Hate actors, don't you? All the folderol and dressing up, it's unconscionably self-serving and exhausting to watch. But seriously, are you having that slice of bacon?"

I slid the plate over. He ate everything. He wiped his lips with a napkin and winked at the waitress when she gave him the stink eye on her way to the kitchen.

"I love this dump," he said. "Want to go for a walk?"

"Why?" I asked.

"So I can bum a cigarette. I like to smoke after a fine meal."

An hour later we were sitting on the sofa in my apartment, naked, smoking cigarettes and drinking Chardonnay. My hair had fallen down in a long tangle over the course of three fucks, from front door to bedroom to kitchen to living room.

"What is this guy hoping to find?" Nate asked. "Tell me more."

"I think he's after a mirror image," I said. "A little brother, a doll version of himself."

"A narcissist," he said. "Easy one." He scanned the room and made an exaggerated frown. "Don't you subscribe to any magazines?"

"No," I confirmed.

"For a journalist..." he said. He took a stroll along the periphery of the living room. I enjoyed the sight of his taut, tan ass in motion. "For any kind of writer, you don't have many books." He stood before the lone bookcase with its secondhand collection of classics.

"I have a few." Feeling defensive and trying not to let on.

"Just the basics," he said with a laugh. "Where did you go to school?"

"Is this a quiz?"

"Yes," he said. "Life is a quiz. What's the guy's name, again?"

I was having second thoughts about enlisting him in my plan. It was a slight mechanism, taking shape in my mind during our second fuck. I'd reiterated and even instigated rumors about Eve. This was different. I would be setting in motion a series of deliberate actions designed to get Eve fired.

"Carl," I said. "His name is Carl."

"I need a portfolio," he said. "That's easy enough. Won't the publisher, Carl, check my references?"

"Not necessarily. It all depends on your charm. He won't question your credentials if he thinks you're cool."

"Well, am I cool?" he asked, still prowling the room.

"You're okay."

"Where do I plausibly meet Carl?" he asked and licked the back of my neck.

"Brunch," I said. "With me. Brunch at Moo's house."

"You'll introduce us?" he asked.

"No," I said. "If you're going to pass as a writer it's crucial for Carl to discover you on his own. No introductions. You have to be fascinating enough to get his attention. All I can do is put you in close proximity. You have to take it from there."

"Fun. Why do I feel like I'm visiting another planet?"

When we arrived Moo was on the front lawn, leaping in the air and swinging a croquet mallet into the branches of an elm tree. Three people I didn't know cheered her on and sucked on cocktails adorned with straws and paper umbrellas. As Nate and I approached Moo waved and laughed.

We entered the house as I had planned, with Nate a few steps behind. Anyone who noticed would assume we were together. Yet later I could plausibly say we were not, and I'd never met him, he was just someone who drifted in around the time I arrived.

Charlie greeted me in the foyer. "Hey there. At last! Come have a drink. You'll need it."

Nate headed off down the hall, asking people along the way where he could find the bathroom.

"By yourself today?" Charlie asked.

"Yeah," I said. "Is that okay?"

I handed him the wine I'd swiped from Vaughn. It was a decent bottle of Beaujolais. Naturally, I'd saved the good stuff for myself.

A Hammerbox tape pounded away in another room at medium volume.

"What is this?" an unseen guest shouted. "Who changed the music?"

Another voice replied, "Are you kidding? I threw that R.E.M. CD out the window."

"Fuck you!"

"Fuck your elevator music. This is Hammerbox! Carrie Fucking Akre! Stay away from the CDs and the tapes! I'm watching you…"

I was surprised to see Steve holding court in the hallway. Two of the minions slouched close to their god, throwing ugly looks at anyone stupid enough to approach.

Charlie steered me past a dining room full of people drinking and arguing about Newt Gingrich. In the kitchen I found another twenty or so people clustered around the counter, picking at something. Closer inspection revealed a side of beef, rare-pink and scarred with claw marks from dozens of forks. A nearby table was piled with cheese and bread and condiments.

"Is this brunch?" I asked Charlie who stood next to me with his drink.

"You missed the pig on a spit. That was the last brunch before the holidays."

"This is weird," I said. "I thought Moo was vegetarian."

"What gave you that idea?"

"I don't know." I really couldn't put my finger on the reason for my impression. "She seems healthy."

"She's Superman healthy," he said. "She's an Olympian. She could kill a man with her thighs."

"I assume you've tested your theory," I said.

"Do I look dead?"

"Maybe you were the exception."

I stood peering down at the ravaged side of beef. There was so much blood I wanted to stare into it. I imagined the outline of my head reflected there. I imagined the guests murdering the cow in the back yard and then hauling it on their shoulders into the kitchen.

"I need to adjust my idea of brunch," I said, and Charlie roared with laughter. Over his shoulder I glimpsed Nate in the doorway, accepting a beer from Carl.

Denny between Bellevue and Olive, the building repainted inside and refurbished. The new owners have slathered white wash over the mold but it's there, yearning beneath the surface.

A security door with intercom system keeps out undesirables. Hardwood floors grace my old apartment. The kitchen has been expanded and combined with the living room in an 'open floor plan,' offering the illusion of more space. The bedroom sports an array of sun therapy lights. Just because *you* live in the Pacific Northwest doesn't mean you have to be subject to little things like weather. The rest of the apartment is stripped back, clean and modern, with the slightly mad look of a woman after a third facelift.

Here you lie, staring at a TV screen, on your $1,500 Danish sofa. Another bad day at the office, thanks to Sadie the Adenoidal Project Manager. She's turned your methodical pace into an issue, and encouraged your teammates to do the same. She's mastered a tone of voice to use when mocking you when you're five minutes late for a meeting, or when you take too long in the bathroom. A smidgen more hostility and you could report her to HR for bullying. As it is, she shames you daily and gets away with it.

Your only release comes from watching these films—a stack of them sits on the $1,100 coffee table—in which women who resemble Sadie are made to run for their lives, pursued by men with weapons. On screen, Sadie scrambles barefoot through a forest until she falls, cutting her hands to ribbons, and turns to find the man with the hatchet standing over her.

Do you feel that? It's a sort of pulsing, not quite a throb, in your right side. You're only twenty-five, so you never visit a doctor. If you did you might discover this congenital condition in time. You've considered a check-up but you just don't have time. Work is crazy, and you have to pay for this place, now a $425,000 condo with your name on the contract.

Sleep well.

Chapter Eighteen

Two weeks later, Eve's reckoning began with a bang. The front door almost came off its hinges when Carl sailed through. We were all sitting around griping and waiting for the staff meeting to begin.

"Where's Eve?" Carl asked. He tugged off his gloves and jacket and glanced around like he expected to find her hiding behind the furniture.

"Should be here soon," Charlie said.

"Probably," I said. "Maybe."

"Why does she, why does she, why doesn't she come in early? She should be excited to be here. What if there's, what if I have good news to share at the meeting? I'm excited about it, and why isn't she here? Never mind. Good news, everybody except Eve! Great news! I met this guy, this whiz kid, this young writer and he's fucking amazing! You won't believe it, he's got credits you won't believe, and he's been looking for a paper with potential, he just moved to Seattle, he turned down offers from the *Weekly* and the *Stranger*, thought those guys would cramp his style, and this is the best thing that could happen right now. Round of applause!"

We applauded. I thought I was suppressing a grin until I caught Charlie watching me.

"Is he going to write features?" Ed asked.

"Features, right, tech, business, anything he wants, he's going to be our news editor and we finally get the fucking Albanian poets and the Everyman Named Chad and the Lady Welders off the cover," Carl said.

Ed grimaced. "I didn't know Eve was looking for a news editor."

"She doesn't, she didn't, when we talked about this weeks ago she promised to make changes. What changes has she made? I don't know, I don't see it. We're still fighting for an audience every issue. So this is where we're going, more timely stuff about business and politics, tech news, political cartoons, all the stuff that's booming. It's our fucking name, right? *Boom City* should be the paper everyone picks up. They don't know what they'll read but they know it's going to be the read of the day. Right? The city's growing and we have to grow."

"What does Eve say?" Charlie asked. His expression told me he already knew the answer. "What does she say about this new guy?"

"She doesn't know yet," Carl said. "If she were on time she would know but she's late so I'll tell her when she gets here."

"You're interviewing him, and she doesn't know yet?"

Carl studied his shoes. He pulled on his jacket then his gloves.

"I hired him last night," he said. "He'll be here in a couple of hours. His name is Nate Shore. Hey, Shelly, bring in a desk and set up a workstation when he gets here."

"A desk? From where?"

"Buy one. Order furniture and have it delivered. He'll need everything, including a PowerBook, put it on my card, take care of it. This is great news, you guys. It's going to put us on the fucking map. Finally! Great news!"

He raised his fist and jumped up like he was trying to touch the ceiling. Then he spun sideways and dashed out the door the way he came in.

Nobody said anything for a minute. We sat there in the wake of Carl's big dream, stunned and uncertain. Moo was the first to stand. She picked up her notebook and headed barefoot back to the sales desk. Gradually the rest of us followed suit and no one suggested going out for breakfast.

In the afternoon the freelance reviewers wandered in on lunch break from their jobs around town. They stopped by to pick up their mail and catch up on staff gossip. A couple of the minions visited with Steve in his cubicle.

We were far enough from our next deadline to be lazy. We pretended to read the last issue of *Boom City* or make notes while we eavesdropped on Carl and Eve arguing in her cubicle.

"This kid is a genius! Look as his pub credits! Read his tear sheets!"

"I read them. He's no genius."

"He's amazing. Why aren't you, why aren't you blown away?"

"Maybe because of the breezy post-gonzo style without any real content, without even the awareness that content matters. It's a style about style, about itself. The first page of every story is a chronicle of the author's day. He's only interested in himself and his opinions. Who writes this way?"

"He does, and the best young writers do. It's context."

"Lack of context."

"Perception, and, and point of view. POV changes. It alters the subject…"

"Duh."

"Excuse me? Did you say, 'duh'?"

"If you wanted a new writer why didn't you say so?"

"I didn't know this was the answer until I met the guy and we talked and then—boom—I knew it."

"Why make him news editor?"

"Listen, no disrespect, you've done a good job but we have to keep growing. There's an explosion of new media, and we're not keeping up."

"He doesn't have a byline printed on any of these samples."

"He was a contributing writer on those. Why are you being like this?"

"I?"

"All I'm doing is, I'm trying to help you."

"You're trying to do the job you hired me to do."

"It's my goddamn paper!"

A silence passed. I guess this was the sound of Eve contemplating the depth of the mess she'd signed on for and Carl staring in disbelief at the middle-aged woman who hated the puppy he dragged home.

"Okay, Eve, look, we've talked. I gave you a chance, I gave you every chance to bring in some topics people my age want to read about, and last week's issue profiled a guy who makes bagels at the market."

"He's twenty-one years old and he thinks ordinary working people should be respected for what they do…"

"That's not a story. It's an opinion. It's a quote. Not even a good pull quote. Do you know the difference between a story and an opinion? This kid, Nate, knows the difference. We talked about what's going on, what's really going on, Eve. We talked about stuff you and I never discuss because, because you're not interested."

"How do you know what interests me?"

"Because I read the paper you edit! You like poetry and metal sculpture and two operas and a boutique in Ballard that sells cheap overcoats. This kid, he fits the moment, he knows what's going on. He's hot, his work is hot, and we're lucky he wants to work for us."

"What are you paying him?"

"What? Excuse me?"

"How did you get this *wunderkind* if so many other papers and magazines want him? How much did you offer him?"

"I'll pretend you didn't ask because it's none of your, this is none of your business, and I'll pretend we didn't have this conversation."

Everyone tried to act nonchalant when Carl strode out of the cubicle and bashed his way into the production room. We heard him roaring at Charlie for a minute. And he never re-emerged. Which meant he must have taken the smokers stairwell to avoid running into Eve on his way out.

When Eve stomped out of her cubicle ten minutes later her arms were full of manuscripts. She stopped at Shelly's desk.

"I'll be working from home today," she said.

"Uh, is that okay with Carl?" Shelly asked. "There's no way for you to check in except if you email to say you're working and nobody can check on you… Um. Not that anybody needs to check. I guess."

Eve didn't return until the following day at noon. By then the new boy, dubbed 'Carl's Young Nate' by Charlie, had been introduced to all of us and had made himself at home in Eve's cubicle, at a slightly larger desk set up by Shelly and accommodated by shoving Eve's desk, coat rack, and bookshelf to one side.

I spent the morning leafing through press kits on the reception area sofa, waiting to see the expression on Eve's face when she arrived. It was worth it. She must have summoned up the will of a Greek mythological hero to keep her face placid, not to break down and weep when shiny young Nate sprang up from his new ergonomic chair, stuck out his hand, and greeted her.

"Yo! Boss lady! We're cube mates!"

At a clean, bright crepe restaurant in Wallingford, the windows are plastered with 'Going Out of Business' signs.

Look at the entrepreneur in tears! My first thought is how strange failure must feel to *you*.

A person your age wouldn't expect to be snuffed out by a rival. You deserve a worthy and important narrative, a test of will spanning years, the struggle to get a brand new restaurant off the ground, followed by astonishing success, piles of money, legendary status in the community. Gosh. How romantic.

Your rival wasn't a dashing, mysterious man who opened a brunch-dedicated café next door. A man you could woo and win over. Silly old you, I think you would have tried. No, your rival is a faceless east coast chain with corporate headquarters in Minneapolis. Your precious crepes can't compete with five different omelets and a signature egg-and-bacon-stuffed baked potato.

When you arrived you expected to take over the city. You anticipated being wealthy one day. You had your eye on a splendid Victorian house in Magnolia, where you would retire at age fifty.

Did you know Europeans have journeyed to this picturesque haven since the 18th century, claiming its discovery and shoving aside whatever was already here? Of course you know but do you consider what this means in such a geographically small city? The effort to make Seattle surmountable and navigable, it took time and money.

Let me share a little history with you.

The hills downtown and leading to Broadway and Queen Anne were carved out, sculpted from the remains of larger hills. For years dirt was pushed away from desirable parts of town to make them accessible; piles of earth and Duwamish bones and buried longhouses, all scaled back from steeper hills no one could climb.

A few mavericks wouldn't go along. Know what the city engineers did? They etched a path right around anyone who refused to sell their home and make way for the re-grades. These spindly peaks of earth topped with stranded houses were known as 'spite mounds.'

What made Seattle seem like an easy conquest to you? Was it the lack of sophistication? It's a ruse. Or was it the price, so affordable compared to the city you left behind? You see, every wave of new residents creates a boom followed by a bust, leaving cheap ruins for new arrivals to pick through. You bought the detritus left by another failed business.

You marveled at the ease with which a smart young person might buy a license, post a sign, and take out an ad in the paper. You ignored the faces of the middle-aged previous tenants. You saw them everywhere, cashing in their discount coupons and buying toilet paper in bulk, and you turned away.

They failed at what seemed simple (the same things you expected to achieve). Now they're drowning in toxic bitterness and pretending all they ever wanted was a nice apartment and a secure job.

You still see them on the bus. If they smile at all it's a mean grin, like a hateful jack-o-lantern watching, waiting for all the newbies to fail.

You failed. Your restaurant failed. Your 'big idea' to offer the best crepes in the city was no match for bacon-stuffed potatoes. And here you are, broke, humiliated, and unable to pay the bank loan.

Open a drawer. The paring knife is best, a delicate instrument. Remember to cut vertically and don't worry about spilling blood in the traces of flour. No one is coming. No one came to your grand opening, or your second, or the third. No one wants the one thing you do better than anyone you've ever known.

Let go. It doesn't matter anymore.

Chapter Nineteen

A month later Nate's first feature appeared. It was a profile of a secretive entrepreneur named Robbie Knudsen who had earned a fortune in five years. His software investments had made him a millionaire. He was about to launch a company he expected to rival Wizards of the Coast, its central product a collectible card game called *Saga of the Titans*.

Knudsen was a quirky guy prone to react to good news by shouting, "Cool beans!" He was proud of having been kicked out of the best prep schools and universities in the country, and he advised bright young people to skip college altogether.

The article was a hit. Readers loved this recluse, Robbie Knudsen, storming around his domestic sanctuary shouting out brilliant ideas.

Three weeks later Nate completed a profile of two anonymous hikers whose weekend exploits involved defacing billboards. The saboteurs claimed they were fighting the corporate advertising that had blighted their hometown of Kirkland with cigarette marketing (until forced by a new ordinance to remove their billboards in 1990). Asked why they continued to rail against a compliant company after the Kirkland ads came down, the adventurous duo replied, "For the thrill, because we can, and because they're all corporate fucks!"

Eve was barely allowed to skim these articles before they went to press. Carl instructed Nate to report to him directly. They spent hours in coffee shops scheming and outlining. Nate came up with one idea after another and Carl signed off on all of it. Pretty soon they were inseparable.

Eve was left alone to read the slush pile. She did this with the grim fatalism of a doomed aristocrat awaiting the guillotine.

Nate proceeded to interview the most obscure, young, eccentric, wildly successful people he could dig up. They were sometimes inspiring, sometimes ridiculous, and always colorful. His writing style was like a teenage Hunter S. Thompson, a speed junkie typing while being sucked off by a groupie. He crammed more adjectives and adverbs into one sentence than most of us could get away with in a whole essay. He raced from one location to another with his yammering subjects, and the background was littered with incidental celebrities. Paul Allen, Courtney Love, Stone Gossard, William Burroughs, and Kathy Acker flew by like stray objects caught in the whirlwind of Nate's expeditions.

Eve complained about Nate's prose style to anyone who would listen. As the circulation numbers climbed steadily and Nate gained a reputation for being the most badass kid in a city of badass kids, fewer and fewer people cared what the editor had to say. For the first time it seemed possible for *Boom City* to succeed, and every one of us felt the rush.

Inevitably, this is when Lee Todd's advice returned to haunt me.

"Take my word for it, Greta. The worst thing you can do is to believe your own hype. If I hadn't been such a fuckwad while I was selling books and getting reviewed in the *Times*, I wouldn't have had so many enemies when I hit the ground."

Of course I cast aside the memory of these fateful words. If Nate (who never acknowledged our previous relationship even in brief, private moments) aimed to make *Boom City* successful, I was going to be included in that success.

In my own fiefdom I was giddy with newfound power and popularity. I would call theaters and demand the best seats in the house, and then skip the show. I rejected production photos I found amateurish or mawkish, and I frequently treated other reviewers to samples of the critique forming in my head during intermission. I advised actors to have cosmetic surgery to correct the tiniest physical idiosyncrasies. I told directors not to quit their day jobs. I was, in short, an asshole. Exactly the kind of pompous boor Lee Todd had been during the good years of his brief career.

"Like I said, Greta, nobody learns anything by example or by warning. Every one of us has to slide down the drainpipe into the same filthy gutter and suck up the shit floating down there before we get a clue about empathy. We're not born giving a fuck about other people. It's when we get our ass kicked by the world that we finally wonder if things could be better, if maybe we could be better. By then it's too late. Because once you hit that gutter, my friend, nobody gives a rat's ass about your opinion."

In the early spring of 1994 I could walk into any fringe theater in town and two or three people would be all over me, fawning and complimenting and begging favor. One person offered a light and another offered a glass of wine, plus a cushion to make my chair more comfy. If I showed up five minutes late, they held the fucking curtain for me.

Some people would have rejected these sycophants. Others would have maintained a friendly yet cool distance. Here's what I did. I accepted all of it. I let a sixty-year-old woman who managed a tiny performance space and did all of her own cleaning, painting, and set-building buy me a one-hour massage at a day spa in Pioneer Square. I smoked the cartons of American Spirits that appeared in my office mailbox, and ate the free meals paid for by actors who waited tables for less money than I made. I was star-fucked by too many people to remember. Okay, seven people. But they were astonishingly able, attractive men and women who satisfied me without reservation, and thanked me for the pleasure. I was not just an asshole. I was a first rate asshole.

All of these perks came my way despite my now habitual trashing of one show after another. Not every aspect of every show. And in my defense, awful as I was, I didn't really lie. Not all the time. Most of the shows were uneven affairs and quite a few of them were horrible things no one should have to see. I watched a 400-pound naked man deliver a one-hour sermon on gluttony while he ate a continuous supply of Oreo cookies. I saw two productions of *The Seagull* and two of *Miss Julie*, and every one of them sucked donkey ass. Now and then I was treated to a glimpse of intelligence and wit, and when this happened I noted it with a relief bordering on hysteria. These rare, positive reviews were the reason I was courted and waited upon.

Inevitably a day came when an invitation to one of Vaughn's shows turned up in the mail. For a shameful five minutes I stared at the envelope and considered throwing it away, claiming it never arrived. But when I got home Vaughn was waiting with a bottle of Chardonnay and that face I couldn't bear, all sweetness in his expectation that I would do the right thing. It was pitiable, the extent to which he didn't know me.

This was a departure for the company, he explained. Yes, they had chosen to adapt an often produced classic, *Hedda Gabler*, but Vaughn had worked closely with a choreographer who designed movement interludes, the story was set in a posh suburb in 1970s America, there was no cross-dressing, and the staging had some touches he referred to as 'radical' and 'maybe a little bit brave.'

"My fear is that I won't do it justice," I said.

"Nonsense," he said. "I've read every one of your reviews and you get better every week. The flaws you point out are genuine, not pet peeves. You have to take more credit."

There was no way out. After months of training myself to zero in on the weaknesses of everything I examined, I would have to write a fake rave. Or tell the truth and break Vaughn's heart. I agreed to attend opening night and went to bed praying for an earthquake and tsunami to cancel all events for an indefinite period of time.

On opening night I sat in the fourth row, center, my preferred spot. Vaughn took his seat in the back row where he could watch the cast and the audience's reaction. There was no curtain, and no change of scenery during the performance.

All of the action took place on the back yard patio of the Tesman home. The interludes were ghostly movement pieces accompanied by subtle shifts in lighting, alluding to past and future events in the lives of the characters.

During these interludes the windows of the house were lit like TV screens, framed with white curtains billowing. Shared scenes took place around a picnic table with pop music playing softly at half speed. Some of the dialogue was mouthed silently in slow motion. When Lovborg died he entered and sat down at the table, and gently rested his head upon it for the remainder of the action. Most startling of all the choices Vaughn had made, Hedda's suicide took place center stage in full view of the audience while her husband, Tesman, and the judge obsessed over the barbecue pit nearby.

When the house lights rose I felt something I'd never experienced in a theater before. I had goose bumps. I wanted to cry and laugh at the same time. I sat in stunned silence with the rest of the audience for one shocking moment, and then we all jumped to our feet spontaneously, applauding like crazy, some of us weeping, some shouting, "Bravo!"

I didn't know what to say to Vaughn after the show, so I gave him a hug then I left in tears. As I walked down the street in the crisp night air my footsteps kept gaining momentum until I was running with my arms out. In the middle of the sidewalk halfway down the block I leapt into the air and let out a wild scream. It was an animal sound of release and joy and passionate comprehension of mortality itself. I had just witnessed a sublime work of art. And nothing would ever take that moment away from me.

Chapter Twenty

I wasn't sleeping well during those days. I would begin to drift, to give in to dullness and emptiness. Then my eyes would snap open and I would sit up in bed, staring at shadows and the black silhouette of clouds.

This wasn't my conscience bothering me. I'd never been terribly worried about being a good person. I tried not to speculate or examine too closely. Yet every time I had a nightmare about climbing a wall or running across a bridge pursued by shadows, my first thought on awakening was, *Lee Todd is dead*.

It wasn't as if I'd been in love with the guy. He was old. His ancient rules for crime writing and his lazy acceptance of whatever circumstances or women came along irritated me. It took a long time for me to recognize why.

Only after I'd scraped by on my lousy pay at the copy center for a couple of years, never even reading the classifieds to see what else was available, and stumbled into reviewing at *Boom City*, and allowed complete strangers to kowtow to me and fuck me in hopes of earning a favor I had no intention of granting, only then did I see how much alike Lee Todd and I might be. I'd mistaken him for a committed writer thanks to his endless aphorisms and advice. In truth he had probably stumbled into writing, got lucky, squandered his opportunity, and fell back to earth where he belonged. Also where I belonged, thanks to my lack of ambition and my inability to get my shit together.

Trying to describe Vaughn's show made me *wish* I could get my shit together. For the first time since I'd entered and lost that stupid literary contest, I wanted to say something that mattered to another human being. I wanted to whisper in the ear of the anonymous public, to entice and entrance with my words.

Eve had failed to make good on her threat to select my shows for me. I hoped it was because of Nate, the nemesis I had introduced into her miserable life. With Nate mocking her every action and Carl criticizing her every decision, I suspected Eve had her hands full.

I stayed home for two days, in my pajamas, writing and revising. I didn't see any other shows and I decided to commit all fifteen hundred words of my section to *Hedda* and to Vaughn's company. I couldn't stop thinking about the show, reliving it in my imagination. I couldn't slow down or concentrate on anything else. I wrote draft after draft until it was exactly what I wanted it to be. I told myself this was a process Lee Todd would never understand. He was a hack, a selfish money-grubber. This was real writing. This was an act of love.

At night I felt the spring chill and kept the windows shut. In the past I was accustomed to keeping them open a sliver to let the fresh air flow. Since Christmas I'd begun to experience a peculiar uneasiness about this habit. Even the thought of a cracked window gave me a nasty sense of being seen and vulnerable, at the mercy of something I couldn't name or describe.

As I said, it wasn't my conscience driving me on. I'd been reading Nate's awful stories with relish, amazed and impressed by his growing success, only bothering to stifle my glee at Eve's discomfort during staff meetings. I was dying to feed Nate stray bits of gossip about her whenever she wasn't around but he avoided me. At first I chalked this up to his undercover dedication. As time passed I wondered what was really driving him. He had long since proven the point I wanted him to prove. He had stolen a paying gig at a grunt newspaper by stalking then charming its publisher. During our preliminary sex he had said nothing about being a real journalist. I had no idea from which orifice he'd pulled his so-called credentials. Editors recommended him but I never knew if these were people Carl contacted or friends of Nate's who contacted Carl with fake endorsements.

What I knew for certain was that the guy wrote like one insane motherfucker. Fast, loose, unconcerned with critical or public reception. He wrote like a kid who had been told every day of his life that he was the greatest writer on the planet.

His energy and stamina and his (false or true) zeal for journalism made Eve seem older than she was, by comparison. Carl and Nate never invited her to their frequent bull sessions and Carl never asked her opinion any more.

Circulation was still climbing, not to *Stranger* or *Weekly* levels, but higher than anything *Boom City* or any of the other wannabes had ever experienced. Nate handled the situation by taking full credit, granting brief interviews to half the publications in town, and predicting we would overtake all of our competitors in the next two years.

As a confirmation of *Boom City*'s growing success Carl was invited to spend a non-holiday weekend with his father. This was the morning I stopped by the office to hand in my review. I had to laugh at the childish joy with which Carl hoisted his jacket on and smiled and buttoned up for the long drive after coyly mentioning his destination.

"It's so sad," Moo told me privately. "The way that man loves his father. And the guy's a monster, a real dick."

I gave my review and profile of Vaughn's company to Steve, who read it and promptly left the office for coffee. I didn't care. Steve had his own process. Soon he would come back, do the edit and hand off my copy to Charlie. If I needed to trim the piece, Charlie would let me know. My plan was to read my mail and decide on a couple of shows and then head home once my word count was approved.

"I'll be in Port Townsend for three days," Carl reminded Shelly, with a nod to Nate. "Should be good weather. Maybe I'll stop by and see that secret mansion Knudsen's building…"

If a grown man could shit his pants and get away with it, Nate would have. That I saw him blanche and shake his head like a sick dog was a complete fluke. I wasn't supposed to be there. But I was there and I had time to take it in. And Nate saw me take it in.

"What am I thinking?" Carl said, oblivious, still wrangling the buttons on his jacket. "We'll be on the boat, we'll be on the boat all weekend. I won't have time for Knudsen! Oh well." And he waved goodbye before dashing away.

I dropped my chin and shuffled through the batch of mail in my hands.

"That guy!" Nate said loudly enough for everybody to hear him. "What a guy, huh?"

It was his usual bluster, a constant echo of Carl's manner. But his timing was off, just a bit. I wondered if he was losing his nerve.

My relief at turning in my first rave review, which was also my first profile piece, and the anticipation of how pleased Vaughn would be, doesn't explain why I failed to read the mood of everyone else in the office. I was killing time shuffling through the latest batch of press kits when Steve tapped me on the shoulder.

"Eve wants to see you," he said. "Right now."

I scanned the reception area. That's when I finally noticed Charlie, Shelly, Ed and Ginny were skulking around. As I glanced at each of them one by one they turned away and pretended to be busy.

"Really?" I said. "I was on my way home. Unless you want me to make changes to my review."

"Now," he said. He had never looked as grim as when he informed me, "She wants you to meet her at Rosebud right now."

I was tired. On the walk to the café I could feel my legs slowing down. My body craved sleep. I barely noted the row of teenage girls sitting on the sidewalk, feet in the gutter, holding one another and sobbing. My mind registered only the ripped flower-print dresses and boots and the twists and barrettes in their hair.

Inside the mauve temple of floral doom I went directly to Eve's table and sat down. In the Nate era she had lost so much of her authority I rarely bothered to extend any courtesy. I was almost giddy whenever I imagined the day when she would finally have to leave the paper.

"What's up, Eve?" I slouched in my chair, still clutching my mail and my bag.

She studied me with a combination of anger and the expression I'd once seen on my mom's face before she stomped on a snail in her rose garden. She reached into the pile of papers before her, extracted a newspaper folded back to highlight an article, and slapped it down in front of me. Her manner shocked me until I gave the newspaper my attention and the first paragraph came into focus.

Over the summer, all the girls traded in their scruffy oxfords for boots, steel-toed if they could afford it. Laced up tight and knotted for security. We wore them with flannel shirts and jeans so threadbare they nearly fell off our hips. We wore them with flower-print dresses slipping sideways to reveal black bras and tattooed thighs. We wore them to cafes and grocery stores, to work and to weddings. We wore them to bed...

Surely my mouth was open when I looked across the table at Eve. Over the preceding months I had allowed my theft of Daisy's essay to recede until it drifted away on a current of negligence. I hadn't exactly forgotten what I'd done but I'd put a lot of people and work between my crime and myself. Gradually it had taken on the nature of a dream or an anecdote someone told to me over lunch. Now here it was in print under my nose. I flinched when Eve jabbed an index finger next to the byline and said, "I take it 'Daisy Parrish' is not your pseudonym?"

Some people would have broken down and confessed. Others would have run away in tears. Here's what I did. I stared at my nemesis, right into her bloodshot eyes, and asked, "What if it is? You can't blame me for freelancing to pay the rent."

Eve could not have been more stunned if I'd dunked my hand in her cup and flicked cold coffee at her face. Then she did something I'd never seen her do before. She tilted her head back and she laughed, a sharp, barking laugh like the sound a sea lion makes to call its mate. The ragged lines across her throat quivered and her saggy breasts jiggled. She laughed the way some people clear their windpipe of phlegm. When she was finished she fixed me with a grimace of pure contempt.

"So you want to add a flagrant impersonation to your list of crimes," she said.

"What crimes?" I asked and I could hear my voice diminishing.

"You are a plagiarist," she said. "The worst kind of criminal. The lowest and most contemptible of creatures."

"You don't know what you're talking about," I told her.

"Is this how you want to defend yourself? With more lies?"

"I mean, I don't know what you mean," I said feebly.

"I knew there was something wrong when I met you the first time."

"You hired me the first time we met," I reminded her.

I was still trying to push responsibility onto this woman I hated. How could it be my fault? I was the person who had been wronged. She had stolen my future, scuttled my plans for a literary career, and now she was accusing me of the worst thing a writer could do—which I had done, of course; nevertheless I was determined not to give her any extra satisfaction.

"You stole this essay. You passed it off as your own. I know it's true because I called the editor of the paper in Portland, and I warned him he might have printed a plagiarized essay. He contacted the author right away. She provided him with every draft she's written. She also said she knew you. She said you were friends, and you advised her not to submit the essay. Now we know why, don't we?"

Every thought I'd had that day began to spin around me, gaining momentum, blurring in the background of the one thing I knew for certain, the one thing that mattered most. Daisy knew. She had been accused then interrogated by her boss. In her innocence she had followed the steps a real writer would follow, she had presented evidence to exonerate herself. Only then had she realized what a liar I was. We weren't two journalists starting out together. She was a writer and I was a thief.

"I didn't submit this for publication," I said. Treading water, as usual.

"No. You put your name on it and passed it off as a professional sample. And…"

I felt all the words in the universe gather around my head like a raincloud about to burst.

"You're fired."

"You have to pay me for my last week, and my last review," I said. It sounded crazy even to me but it was all I had left.

"I don't have to do anything," Eve said, her lips drawn into wicked, thin lines. "I told Steve to throw away your last review. You're lucky I don't print a public apology to all the people you've maligned."

"You're a fucking bitch, you know that?" I said.

"You're a fraud," she said. "Go home."

A greenbelt in Ravenna, near dusk, trees shot through with orange-gold rays, leaves rustling and the faraway howling of a neglected dog.

Oh, my goodness, look at both of *you*. Geared up and ready for duty. Tiny flashlights, whistles, and water bottles, and where did you get the dun shirts and camouflage khakis? Are you on safari?

No, wait a minute. You're on a date, a married date. You're stomping around out here in the cold on a good-citizens-doing-good-things date.

Your neighbor, the one who lives in the renovated bungalow surrounded by kitschy clocks and pricey lawn furniture, gave you a phone number to call. Homeowners are doing it for themselves, pitching in to clean up the metro area. Tidy the greenbelts in your neighborhood by gathering plastic, bottles, tin cans, pots and pans, clothing and backpacks, and throwing them away. If you throw away their belongings, do you expect the homeless people will follow? Will they disappear and move on to someone else's neighborhood? Is that your ultimate fantasy here?

Swinging your garbage bags full of clothes and food, you stumble over some roots, right yourselves, and giggle. This is exciting work, isn't it? Better than the couples golf lessons and much better than movie night. Know why? It's the element of danger. You're like children stealing change from an elderly aunt's purse. What can you get away with and not get caught by those horrible, cranky old men living in tents and boxes all around your otherwise adorable neighborhood?

Tell you what, why don't you kiss for luck? That's right. On the lips, the way you used to kiss, before you bought an over-priced house in a dull part of town and worry became your only pastime.

What do you have to worry about? The mayor wants you to pay higher property taxes, for one thing. More taxes to fund shelters for the homeless people who keep sleeping on your lawn and shitting under your shrubbery.

Tell you another thing. All of this skulking around is hot. Go ahead. Kiss and make it count, tongues exploring, garbage bags dropping to the ground, hands feeling for purchase and pulling at khaki, sinking into the leaves with a final, mad giggle.

Feel that? It's thrilling because it's wrong. It's so wrong it makes you hard and wet, respectively. Ordinarily you wouldn't dream of fucking here, in the leaves, practically on another person's doorstep. All right, there's no actual door to his tent, and that's what makes him a vagrant while you're a good citizen. Feel free to tumble over, sucking lips and dipping fingers into orifices. Go on. Enjoy acting like randy teenagers getting away with something.

You're so taken with yourselves you never hear the snap of twigs and the snick of a pocketknife opening. Oh, you won't understand what's happening because such things don't happen to lovely people like you. But just in case you ever wonder, your murderer has a name, Griffin, and this is his home, and here you are the intruders.

Chapter Twenty-One

There wasn't much to do at my apartment. Wash my three plates. Wipe the wine stains off the coffee table. Stare at the shitty orange carpet and pretend I would clean it if I had a vacuum cleaner. Ignore Vaughn knocking at the door and calling my name.

On the way to my apartment I'd seen couples and small groups of people embracing, fighting back or giving in to tears. Sitting alone by my window above the street I lit a cigarette and watched the drizzle. Several kids gathered in the ATM alcove. One boy carried a bunch of wildflowers and he passed some of them to the others. A girl stood at the edge of the sidewalk leaning out into traffic as though deciding whether or not to fling her body into the street. One of the boys from the group went to her, put his hands on her shoulders, and drew her into his arms.

"What the fuck?" I said out loud.

"Oh no! No, no, no!" The words bounced up at me from the pavement. The barber from the shop below stood down there, shouting and weeping in the rain.

From these clusters of random individuals, word spread in all directions, first across the city and soon across the world. Traffic didn't stop. Restaurants didn't close. Performances weren't canceled. But everywhere, all afternoon and night, people would stop in the middle of a meal or a show or a concert and ask for a moment of silence or offer a tribute of some kind. I heard a company called Run/Remain began their performance with a solo dance, hard, passionate and heartfelt, to "Smells Like Teen Spirit." I wouldn't know for sure because I sat at my window all night lost in the wasted desires of my pathetic existence while half of the city around me mourned.

In the days following the discovery of Kurt Cobain's body there were thousands of tributes. Many were sincere and many were just a way to steal some of the spotlight. People who knew him divided into those who were stunned that he would commit suicide and those who had seen it coming. There were the compassionate observers who wished the best for his family and friends. There were the vicious curmudgeons who wished it had been someone else, someone they disliked. There were suicide experts and conspiracy theorists, followers and critics, and there were the few inevitable copycats. Guess which of these topics *Boom City* decided to feature and mock?

I crawled back to Copy-Z after applying for work at almost every paper in town, and after receiving not so much as a phone call. By this time Tam was the new manager, and she was happy to have me back although she said our old scam wasn't allowed on her watch, and she never left me alone in charge of the till.

As soon as a couple of actors found out where I was working, theater folk started dropping by on a regular basis. They practiced their skills, playing out scenes in which they were shocked to see me in what they referred to in hushed tones as 'reduced circumstances.' They expressed their best wishes for me in my awful situation and invited me to come and see them in their latest shows. 'Just ask so-and-so at Will Call for a discount ticket. No problem!' Their icy, over-pitched laughter followed them down the street. Or they would come in with a set of flyers and posters and spend an hour deciding on sizes and colors before snapping the originals shut in a folder and heading off to another copy center.

One day I was clearing sample pages off the counter when I saw Charlie walking past the shop. I waved and caught his attention. The way he glanced at me, as though he'd seen a fly buzz past or heard a ghost whispering and then turned away and walked on, was far worse than Eve's condemnation.

Until I saw Charlie that day I'd been thinking I was back where I started. I thought I was nothing again. But this was worse. I was less than nothing. Nothing still has the potential to be something. Nothing might wake up one morning and do something surprising.

Back when I was nothing I thought I'd given up but it wasn't true. You never really give up until other people give up on you. When you see someone who liked you or liked what he thought was you and he looks through you, past you, as though you're another window, then you're less than nothing. I was nobody and would be nobody forever. This is what everyone I met conveyed to me, with and without words.

In this half-world of existing and yet being nothing, I daydreamed a lot. It helped to pass the time while the machines around me churned out thousands of photocopies...

I was on a break one afternoon. I was reading the latest issue and grinding my teeth when Vaughn walked in. He strolled slowly, dramatically, up to the counter and hit the service bell. Tam stuck her head around a corner of the machine she was running and nodded.

"I'm here to see Greta," he said.

Tam went back to what she was doing. I gave Vaughn the best greeting I had, a lame little wave.

"I'm so pleased to see you're alive," he said.

"You could call it that," I told him.

"Don't be a smart aleck," he said. "I was worried. Why wouldn't you answer the door? I had to call the office to find out what happened. Boy, those are some rude people you work with."

"I don't work with them. I make copies."

"Right," he said and reached for the newspaper in my hand. "But you're still following their antics, I see."

"Who isn't? Pretty soon they'll be as popular as the *Stranger*. I knew them when. Lucky me."

"Please! They wish they had your wit and your talent." He took the paper from me, folded it, and tossed it into a trashcan next to the counter. "Do you believe the article that kid wrote about copycat suicides? People are in mourning and he's being satirical."

"It sells papers."

"It's disgusting."

"People are disgusting," I said.

"Oh, come on. He's an upstart, a snotty child. He'll never achieve anything."

"He's a con man," I said. "He'll probably make a fortune. Listen. Sorry about the review of your show, Vaughn."

"Is this why you've been avoiding me? Are you serious? You think I care about a goddamn review? Honey, you have to stop kicking people away or you'll be alone all of your life."

I leaned against the counter and watched the rain through the shop window. Vaughn put one hand over mine.

"You're having dinner with me tonight," he said. "No excuses. No pretending you're not home."

"Okay," I told him. "Yeah."

I was tidying up as well as I could in my shitty apartment that night when there was a knock at the door. Remembering what Vaughn had said, I didn't hesitate. Only it wasn't Vaughn. It was Daisy, draped in fake fur and silk scarves, eyes flashing.

"Shit," I said.

"Uh-huh."

"I was going to call you," I lied.

"If you were going to call me you would've fucking called me."

"Yeah," I said. "I know."

"What the fucking fuck?" she shouted. She stepped into the room and I closed the door. She was going to get loud and I didn't want to add angry neighbors to the growing list of awful things in my life.

"Daisy," I said. "I'm sorry. Really sorry."

"What an eloquent apology. Did you write it yourself?"

"Really, really sorry," I added.

"What the fuck is going on? I come to you for advice and you steal my fucking words! Do you know what this means to me? Words are all I have! My words *are* me, Greta; they're everything I am! The way I write is *my voice*. If you take my words, you take my voice! You silence me. You rape me. You make me nothing. Do you understand?"

"Yeah."

"Do not say you get it if you don't. Please don't lie to me," she said.

"I'm not," I said. My throat felt raw. "I get it. I know what I did."

She shrugged and faced the window. She shook her head.

"Jesus Fucking Christ!" she shouted so loudly the windowpane rattled. "All the way over here I was planning to kill you. With my bare hands I wanted to rip out your *spleen*. You know? Rip it out and eat it! Like a fucking *mad dog*."

Her shoulders shivered and I knew she was laughing. Letting it go and laughing the way I would never have done. Because I wasn't her, I wasn't golden and talented and sure of the words that belonged to me. I would have been petty, spiteful, shitty to the end, but she was laughing.

"I'm sorry," I said again.

"I'm going to stitch that on a pillow and give it to you to sleep on," she told me. "You're a fucking maniac."

She threw her arms around me. I inhaled the honey and wildflower and rain scent of her body. She groaned, deep and throaty like an animal finding a lost cub, anger and joy inextricably spun together in her soul.

"Come on, let's drink," she said. "Everybody's dead. Let's drink."

"Vaughn's coming over," I told her. "He's bringing dinner."

"Great," she said. "I'm starving! Your food is my food now, Greta. Your apartment is mine, too," she said and laughed for a long time.

When Vaughn showed up with red wine and manicotti we stuffed our faces. We listened to his horror stories about high-strung stage managers and ingénues with allergies. We laughed. We drank. We sang songs into the night...

Yeah. Some people would end right there. Others would go on to describe how adversity only increases one's appreciation for friendship. Most people would enjoy that story more than the truth.

In fact, Daisy never called, never stopped by while she was in town, never returned my phone calls. And the kind words and solicitations I've attributed to Vaughn never happened. He didn't stop by the copy center and he never invited me to dinner. I read about Nate replacing Eve as editor at *Boom City* while I was on a smoke break, alone, in the alley.

Vaughn got busy with another project around the time I was fired. I told him my profile of his company wasn't going to appear in *Boom City* (or any of the other papers to which I subsequently submitted the review, by then long outdated). Vaughn didn't say he was disappointed. He didn't pass along any gossip he'd heard about me or why I'd been fired. He just drifted away. The last time I saw him he was chatting on the stairs of our building with a woman whose performance I'd unfairly mocked in a production of *Who's Afraid of Virginia Woolf?* She rolled her eyes and laughed when I edged past. Vaughn waved hello and turned his attention back to the actress.

I spent most evenings watching the street from my living room window, invisible to the world. At this point some people would begin a new adventure. Others would reflect and find a measure of inner peace. I did neither of these things.

Deep beneath the city, in a tunnel corridor drilled by a machine named Bertha.

I wish I'd brought a hardhat. Not that I needed it, but the atmosphere makes me crave authenticity. Wow. This is every bit as impressive as the news articles make it out to be. And loud, for fuck's sake. It's loud! How do *you* put up with it? Earplugs can only muffle so much. Are yours custom made?

There's the bitch, way up ahead, Big Bertha, pounding her way through the underpinnings of the city. Drilling through dirt and rock and bone. What a gal! She's 326 feet long and she weighs over 6,000 tons. Expensive date, too. She's worth $80 million. She's a hell of a girlfriend, isn't she?

If I were you I'd go mad. Would you like to lose your mind for a while? It's easy to accomplish. Ruminate about your ex-wife and your ex-children, for a start. Remember how you almost took that job in the Midwest, the one that would have made your family love you. Instead, you're doing the worst work imaginable for a lot more money and an empty apartment. Makes you wonder, and drift, and cry.

Tell you what. How about a vacation? Because in a few hours your girlfriend up there, she's going to slam up against a steel pipe left over from 2002, and this whole operation's going to come to a shrieking, grinding halt.

When it happens you'll be laid off. You'll have hours and days and weeks to lie on the couch thinking about how lonely you are. You'll call your ex in the middle of the night and she'll hang up on you. Your kids will forget your birthday. Your best friend will kill himself after checking in to the Disneyland Hotel in Anaheim, and only you will know why.

Tell you what. Set all of it aside. Step back and watch your life as though it were a cartoon. Does it amuse you?

On one of those long nights on the couch, reach over and grab the Swiss Army knife from the table. Pull open the corkscrew. Run your fingertips over it, following the spiral to the vicious tip.

Nestle in the cushions and tilt your head back. All it takes is one swift, sure jab to the jugular. The pain will be excruciating, stunning, unlike anything you've ever imagined. But then all of the terrible nights will slip away. All of the unanswered calls and unspoken words of affection will fade. Your blood will pulse and flow, warm, metallic and sweet. Your eyelids may flutter but this is only a nervous spasm, not a desire to stay alive. Let the blood flow down your throat and onto the floor. You've been looking after ungrateful people most of your sad life. Let someone else clean up the mess for a change.

Chapter Twenty-Two

I didn't think Carl would answer the phone. But I knew exactly where to find Eve. And I had nothing better to do on my day off.

The morning was mild gray with bright and cloying notes of cherry blossom in the air. Walking down Pike to Rosebud, I noticed for the first time how briskly other people moved. I had laughed at the lazy, ambling pace of the locals, and somehow I'd missed this change from idleness to a sense of purpose. People were not on the street to wander and mingle. Each pedestrian seemed to have a clear destination. Were they really moving faster, or was it my perception, my sense of being outside everything?

The shift from daylight to the cloistered murmuring shadows of Rosebud had never been as jarring. I squeezed my eyes shut to adjust. When I opened them I spotted Eve immediately. The court had moved on but the queen refused to relinquish her throne.

She didn't look up from the book she was reading until I reached her table. Her expression told me nothing.

"What do you want?" she asked.

"Want?" I took the unoccupied chair opposite her and rested my elbows on the table. "What else could I want? Carl fired you, right? He gave Nate your job. Doesn't that make my life just about perfect?"

"Why?" She studied me. "Why does it matter to you? My life has nothing to do with you, or Carl, or the children he hires."

I laughed. It was a nasty, snorting sound.

"Carl didn't hire me," I reminded her. "You did."

"One of many mistakes," she said.

"Good. You admit you did a lousy job."

"Admit?" She let the word hang in the air. "Are you trying to interview me? Are you still pretending to be a writer?"

"I wouldn't write about you," I said.

"Another difference between you and the woman you plagiarized."

It's always a disadvantage in any exchange with your enemy to be confronted by unexpected news. My blank expression prompted a nasty grin, transforming Eve's lines and dark circles into the visage of a mischievous demon. She might have been a gargoyle crouched atop one of the old apartment buildings on Capitol Hill.

"You're a foolish young woman," she said. "You keep trying to convince someone you have talent."

"Keep trying?" I was still wearing a stupid expression.

"The awful short story you submitted to the Citywide Arts competition?" She made a little clucking sound with her tongue. "Yes, yes, I recognized your name when you applied for a job. Your fiction submission was memorably bad."

"You never said anything."

"Why would I?" She sipped her coffee. She had all the time in the world. "You wanted a job and I thought you could handle it. You could have started slowly, with 250-word reviews, and you might have improved your skills. I was willing to take the chance, to give you a start."

"Well," I said. "Thanks for that." I could see she wasn't at all intimidated by my sarcasm.

"Writers earn their reputations," she said. "They don't become famous just because a few people are conned into taking them seriously."

"Oh, is that why Nate's turning into a celebrity and you're out of a job?"

She scanned the room. Taking in the couples arguing in whispers, the hung-over office workers guzzling caffeine, the actors, dancers, and writers gathered in clusters to plan projects and trash rival artists.

"Apparently the new editor of *Boom City* is in touch with the zeitgeist," she said.

"What would that be?"

"Style over content," she said. "Over-energetic wordplay. If he wrote fiction, he might have potential."

I made my move. Sliding her books aside and leaning in, my elbows still resting on the table, I said, "Our young Nate is writing some of the most popular *fiction* in town."

"What is it you hate so much about women?" I once asked Lee Todd on a hazy night when we lay awake, naked on top of the sheets, smoking and drinking. It was one of our rare extended conversations.

"Obviously, I don't hate women," he said.

"I don't mean in bed. You know what I mean."

"Greta, I've been married three times. The one and only thing I know for sure about women is this. They don't know when to quit."

"Quit what?" I asked.

"See what I mean?"

After I explained Nate's status as a liar and a charlatan, Eve grabbed her books and bags and stormed out of Rosebud. I had intended to be cool about it but once I got started—once I saw the range of emotions playing across Eve's face—I couldn't stop. She was my enemy and Nate was hers. I knew she would use everything I told her to bring him down. When she ran from the table I imagined she was on her way to the nearest pay phone. I assumed she would track Daisy down in Portland and give her the tip of a lifetime.

Boys can get away with anything as long as they're brash and charming. Some of the places and sources Nate mentioned in his articles couldn't exist but his readers had grown accustomed to his breathless style, and his habit of tossing off and not following up on colorful details. No one asked how he could locate his idiosyncratic interview subjects when the most reliable journalists in the city had never profiled, never mentioned, never even heard of them. No one had called him out. His fans didn't doubt him for a minute.

I was twitching like a trigger finger. It would be delicious, watching Nate's newfound career go down in flames. He would be ruined and *Boom City* would be the biggest joke in town. Daisy would have an award-winning article and she would owe it all to me. Sure, it might also make Eve feel vindicated but I couldn't worry about that. If Daisy wouldn't speak to me and Carl had forgotten who I was, I needed Eve to be a catalyst.

After all, I would never lose the sweet satisfaction of seeing her shock and sadness when I confessed to sending Nate to the paper. In a flicker between disappointment and determination, I saw her sleepless nights, her single meals, and her drunken phone conversations with acquaintances, bored and skeptical, who probably advised her to move on. She was stuck. The city kept spinning around her but she had no will to join any of it. Until I gave her the information she needed to ruin Carl and his pet.

I told myself I was primarily interested in justice. Lee Todd would have seen through my high-minded internal speeches.

Every day I spent running those loud, filthy copy machines was a new lesson in bitterness. For a long time I'd lived like a cast-off girlfriend still wishing the man of her dreams (who was nothing but a bald guy in ugly shorts) would pay a visit. But the morning I confessed to Eve, everything felt different. I pretended this was due to a lightness of heart since I'd done the right thing. In my secret heart, though, where I lived most of the time, I knew the lightness, the glee, was pure spite. The people I'd known, the ones who had praised and then rejected me, were on their way to unemployment, thanks to me.

At home I poured a glass of wine and kicked off my shoes. I smoked and tried to read but it was too hard to concentrate. My brain buzzed with excitement. I knew Daisy would soon be investigating Nate's stories. All I had to do was wait for the news to break. Daisy would expose Carl and Nate, and become famous in the process.

Eve might think she was going to be exonerated but her failure to spot Nate's fabrications would further damage her reputation. Maybe Carl and Eve would fight over who was to blame. Maybe they would sue one another. All of the possibilities were delightful.

All I had to do was wait. A normal person would have waited.

"The killer inside isn't a psychopath, Greta. It's that plain, old, regular-sized bastard...vanity. The need to be noticed, not even respected exactly, but noticed, acknowledged. We all have the craving and we have to conquer it."

I had failed to conquer it. (So had Lee Todd, in my opinion, despite his words of advice.) Despite all I had done and how badly I'd screwed up my only chance, an ugly voice inside kept piping up with cruel observations, pitching pebbles at windowpanes, demanding to be noticed, demanding to be heard.

"Trouble," my mom had said all those years ago. "Always trouble."

Chapter Twenty-Three

On Friday morning I wasn't looking forward to the weekend. Two co-workers were feeling queasy. If they called in sick my Saturday would turn into a workday. On Sunday I could sleep in and then wander around.

I thought of Daisy and a hundred scenarios of forgiveness flashed through my mind. I told myself she was busy researching Nate and writing the biggest assignment of her career, thanks to me.

I looked out the window and saw Vaughn downstairs on the street. He ducked his head and dashed toward Broadway, probably to catch a bus to the wine shop. No one had taken note of his wonderful production of *Hedda*. The show had closed after three and a half weeks, its one snippy review in the *Times* failing to boost ticket sales enough to complete the run.

My morning routine included one luxury, a dark and fragrant cup of coffee from a French press. I was dressed for work, sipping coffee, trying to remember where I'd left my pack of American Spirits, when I heard a knock at the door. I assumed it was a neighbor or the landlord. I pulled the door open and took a step backward, farther into the room.

There was no one at the door. Only a peculiar smell, a smoky aroma like a burned-out campfire. I stood in the middle of the room for a minute, trying to remember what I'd been doing just before that. I couldn't recall. I pulled on my jacket and went to work.

Tam was as irritable as ever, and as paranoid. She made a habit of reconciling the register and the sales slips twice a day since she'd become manager. It wasn't only that she didn't trust me, she trusted no one.

That Friday she was especially wound up, dashing from the counter to the machines and back, checking her watch and swearing. She didn't even break for a smoke.

The customers were the usual battery of dullards and assholes. Most of them couldn't figure out how to make a stack of photocopies if their lives depended on it. Despite this we had new competition from a self-serve copy center a block away. Their prices were starting to attract students from Seattle Central and Cornish. Tam was devising a plan to advertise with flyers at all the law firms downtown but I'd heard Xerox was taking over the market with their in-house operators. Pretty soon I wouldn't even have a job making copies.

On the way home the sky grew overcast. Rain spattered the sidewalk and I was filled with an inexplicable dread, a desire to be anywhere other than where I was. It was Friday. Vaughn probably had a date. No one would be waiting for me at home. I hadn't heard from Daisy or Eve, not that I expected a call. I just didn't know how long it would take for the story to appear in the Portland news and get picked up by the Seattle dailies.

I tilted my head back and let the raindrops fall on my face and inside my shirt. I heard a rumble of thunder. I studied the clouds. Across all of the rooftops on Denny and Olive Way shadows went slithering down, cast by clouds and suddenly broken free, sliding onto window ledges and under doors, slipping away into sewer grates with the rain.

Trick of the light, I decided. Or maybe it was exhaustion. I needed to get out of Seattle. There had to be other places where I could get a job as lousy as the one I had, warmer places where people smiled because they weren't drowning in rain and envy. Maybe I could crash on my mom's living room floor until I figured out what to do next.

Meanwhile I wanted to sit down. I only had two dollars in my wallet, but I decided it would be worth the price to catch the bus for the last six blocks. The stop was deserted. I sat down on the bench and I must have dozed. When I woke up a bus was pulling away from the curb. I ran and shouted, arms up, heart pounding. The driver ignored me. I was soaking wet and there was no point in waiting for the next bus.

I gave up and trudged the last six blocks, stomped up three flights of stairs to my lousy, cramped apartment. All the while noting the familiar scent of mouse turds and tomato soup, I opened the door and stared down at a dead body. My body, right where I'd left it.

Part Three

"No self-respecting crime fiction writer uses a dead guy for a narrator. Don't say, 'Sunset Boulevard,' because that was a movie and it was satire and if you can't tell the difference you should get out of my class before you say anything else. And don't tell me you're making 'an artistic choice.' It's nothing but a tip-off to the reader that you don't know what the hell you're doing." – Lee Todd Butcher, RIP

Chapter Twenty-Four

When I was alive I thought my circumstances couldn't get worse. Introspection was less maddening back then. Examining my shitty life was easier when I had gobs of it left. Of course there's still plenty of time but the illusion of moving forward is gone. The fantasy of my existence as a matter of more significance than my non-existence is over.

I've made numerous returns to my apartment, watched it become a refurbished condo 'with vintage appeal.' I was never socially active and all of the places I frequented are gone or unrecognizable. So it goes with most cities but this one changes with a vengeance. If you love something, count on it being demolished and replaced.

There isn't any of my life in this universe. There isn't any of my self in a form anyone who isn't crazy would recognize.

Certain realities have come to light gradually. What I expected, whatever it might have been, hasn't come about.

In the moment when there was still blood on the mantel and the scent of perforated skin in the air, I liked to think I had the potential to make sense of what happened. I pretended to be in charge of the moment of my death, if nothing else. What the fuck did I know?

The one thing that made sense to me was the anger I continued to feel toward Eve. She was my nemesis. My confession had been a gift, a chance at redemption. She had failed in her mission, so I decided to kill her. I assumed she had killed me because she hated me. Unable to convince Carl or Daisy to investigate Nate, she bought a gun and made my death look like a Cobain-obsessed suicide. This was the final insult, and one I was not going to forget.

In those murky days immediately following my death, some events were not clear. Others became indelible. Nothing was more obvious than the obsession with which I'd filled my days when I had them to spare, when I thought I had thousands of them ahead of me.

At last I was able to enter the office as I pleased, without incurring the wrath of Carl or the glare of Shelly. Each time I crossed the threshold I was seized with an adolescent desire to wreck things. I would rip open a cushion, unload staplers, leave a rug corner rolled up to trip someone, never staying long enough to watch my pranks play out.

On my first visit I stuck matchbooks under one leg of Shelly's desk, leaving it with a wobble I knew would drive her mad until she figured it out. Nate was absent from his cubicle. The desk that had belonged to Eve was shoved into a corner with dead plants piled on top of it roughly in the shape of a wreath. Her snobby postcards featuring famous writers and their famous quotes were gone, replaced by Nate's marked-up calendar and his collection of fan letters.

Of course the most likely place to find Eve was always the same. Rosebud.

I heard the low murmur of small talk around me. I checked the corner table and then scanned the rest of the café. No sign of her.

I knew only the general neighborhood where she lived. The bridge connecting the weedy part of north Queen Anne to Fremont was crowded with traffic. Seattleites drank like fish on the weekend. My guess was Eve would be at one of the bars.

Unlike other neighborhoods, Fremont isn't on a square grid. It has a center resembling a small heart with arteries and veins branching off toward Ballard, Phinney Ridge and Wallingford. The Fremont Bridge stands east of the massive George Washington Memorial Bridge, which everyone calls the Aurora Bridge. Beneath the north end, tucked under N. 36th Street, there is a massive stone sculpture, its face, arms and hands emerging from rock, left hand clutching a Volkswagen beetle. The Fremont Troll is typical of local public art—humorous and inoffensive, a tourist photo op. (Even the nearby statue of Vladimir Lenin is routinely decorated with rubber ducks and plastic flowers.)

That night I found Eve sitting atop the troll's right hand. Despite the upturned flask, or maybe because of it, she served as a secondary background feature to the German-speaking family taking pictures. She was wearing mom jeans, a clean black T-shirt, and torn-up All-Stars. The shoes made me wonder if she made a habit of drinking in this spot. Did she scramble over the knuckles of the troll and sit there all night under the glare of his shining hubcap eye? No, I knew she didn't. I knew she had wandered down the dirt path after she ran out of money at the Triangle Pub. I knew she had every intention of staying, camping out and sleeping on the back of a giant stone hand.

"Crazy bitch," I said. "You crazy, murderous bitch. I gave you a chance to redeem yourself and you killed me."

"What's it?" she said. She groaned and turned her head.

The German family moved along to the next site on their itinerary. The mom was especially anxious to leave, the novelty of the drunken American lady communing with a troll having worn off.

"Now would be a good time to jump," I said, estimating how many feet Eve would have to drop to fatally crack her head on the ground.

"Fuck you!" She sat up.

"You can see me?" I asked.

"Fuck you, Seattle!" she screamed. Her voice reverberated in the cavern formed by the bridge and dissolved in the roar of traffic overhead.

In the space between the troll's arched back and the bridge, a thousand pairs of eyes opened. They peered at me but I couldn't tell whether they could see me. They blinked and began to draw closer together, centering on the spot above the troll's hubcap eye. Bright dots like fireflies, they merged and drifted down until they covered the troll's eye. With a sound as quiet as a sigh, it closed.

Eve lay back and sprawled across the troll's right hand, a middle-aged Fay Wray luxuriating in the company of her oversized paramour. The silver flask rested on her stomach. She drew a shuddering breath and the flask fell and clattered over the rocks. My nemesis had never looked older or more ridiculous, bawling on her back, alternately crying and screaming obscenities to the oblivious night traffic above.

In my new state I understood she was nothing, this woman. She was a figment of her own imagination, cobbled together and barely making it through the day. She had no family, no friends, no allies, no awards, no career, and nothing to believe in. She didn't kill me. She was the person I might have become if I'd gone to a real university and dribbled my years away editing prestige magazines with a readership smaller than the occupancy of my apartment building, and accepted a job at a weekly paper out of desperation and vanity. She was dying from neglect and loneliness. She wouldn't last another decade.

I picked up the flask and found it contained another swallow of whisky. I poured the last drop into Eve's mouth. She let me cradle her head in one hand and press the metal spout between her teeth. She didn't fight me when I forced the flask deeper and deeper into her mouth until her pupils dilated. I waited and held on while the irises grew dim.

I left her lying there. The woman eating a silver bottle under the eye of a troll would make a good photo for the dailies.

Chapter Twenty-Five

"I didn't give you enough credit, kiddo. I knew you were tough as nails but I thought you might grow out of it."

I froze. This wasn't a memory. This wasn't an echo in my mind. I was sure of it. The voice was real. Lee Todd was following me. If I glanced over my shoulder I'd see him in a suit and tie for the first time. But I didn't need to look. I knew.

"Jesus Christ," I said.

"You killed her," he said. "Was that necessary?"

"What are you, my fairy godmother?" I asked. "Are you going to follow me around now?"

"You would hate that, wouldn't you? Some old bastard trailing your ass everywhere, reminding you what's wrong with you."

"Great," I said. "Yeah. Because you're so wise, you have the right to judge. Fucking loser. You drank yourself to death."

"I did not!"

"You fucking did."

"I fucking did not."

"Read your own obituary sometime," I said. "I read it." He grinned. "Only to make sure you were dead. I read it for a laugh. You died in a hospital bed in Seattle with cirrhosis of the liver."

"You're not any better than you were in my class when it comes to digging up facts," he told me.

We stopped under the gray-white arc of the streetlamps. The bridge shone in the background through drizzle and fog. Cars whooshed by. A homeless man shivered under a thin blanket near the overpass. Two 20-something guys walked a wide circle of disgust around him.

"Man, the nights are crap here." Lee Todd observed.

"Yeah, it's grim," I said. "Rain's a given. I grew up with rain. But the people..."

"Misery on a fucking stick," he agreed. "You should've met the nurse who murdered me."

"Murdered?"

"I'm flat on my ass in one of those beds they keep adjusting every couple of hours to make the patients 'comfortable.' I've got an IV in the back of my hand and my skin is swollen and waxy and I can barely breathe.

"All of a sudden, in waddles this mushroom of a nurse, her face and neck like a toad's, with auburn hair pinned up tight under an old fashioned cap. I should've known something was up. Nurses don't dress like that anymore unless it's Halloween or they're part of a dominatrix game.

"Anyway. My abdomen was on fire, burning like Satan's dick, so they had me on painkillers. This bitch reaches over, pinches the IV and pulls it out, replaces it with another tube. I can see what's rolling into my veins and it's light blue, you know, it's pure as fucking shit.

"This roly-poly twat leans over me. She's so close I can smell the drugstore perfume between her tits. She stares into my eyes until she can see that I *know* what she's doing. And she smiles at me. Shows me her tiny, square, yellow teeth.

"I mean, I've heard of angels of mercy but trust me on this, Greta, that bitch wouldn't have known mercy if it fucked her up the ass. She murdered me in my bed and she enjoyed every second of it."

I almost felt sorry for him. Almost.

"You were dying anyway," I said and started walking again.

"See what I mean?" he said. "Hard as nails."

"Why should I be otherwise with you? We weren't in love or anything."

I could hear him chuckling, a low rumble. He caught up with me and kept pace.

"*You* weren't in love," he said.

"Please go to hell, okay?"

"Believe me, if that were an option I wouldn't be here," he said and lit a cigarette. "Say, who's that woman you just did away with?"

"None of your business," I said and then thought better of it. "Can't you tell? Can't you look at people and just...tell?"

"Nah," he said with a shrug. "Who wants to know everything? It's all crap anyway."

"I forgot how much I dislike you," I told him. When I turned to see his reaction, he was gone.

In the weeks following my death the police made all the assumptions I expected. I was just another sad girl, a loser in the City of Losers, a copycat caught in the wake of a famous musician who famously committed suicide. There was no real investigation.

I wasted a few spiteful hours wrecking car batteries at the nearest precinct. Maybe I wouldn't have been so cynical about Seattle law enforcement if I hadn't spotted Cobain riding the #39 to Seward Park one afternoon, smiling like a kid at the circus.

Foul play *was* suspected in the death of Eve Wallace, former editor of *Boom Town*. (The weekly papers got the name wrong.) Circumstances implied Eve was murdered during a mugging. The German family lost their camera overboard on a ferry to Tillicum Village. Not that the roll of negatives inside would have identified the person who murdered Eve. At this point I was just being mean. The kids cried when they found out their troll photos were gone, and this was fairly satisfying.

Following my conversation with Lee Todd I paid closer attention to the shadows adhering to rooftops and windows and slithering over cobblestones in the alleys outside Pike Place Market. There were times when I could almost say for certain I recognized an outline but it was hard to say for sure. The shadows moved in concert with one another, with a mute grace I doubt most of them enjoyed in life.

I spent a lot of time thinking about Eve. Not guilty or wishing I'd done things differently. Wondering why I didn't feel a sense of completion or a rush of satisfaction, wondering if these feelings were beyond my current state.

I was smoking and pondering these questions on the #7 when the answer occurred to me. First of all, it only took that single glimpse of Cobain to convince me to try the bus again. During non-peak hours seating was great, and I found the warm chugging movement comforting. I realized half the people I'd been ignoring inside the Metro line were just like me. We didn't acknowledge one another. We simply rode the lines we liked, taking in the scenery and waiting for a chance to trip a teenager or a curmudgeon on the way in or out of the bus. Small pleasures, as they say.

So I was sitting in my favorite seat on the #7, on the left and three rows behind the driver, when I spied a discarded issue of *Boom City*. On page six Nate had had the balls to write a brief satirical tribute to 'the fallen women' of the publication. Eve was portrayed as a mental case, a sad spinster meeting men for illicit public trysts, implying she'd finally crossed paths with someone she couldn't handle.

My story was pure invention although there were quotes from Vaughn and his friends, no doubt taken out of context, probably acquired with lies about the nature of the article. I was this club-hopping slut who was fired from the paper for stealing another author's work and couldn't deal with the combination of professional failure and the death of my grunge idol.

I shrieked when I read the last part. I yanked the stop request cord and stomped off the bus at the next corner. The door folded open and the live occupants only nodded and returned to their sleepy state when they saw no one depart.

"What the fuck?" I yelled.

"Look at you, giving a shit about something," said Lee Todd, trailing after me.

"What the fuck?" I said again. "Were you on the bus?"

"How would I know?" he said.

"What the hell is going on? Why hasn't Daisy exposed this guy's fraudulent ass? Why is he still editing *Boom City*?"

"All good questions," he said. "I guess you can stand on the street and scream about it, or you can find the answers."

"Look, gumshoe, get out of my face and leave me alone," I told him.

Daisy lived in Portland. Try as I might I couldn't get there. It seemed any place or person outside the 'greater metro area' was beyond my capacity. So much for ever seeing my parents again. I ruminated. I drank. I wondered how to find the answers I needed. I thought about murdering another person, and in the next moment I was standing before a door.

When I entered Carl's apartment the odor of gym socks and rotten pizza almost knocked me off my feet. I held my nose and kicked a few takeout food cartons aside.

In the bathroom the shower stall was rampant with mold. The kitchen was unthinkable. I pushed open the bedroom door with one foot and stepped into a jungle of clean and dirty clothing. The only clear spot was in the center of the bed where Fucky-Face lay snoring, naked. This was surprising but not as surprising as the sight of Eve crouched on top of the bed, her gray-white face pressed against the face of the sleeping woman.

Some dead people would have run away. Others would have evaporated. Here's what I did. I tapped Eve on the shoulder and asked, "What the hell are you doing here?"

She studied me with bloodshot eyes. Her hair was swept up in a French twist. "Mind your own business," she said.

"Who did your hair?" I asked. Not that I cared much but now, for the first time, I wondered what I looked like. I knew how I saw myself but how could I be sure Lee Todd and Eve didn't see me with my face blown off? Then I remembered, I'd seen Cobain's face; I'd recognized him.

The killed came back intact while the self-murdered slithered like black oil across rooftops and between cracks in the pavement. It seemed to be the only rule in my current state.

"I like it this way," Eve said. "Why are you wearing false eyelashes?"

"Really?" I was startled and then pleased. "I always wanted to but I didn't have the nerve. Are they flattering?"

"Are you serious?" she asked. She turned her attention back to Fucky-Face. "Can you believe this woman, this *bitch*? We were friends. I told her everything. She got a position at Microsoft on my recommendation! We used to go out for cocktails at Happy Hour. I kept trying to figure out who was undermining me and making up lies. Who was telling Carl I didn't read the slush pile and I didn't have back-up features ready in case an article fell through? I was crying on her shoulder for months and she was screwing the publisher. Bitch!"

Eve reached out to the nightstand. She hoisted a fat crystal ashtray and dumped its contents on the floor. She raised it above her head with both hands, aiming for the center of Fucky-Face's throat.

"You don't want to do that," I warned her.

"Yes, I do. And then I want to push Carl out a window, and staple Nate's mouth shut."

She raised the ashtray again.

"Eve, I know you're pissed off but this isn't going to work. You kill Fucky-Face and pretty soon she'll be prancing around here in stilettos and a push-up bra. You'll never get rid of her."

"How do you know?" she asked.

I mulled this for about five seconds. No way was I going to confess. I didn't know what Eve would do if she knew I'd murdered her.

"Because you killed me and I'm still here," I said. It seemed like the right time. And then it all fell away, everything I'd believed up to that point.

Eve was shocked. She lowered the ashtray and let it drop on the bedspread among the underwear and magazines and sex toys.

"What are you talking about?" she said. "I didn't do anything to you. I read about your suicide in the *Times*."

"No," I said. Keeping my voice steady, choosing my words carefully. "I told you Nate was a fraud. You told Daisy and Carl, and then you shot me in my apartment."

Fucky-Face let out a chortling noise, a blocky snore, and rolled onto her side, still sleeping. Eve moved closer to her.

"Why would I do that? How? I've never owned a gun in my life," she said. "How would I shoot you? Who's Daisy?"

Clueless. Absolutely without a clue. I was glad I'd killed her.

"Daisy's the reporter whose essay I stole. You called her with the story about Nate. You told her to investigate…"

"No," she said. "Carl. I only told Carl." We stared at one another, puzzling out the odd turn of events.

"Carl killed me?" I asked.

"And me," said Eve. "To save his crummy little newspaper. If anyone found out about Nate, it would ruin Carl. The paper's finally taking off and this would make it a joke, a bad, stupid joke." Absentmindedly she reached over, pinched Fucky-Face's nose, and held it shut.

"Eve, I thought you were a murderer."

"Not until today," she said.

Fucky-Face's mouth opened and Eve popped a rolled-up sock in it. We watched Fucky-Face's pallor turn pale blue and then purple. Fine pink lines crept beneath the skin around her eyes. At last she stopped breathing. And for the second time since I'd known her Eve threw back her head and laughed.

Chapter Twenty-Six

Given all of our options, I wouldn't have chosen Rosebud as a place to celebrate. The Comet was more my style. All right, that's a lie. I was one of those people who called it the Vomit because of the beer and puke scent ingrained in the wood counters, tables, and floor. To me the Comet Tavern was a stinky haven for locals obsessed with authenticity.

Always a creature of habit, Eve insisted on her old haunt. And since it was available she chose her favorite table in the corner.

"I can't even tell you how much I hate the floral décor in this joint," I said. "How can you stand it?"

She turned to her left and considered the wallpaper. She turned to her right and considered the curtains and cushions.

"Oh, yes," she said. "You're quite right. This is ghastly."

"What, you never noticed before?"

"No," she admitted. "I came here for a pastry and coffee, and to read the freelance submissions. Nobody bothered me.

"Holy shit, Eve," I said. "Come on. We're going to B & O."

The black tiles and delicate coffee cups gave me a tiny flutter of excitement, not a feeling but the memory of a feeling, a caffeine *frisson*. The slightly shabby European atmosphere was pleasing to me and, apparently, to my guest. Ditto the crisp white linen tablecloths and napkins, the sturdy silverware and the marvelous view of a bustling corner on Capitol Hill.

"How long has this been here?" Eve asked.

"Forever," I told her. "You should get out more."

"Everybody says so."

"I have to ask you one thing before I visit the ladies' room," I said. "Listen…"

"What do you do in the ladies' room?" she asked.

"Never mind."

"Tell me," she insisted.

"Talk to people," I said. "I talk to people while they're looking in the mirror. I listen to what they're thinking, when they think they're not thinking. Staring into their own eyes, drying their tears, convincing themselves tomorrow will be better—it's the best time, when they're vulnerable."

"You can tell what people are thinking?" She blinked.

"Forget I said anything," I told her. "I'm sure you have talents of your own. Maybe you can fly or something."

"Listen," she said. "Are you sure you didn't kill yourself?" She cast a longing smile at a plate of spanakopita and sighed.

"Did *you* kill yourself?" I asked. I was playing a dangerous game and I knew it, counting on her not to figure out what really happened under the bridge in Fremont.

"I don't know," she said. "I was trying to drink myself to death, and I died. I was in a blackout. Maybe Carl bought me my last drink. Or maybe he followed me and finished me off. The details don't make much difference, do they?"

"Your friends and family might want to know the truth."

"Now you credit me with having friends. You've changed." She reached out and nimbly picked a triangle of spanakopita off a woman's plate. She bit into it and nodded. "This is good. You should try it."

"Smoking's fine with me," I told her. "Cigarettes, weed, coffee, and the occasional glass of wine." I thought of Vaughn and realized I hadn't tried to see him since I died. Poor Vaughn. He probably discovered my rotting corpse and called the police. Did he think I'd offed myself out of a sense of failure? Did he think I felt guilty about the profile and review I botched?

"The scenery's changing," said Eve. Her gaze was turned toward Malstrom's Market across the street, a little convenience store where I used to buy single cigarettes when I was broke.

"Yeah, some objects move," I replied sarcastically. I was really wishing I hadn't found her in Carl's apartment.

"No, this is strange," she said. "In the traditional sense. Try staring at one spot for a minute. Sit perfectly still and try to watch one thing."

I started thinking of ways to ditch her. But for the moment I indulged her and directed a steady gaze at a telephone pole on the far corner of the intersection. Rusted staples and bits of paper ran from knee height to about five feet, the remains of posters city workers had torn loose and thrown away.

Nothing happened for a minute but then I blinked and a small flyer appeared, pinned to the pole about four feet off the ground. I flinched and Eve laughed.

"You see?"

"What the hell was that?" I asked.

"You tell me," she said. "You've been here longer than I have."

I didn't know what it was and I didn't like it.

"Have you noticed sometimes it's afternoon and when you go somewhere else it's night?" she said.

"Time passes," I said, sarcastic again and aware of how many of my attitudes were a defense against things I didn't like or couldn't get.

"Time 'passes' in jumps and starts," she said. "Sometimes it flickers and does a fast-forward like a VCR."

"Quit fucking with me or I'm leaving," I said.

"I'm not causing the phenomenon," she said. "I only thought I'd mention it. In case there's something you want to do. Better do it soon."

She winked at me. It was the scariest thing I'd seen since she laughed while killing Fucky-Face.

When I parted company with Eve she was boarding the #43 headed to the Arboretum, a gushing pile of gardens along the shore of Lake Washington. I'd only visited the place once. Like every other thing in the northwest, the Arboretum was picturesque, its real beauty somewhat ruined by too many quaint touches. I didn't ask Eve what she would do when she arrived. All I wanted was to be alone, to wander for a while and then track down the one person with a good reason to murder me.

Carl wasn't home. Fucky-Face's body was gone. Likewise the detritus stinking up the apartment last time I visited. Every surface, from the kitchen floor to the bathroom sink, was immaculate and shining. This could not have been Carl's doing. It was a professional job.

On the living room table in a cardboard box I found a pile of coupons. Not exactly coupons, more like IOUs from advertisers settling bills with freebies. Apparently Carl accepted these trades as payment, the kind only he benefitted from. There were two from a bar and grill called Toffy's, three blocks from Carl's apartment. I figured Toffy probably used the barter system a lot.

I was right. Tucked into a half-circle booth in the back, Carl was eating clam chowder and a halibut sandwich, and reading the *Rocket*. He had a pint glass of ale. I noted the vacant seat across from him, slid into the booth and made myself comfortable.

"It was *you*, wasn't it? You're such an asshole," I said to the side of his face. "Why don't you drown yourself in your chowder?"

He read a paragraph in the paper and chuckled. I noticed his blond hair was cropped short. It reminded me of someone.

"Doesn't matter how you wear your hair," I said. "You'll always be an asshole."

"Yo! You look like you could use another pint, dude."

Nate held a glass of ale in each hand. He was beaming with boyish fun and stupidity. His close-cropped auburn hair made the two look like fraternal twins. When Nate slid into the booth I moved over and sat between them.

"Thanks, dude!" Carl beamed back at him.

"What's up with the hippies?" Nate asked with a nod toward the *Rocket*.

"Same old," said Carl. "Jesus, these guys are just, these guys are doomed! The *Stranger*'s taking all their business and they don't even see it, they don't have a clue. It's just, it's just crazy!"

"They'll sell, if they're smart," Nate said. "Let some Midwest weekly absorb the whole thing."

"Oh yeah," said Carl. "Yeah. Hey, this chowder's the best! You should order food. It's on me."

Nate shifted in his seat and grinned. I marveled at how deftly he played this role. I'd given him all of my petty observations of Carl and the *Boom City* staff, and Nate (or whoever he was) had constructed a perfect dude. He had the flinty intelligence of a boy wonder and the insouciance of a kid brother. He fit the part Carl wanted him to play; he was exactly what Carl wanted him to be.

I remembered how Nate had sidled up to me at Ileen's, a virtuoso grifter adapting to his target. I was alone and then suddenly he was there, somehow both obvious and unobtrusive. Where had he come from? I wondered if he had seen me and scoped out my situation, my advantage. For all I knew he might have been following me for days before he found the right moment to create our 'accidental' meeting. He might have judged me to be an easy way into a job he really wanted.

Or had the whole stupid joke occurred naturally? Had he seen me, hooked up with me, listened to my idea for a mean prank, and run with it? His animal grace, his good looks bought his way in. He was brash and cute and a little bit snotty. Everybody made way for him. Maybe he decided to go along as far as the joke would take him. If no one questioned his articles, his sources, or his intentions, he could do as he pleased. Right now he was playing the perfect asshole, for Carl's amusement.

Nate raised his hand. He called to the waitress.

"Yo, mama!"

This made Carl double over with laughter. When he recovered he shook his head, one of those 'boys will be boys' acknowledgments.

"Yeah, can I get a bowl of the chowder?"

"On the house," Carl reminded her. "It's on the house. Ask the manager. I'm the publisher at *Boom City*. It's on the house."

The waitress regarded both of them with contempt bordering on violence. She walked away without saying a word. Her back and the way she slouched at the counter said she'd like to shove a bowl of steaming chowder up Nate's nose.

"Wow, dude, the service here is the worst," he said.

"Great food, though," Carl said.

"Food's okay, service deserves a one-star review, if you ask me. I can assign one of the minions…"

Ah yes. It made sense, Nate trying to take over Steve's informers. I wondered if any of the minions had defected. Nate couldn't offer them a job, or even a mention. Their need for recognition was at war with their need for discretion, and only Steve understood this. A listing in the masthead would have been thrilling but a public display might blow their cover and get them fired from their day jobs.

Knowing how precarious their position was, Nate could easily control them. He could destroy them if he wanted. In his new capacity as Eve's replacement he could steal the minions from Steve and use their gossip any way he liked. How could they say no to extortion? Nate could tell the world who they were and what they had done to their employers, co-workers, and friends. He would never coddle them as Steve had. He would ruin them and make them hate themselves even more.

"Nah, come on, don't review Toffy's. They advertise with us," said Carl. "They do business with us."

"They do business with *you*," I said. I knew he didn't share those IOUs with anyone except Nate. They probably ate lunch for free every day while the rest of the paper's staff scraped by on minimum wage sandwiches, at least the employees who didn't have trust funds.

"The advertiser's king," said Carl. He gave Nate an uneasy look.

"I thought the reader was king," said Nate.

I was close and listening, but Carl was tough to read. His thoughts skittered and disappeared like cats, then jumped up out of the darkness and ran away. He had done terrible things, worse things than shooting an ex-employee in the face with one of his father's unregistered handguns; worse than wrapping Fucky-Face in cellophane and handing her over to his father's personal assistant for disposal in a Bremerton construction site.

Carl had traveled the world. His stories were a jungle of real events and anecdotes, false and true starts. Back roads flashed by at night, redwoods and fir trees crowded the edges of memory, shadows looming, a naked man hammering away in the trunk and screaming for mercy, the blood-stained fur of a white Labrador soaking up mud, someone named Kip running toward a lake in the rain...

"Tell me about the festival, the festival chick, the chick you're writing about," said Carl.

"She's no chick," Nate told him. "She's about forty."

"Okay, okay, what's the, you know, what's the deal?"

"Charlotte Franklin," said Nate.

I recognized the name. She was a real person. My guess was, he occasionally chose actual subjects so the game seemed less risky, more manageable. Anyone investigating would have to wade through a lot of material to find the verifiable lies.

While Nate was cutting a path of extortion and fraud, and Carl was busy disposing of anyone (me) or anything (Fucky-Face's body) that might wreck his newspaper and embarrass his father, Daisy was reporting on mushroom festivals in Portland. Thanks again to Eve. I'd given her a chance at redemption. All she had to do was tell someone to investigate Nate's background and my murder, and what did she do instead? She blabbed the whole story to Carl and told him she got it from me. Crazy bitch. She didn't pull the trigger but she certainly got me killed.

If anyone had done a little fact checking, there was enough damning information in Nate's articles to send his nascent career skittering across the rocks. My personal, impossible desire was to see him break down and cry in front of Carl, cry and beg for his job and sputter like a baby. This would be satisfying in so many ways. Carl would never trust another boy wonder, and his paper would be ruined. Fair enough. But I was wiser than I used to be and getting wiser by the minute (however long those lasted any more). I knew the two men sitting on either side of me had less than a soul between them. They didn't break down. They didn't cry. They were tougher than tough guys. They were assholes.

I'd put Eve out of her misery and gained nothing from the experience, except Eve's unwanted company. I figured there was no point in murdering Carl. Destroying his dream would be better. Checking back now and then over the years to see him grow fat and old and lonely would be better in every way.

"Miz Franklin started this dance festival five years ago and she promised to pay the artists but she only paid the first year," Nate explained.

"Good, okay," Carl said. "Good. We're warning local artists…" He put his elbows on the table, clasped his hands and put on his most serious expression. "We're the good guys here."

"Right, yeah," said Nate. "She's completely disorganized. I met her and she's so scatterbrained she asked my name about five times."

Carl laughed. "That's, yeah, she's a nut, I heard from somebody she's a nut."

"She's batshit crazy," said Nate. Carl burst into laughter again. "She wears these tiny paisley dresses and you can see her gut spilling over the underwear. It's disgusting. You wouldn't believe it. Like she's a teenager in her mind. Obviously high and clearly half-drunk…"

"Jesus!" Carl rubbed his hands together. "Cool! But we're not saying anything libelous. I mean, the focus is on, the focus is her mismanagement of the what-do-you, what-do-you-call-it…"

"Movement festival," Nate said. His chowder arrived. He took a big swig of ale. When the waitress left he made a show of watching her ass. Then he lifted his eyebrows at Carl, who laughed and shook his head.

"Maniac," said Carl. "You're a maniac."

"I'm a maniac with a bladder the size of that waitress' left nipple. I'll be right back." Nate scooted out of the booth and headed to the men's room.

The second he disappeared Carl stopped shaking his head and chuckling. He turned his attention to the street beyond the windows extending the length of one wall. Frowning and rubbing his hands together, he studied the girls in ripped jeans and combat boots, the boys with sloppy hair and lopsided shirts, and the homeless guy holding a sign. He didn't see what I saw—Fucky-Face in nothing but a pair of soiled underpants, staring straight at him through the window.

She remained through another beer after Nate returned, through a round of locker room talk about all the parts of a woman's anatomy Nate and Carl found least and most offensive, through a brotherly handshake and goodbye, until Carl threw a dollar on the table as a tip, wandered outdoors, and headed toward his apartment. When he turned the first corner a block away, Fucky-Face was right on his heels.

Chapter Twenty-Seven

The phenomenon Eve pointed out to me quickly became an obsession. I didn't have the nerve to study a clock but the signs were everywhere. For example, I'd watch a guy cleaning the bathrooms at the Broadway Market. I'd see him mop the floor and gather his supplies and leave. Moments later the floor was decorated with urine or piss and no one had entered the bathrooms.

Before this I'd never paid attention to how suddenly the weather changed from overcast to downpour to clear skies to drizzle. I was used to the shifting light and temperature. Once I took note I realized the cycle was faster than it used to be. Everything had this shuddering quality. I'd stand in an espresso line and watch the sluggish barista describe the past week of her dance classes to an acquaintance while ten people shifted weight and rolled their eyes. Suddenly the barista would twirl and skip and jump, demonstrating moves she must have shown to three or more customers. And just as suddenly the line would form and time would drag again.

For this reason I had no idea how much time passed unless I checked a newspaper. I don't know how many days went by after I saw Fucky-Face stalking Carl. I wondered how soon his name would appear in the news. It might take weeks, or his death might occur in a matter of hours. The beauty was, I didn't have to lift a finger.

"You know, there's a reason most fictional detectives lead a frugal existence. You can't drift and succeed. Assholes survive better than non-assholes because they're driven to be successful and they'll do what it takes, no matter what. You can't wander around looking for the truth and expect a reward.

"The pursuit of happiness is a so-called right elevated and protected by the Declaration of Independence. The pursuit of truth is a whole different thing. You can chase the truth down some ugly backstreets, never reach your destination, and get your teeth kicked in for the effort."

"Says the guy who died with a face like a tangerine," I said. "You didn't get kicked in the teeth. You drank yourself to death."

"I was murdered."

"Oh, right," I said.

"Why don't you go quietly?" Lee Todd asked, now dressed in a white linen suit and sporting an out-of-season boater with a black silk band.

"Go where?" I asked. We were riding the #7 again because I liked the crowds of people who thought they had a purpose, bustling to work and back, hurrying to meet dates and pick up children, dashing to the market for dinner supplies, all so exciting and busy and pointless.

"Nowhere," he said. "Blissful, beautiful nowhere. The first time I glimpsed eternal death was during surgery. For a while after you wake from the anesthesia, whenever you dream it's this nursery world full of stuff you can't figure out, a big Technicolor acid trip with painted people and giant talking animals and flying robots. But before you wake up, while you're under, it's nothing, Greta. It's a big, gorgeous blank. When your mind stops chasing answers, and comes to rest, it's all a beautiful, dark emptiness."

"I'm not feeling any of this," I said. "What is it supposed to feel like? I found out who really killed me, and nothing changed."

"You let that woman kill a guy."

"That guy murdered me," I said.

"Do you know what she did to him? Did you see it? Did you read the story in the newspaper?"

"Don't care anymore," I said.

"Okay. So why follow people? Come on. Don't lie. I know what you're doing. A whisper here and a little push there…"

"Most of the ones I choose are already suicidal. All they want is a word of encouragement, to let go and fall."

"Oh, please, don't play the altruist," he said.

"I do it for myself, too. It feels—almost like a feeling," I told him. "It's better than floating empty all the time."

"Some of us find things to do."

"Great," I said. "Spend eternity trying on expensive suits. You're practically a goddamn TV angel."

"Okay," he said. "Okay. I gave it a shot. (Pun intended, by the way.) I tried to help."

"You don't have to help me. I don't need you, or anybody."

"I know," he said. "I know. Tough as nails, that's you. All right, then, Greta, take care of yourself."

"Will do," I said. His sad smile told me something was going on, more than the usual friendly brush-off before I'd see him again at some random bus stop.

"What's the deal?" I asked.

"I found her."

"Who?"

"The woman who gave me an overdose in the hospital," he said. "She wasn't a real nurse and I only saw her once, so it took time to track her down."

"Do you feel better, now that you've returned the favor?"

"Oh, no," he said. "I didn't kill her."

I needed a cigarette for this one. Lee Todd lit one for each of us.

"Why not?"

"She was a mess," he said. "I tracked her from a hospital parking lot..."

"Is that where you've been hanging out?" I had to laugh. "For how long?"

Lee Todd pushed the boater high on his forehead. It was ridiculous.

"I was hoping to solve a mystery," he said. "Assuming this pale, sad woman was masquerading as a nurse and murdering patients for a reason, for some kind of profit, beyond pleasure— that was my mistake.

"In outdoor light, even in the rain, I could see her uniform was frayed at the hem and seams. She had a dirt stain on her right hip. She walked stiffly and she grunted when she climbed into her car. She was in pain.

"The backseat was full of takeout food cartons and aluminum cans. I took the passenger's seat and watched her drive. She was one of those people who sing along under their breath to every song on the radio, too shy to really belt it out. Probably somebody told her, once upon a time, she had a terrible voice. She did, too. She sang off-key. She smelled like French fries and dog hair.

"Her house was rank but also bare and cold and ugly. She watched TV from a futon and fell asleep on it. The yard was nothing but dirt and gravel."

I couldn't believe it. "You let your killer live because she had a crummy house?"

"Yeah," he said. "And a crummy life, a crummy car. Nobody wanted to spend even one minute with this broad. I'll bet nobody had touched her in twenty years. I felt sorry for her."

"You're insane," I said.

"I'm fading."

"Sorry?"

"Haven't you noticed?" he asked. "You're getting bolder, more distinct, all the time. I'm fading. Greta, I think this is how it's supposed to be."

"Fading?"

"Letting go. We're meant to let go. We're not supposed to be here."

I hated the idea. It sounded like my life—standing back, slipping out the back door, living in shadows, and never getting anywhere. Now that I was dead, my impulse was to move, to reach out, to catch one of these fast-paced bodies by the elbow and send him hurtling down the stairs. I was becoming a fan of the sounds a person's demise could make—the splash and burble, the final shriek of recognition, the crack of a skull on the pavement—all of it was deeply satisfying and more intimate than any relationship I'd ever known.

"If you need me after this, you know, I won't be here," he said.

"Good," I told him, and exited the bus at the next corner.

I didn't thank him. I didn't say goodbye. I didn't owe him anything. I just left him there, surrounded by strangers, to finish fading away.

Eve had fallen in love with the Japanese garden at the Arboretum. By the time I ventured there to check up on her, I couldn't have lured her away if I'd wanted to. I swear it was because the woman didn't get out nearly enough when she was alive. She was more reclusive than me, and that's saying a lot. Her first time really playing outdoors, without anxiety or responsibility, she was hooked.

In the Japanese garden her favorite thing was creeping up on tourists with a cold breeze or a whooshing noise. She perfected the art of making people feel like the air was passing right through them. It freaked most of them out, especially when it was followed by a woman's reedy voice wafting up from the bamboo under the footbridge calling, "Where are youuuuuuuu?"

I considered telling her what Lee Todd had done, how he had chosen not to kill anyone, and now he was free, or blank, or whatever it was that wasn't lingering here anymore. But what was the point? Eve had killed Fucky-Face out of spite, thanks to me. I didn't help but I didn't try to stop her. It was done, Eve was a goner, a loser, a spirit attached to a place with nothing to do except mess with the living.

I don't know what happened to her after that. For all I know she's still there, scaring the shit out of children and ruining their parents' vacation.

The next time I checked up on Nate he had a ridiculous suntan and a new condo. Apparently he had become the voice of his generation, unashamed of ambition, unapologetic about his intentions. Why apologize when you've got a book contract and a journalism award for a series of articles about software kings in Silicon Valley?

In his penthouse in a newly refurbished art deco building downtown every surface gleamed. The polished wood floor didn't creak. I know because I tried every inch of it. I also tried putting a crack in the marble kitchen countertop but it was a waste of time.

"He was just, he was a great guy, a great guy to work with, and a great guy to know," Nate told the dailies and the reporter from NPR when he was asked about Carl. "Honestly, I thought he would be the next, you know, the next Rupert Murdoch. He was such an energetic guy, and he had a lot of *potential*. Seeing him end up like that was a shock, yeah, it was a tragedy for Carl and for his family, and for all of us, really. Goes to show, you never can predict how life will turn out, right? Make the most of it, seize the moment, all of those clichés, you know? I was just lucky — I felt lucky — no, I *feel* lucky to have known him. Very lucky, every day, and grateful, you know what I mean? And I can't thank him enough for the boost *Boom City* gave to my career at a crucial moment."

In whatever amount of time had passed since I let Fucky-Face murder Carl, all the wrong things had taken place, one after another. Carl's death — he was found at the bottom of a stairwell with his head turned completely backward — destroyed his parents.

Daisy returned from Portland to write an investigative piece but Carl's father threatened a lawsuit her paper couldn't afford to fight. Daisy tore through her notebooks, interviewed a hundred people, followed my tracks and Carl's and Eve's, to no avail. Understandably, she couldn't make sense of the incredibly stupid events of spring, 1994, in Seattle, and soon enough a much bigger news story would break. A real celebrity running from the law, a slow-speed chase on the freeway in California, and every journalist in the country had to follow.

Eventually Daisy joined her brother on an expedition to Alaska, reporting on the melting polar ice caps and its effects on wildlife.

Fucky-Face was never found and her friends argued for years about whether she was dead or had simply run away from her sad life to start fresh somewhere else. This was partially true. The new Safeway and adjoining parking lot in Bremerton became her forever home. Sometimes I envy her. At least she got out of the city after she avenged herself.

Actually, she had help. Fucky-Face's physical transportation was managed by two men in black sweat suits. At one a.m. the day after her death, these men tossed four plastic trash bags into the solidifying foundation of the new Safeway in Bremerton, fifteen miles east of Seattle, the other side of Elliott Bay. But this was not all of Fucky-Face. A fifth trash bag fell from a return ferry that night. The bag slipped into the bay and quickly sank. Weighted with broken marbles and rocks and shaped like a small handbag, it settled down deep with the rotten canoes and tide-stripped skeletons of ancient Duwamish, a name which roughly translates into 'the city dwellers.'

Thanks to the news reports, Vaughn became certain I had killed myself. Nothing could change his conviction that I was harboring dark secrets and suffering from this or that condition. In the spring of 2002 he launched a new show, nothing like his previous work, a drama about a 20-something struggling with mental illness. It was his first big hit. He won a local award, and then a regional award. A producer contacted him and offered to take the show to New York. There was a workshop followed by a production. In 2005, through absolutely no fault of my own, I was the toast of Broadway.

Speaking of toast, *Boom City* dwindled and died over the summer of 1994. Nate dumped the paper when Carl died, and moved on to bigger prospects. At first Carl's father couldn't bring himself to shut the place down. Steve tried to keep it going with the O.J. Simpson story but he had too much competition. Pretty soon, even the people who used to pick up the paper as a joke moved on. There were much better papers on offer, and 24-hour broadcast news was more exciting.

Steve took a job maintaining the database in the circulation department at the *Weekly*. He stayed in touch with the minions, and mourned the death of each one over the years. The ones who did away with themselves became part of the sludge, the black fungus only the dead could see, crawling up the sides of old buildings, murmuring in tongues, still unloved and misunderstood. Only the creeping tide of new construction can put them to rest, their remains scrubbed away by bleach or sealed with cement.

Nothing gave me the satisfaction I was seeking. Some people call it closure. Others call it revenge. Here's what I call it. My whole life was one stupid fucking anti-climax, like most lives, if you think about it. The cycles of birth, screwing around, and death are random, meaningless events. People pray, or fuck, or traipse all over the world making a mess and calling it adventure, and these things give them the illusion of meaning. Having a baby, or ten babies, is nothing but a shield against the void.

People who wallow in comfort, in good wine and delicious cuisine, are a little less stupid than everyone else. At least they squander their lives doing what feels good.

Artists are nothing but expert time killers, filling up the hours by entertaining themselves. But the ones who think they're changing the universe are truly delusional. Writers who believe communication makes any difference are the most delusional of all. Every day people find better, faster ways to communicate and guess what? The same percentage of humanity remains ignorant and hateful. We still torture and murder for profit. We still rape and steal, and we step gingerly over people who are starving to death so we won't get any of their shit on our shoes on our way to the espresso stand.

In case anyone wants to chalk up my shitty attitude to bitterness, let me be clear. I don't blame anybody. Not anymore. The man I tried to prove wrong thought enough of me to hang around and offer me words of advice I didn't follow. The woman I wasted time hating was barely aware of my existence. Even now she's busy spreading a fistful of thorns across the footbridge at the Arboretum, and tripping children with broken bamboo stems. The man who killed me in cold blood was murdered by a ghost wearing stained underwear.

The worst thing Eve did was to reject the best I had to offer. Last I heard that wasn't a killing offense. No one was out to get me.

Nothing stood in my way. Life was mine to fuck up, and I fucked it up good. Here's the proof.

Years ago, in one of my restless moods, I hid outside an elementary school on Capitol Hill near Volunteer Park. Indoors the scent of chalk and finger-paints, outdoors an extended canopy of cherry blossoms, like a tunnel of bright aromatic light. I crouched on the mossy steps and waited until the last child emerged from the brick building.

She was strangely familiar, with her lanky stride and her shoulder-length dark hair. She exuded light, a sense of wellbeing and curiosity. With her backpack stuffed full of art and science homework, stopping at each new marvel—an overturned sidewalk stone where ants streamed toward the nearest lawn, a garden gnome clutching a bunch of weeds—she was irresistible.

She followed the curve north, bypassing the park. Soon we were crossing 10th Ave. On a side street the repaired asphalt and concrete gave way to a cobbled path. She reached up and unbolted a gate covered in ivy. When she pushed the gate open another world appeared. A wild and splendid garden surrounded us with a heady aroma of flowers and the sparkling greenery of a barely tended yet naturally beautiful lawn.

The gate creaked shut behind us. Up ahead lay a large, rambling Tudor-style house. The windows and the backdoor stood open. Wafting in our direction, the unmistakable scent of bread baking. The second the smell reached her, the girl took a skip forward and let out a weird cry.

I stopped there, puzzled. I watched the girl proceed across the grass to the backdoor. I kept trying to figure out the nature of the sound she made. Was it fear?

While I was wondering, a woman stuck her head out one of the windows and called out, "Sally! Sally, Sally! Over here!"

The voice hit me like an old song on the radio. Reaching past the present to my youth, my life, all of my wasted days. Moo! It was Ginny Moo calling out.

Through the backdoor a tall, slender man with close-cropped salt and pepper hair and a trim beard emerged. He reached out for the little girl, who dropped her backpack on the ground. The man swept her up in his arms and cradled her, both of them giggling and shouting. Moo looked out and laughed at the sight of her husband Charlie and her daughter Sally.

I stood there on the lawn and watched them swirl in circles. Charlie tossed Sally in the air, caught her, and gently set her on her feet. He picked up her backpack and slung it over his shoulder. The two clasped hands. Charlie had a peculiar expression, as if he'd picked up a bad scent on the breeze. He put one hand against the back of his daughter's head and ushered her softly into the house, closing the door behind them and locking it.

Only after Moo's face disappeared from the window did I understand the sound the girl had made when approaching the house. It was joy! It was a feeling of delight and anticipation, as pure and wild as anything I'd ever heard.

Chapter Twenty-Eight

This really is a boom city, isn't it? As long as the tectonic plates grinding away beneath the surface don't slip and fling Seattle into the Pacific, it's only going to get bigger, prettier, louder, and more expensive every year, like most cities.

The light rail is a welcome addition, replacing some of the deadwood, the houses once occupied by families, later marked for demolition and protected (for their eventual demise) behind tall fences and barbed wire. House after house was knocked flat, the detritus of generations hauled away to make room for the train station on Capitol Hill.

I like the train. Clean, fast, fun to ride even during peak hours. Too bad it's such a short ride but that will change quickly too. Soon everyone will take the train and won't that be fun? Every stop is a new opportunity, for those who are not quite satisfied with their lives, and not quite happy in the midst of all this glitter, greed, and beauty. For the moment the train is sort of the monorail of its era, a bright novelty and a promise for the future, reminding residents they live in a place of aspirations and ideals and continual alterations.

Public transportation is the most fun. Once in a while, though, I enjoy climbing into a car beside a driver trapped in the awful freeway traffic. The moment is intimate. Cold rain outside, heat and rage and despair inside, fogged windows separating the busy world from a single, sad resident. I whisper between the lines of a song on the radio. "Go on and hit the gas. There's a truck stalled up ahead. Get it over with..."

The bus tunnel drilling made for some chilling encounters. It's hard work underground. For now, the drilling is at a standstill. Stop and start, stop and start, shutting down and then gearing up. Nobody said progress would be easy.

Who proposed a Ferris wheel in the middle of the city? What a sweet idea. It's as cool as cotton candy at a shopping center. You can exit your sparkling new high-security condo, buy a gelato, and ride the Ferris wheel without leaving your neighborhood, like a child, a 25-year-old working child. I find the seating compartments particularly enjoyable. Think of it, sitting there in the enclosed space high in the air with a view of the teeny Space Needle and the gray sludgy clouds over Puget Sound. Suddenly there is the distinctly cool hand, a low whisper, a bite on the cheek—and absolutely no way out.

I'm surprised to find I have a real affection for the fish odor of the market. I like the cold water splashing on tiles and meeting a strange heat, the density and headiness of the human swarm, brisk shadows flashing through the labyrinthine corridors. It's timeless, the atmosphere of travelers and shoppers; craftsmen selling gorgeous gifts and cheap trinkets; the homeless seeking quarters dropped on the filthy tiled floors, grasping for dimes with black-nailed fingers.

People marvel at it, love it, yet they wonder about the occasional dizziness, the too-crowded feeling reported by tourists who have become ill at the market and blame the proximity of so many bodies, so much bacteria. In the underground halls of the market where they shop and dine at night, and on overcast afternoons all year round, the visitors dress in layers and consider moving here for good. Many of them do move here, lured by tech jobs and pretty images online.

Nothing is more delectable than the stink and sweat of the market. I like to glide between shoppers, sometimes pinching or slapping an uncovered scalp, or brushing past and slamming an elbow into a rib. For the most part my market activities are harmless, and these moments of intimacy are benign; I don't always follow a shopper or a seller home. As I go on, I find the market, just the wandering and harmless mischief, necessary to keep my memory of something real.

I didn't apply for this job. I didn't plan to live here forever. I didn't plan anything. I simply followed my instinct. Here, surrounded by bad memories of my life, I fill the void in my own way. At times I only watch accidents, and at times I make sure the right conditions are met. I'm not seeking anything, only killing time. But there are days and nights when I have a tiny sense of belonging, of serving a purpose. In the city of rain and serial killers and suicide, I'm almost at home.

On good days, really good days, I find someone not quite shunned but shut out by choice. I spy a loner or a person seeking the same refuge I find in the anonymity of crowds.

The sea coils and churns beyond the glass, and fathoms beyond our vision creatures are shuffling through darkness, instinct guiding them to satiate a hunger for which they have no words. Isn't it the same here on the land? Here I am, wandering, watching, and waiting. Once in a while I still hope for an opportunity to tell my story (the only one I'll ever know) to a fellow wanderer, a lost cause, a future death in the making. Once in a while I spy one, a seeker of real or imagined solace—someone who doesn't know me, who is yet drawn to the quiet corners and abandoned alleys where I like to roam—someone lost without knowing it, someone hungry for things that will never exist—someone a lot like *you*.

The End

Black Static reviewer Peter Tennant rates S.P. Miskowski "one of the most interesting and original writers to emerge in recent years." Her debut novel *Knock Knock* and novella *Delphine Dodd* were Shirley Jackson Award finalists. Her short stories appear in the magazines *Supernatural Tales*, *Black Static*, *Identity Theory*, and *Strange Aeons* as well as in the anthologies *The Madness of Dr. Caligari*, *Little Visible Delight*, *October Dreams 2*, *Autumn Cthulhu*, *Cassilda's Song*, *The Hyde Hotel*, *Darker Companions: Celebrating 50 Years of Ramsey Campbell*, and *Looming Low*. Her writing has received a Swarthout Award and two National Endowment for the Arts Fellowships. Dim Shores published Miskowski's "Stag in Flight" as a limited edition chapbook with illustrations by Nick Gucker. Her novelette *Muscadines* is included in the Dunhams Manor Press hardcover series with illustrations by Dave Felton. Her short story collection *Strange is the Night* is forthcoming from JournalStone.

CPSIA information can be obtained
at www.ICGtesting.com
Printed in the USA
BVOW08s1425110817
491730BV00004B/21/P